Rowe is a paranorm

❧ ❧ ❧

Praise for No Knight Needed

"*No Knight Needed* is m-a-g-i-c-a-l! Hands down, it is one of the best romances I have read. I can't wait till it comes out and I can tell the world about it." ~*Sharon Stogner, Love Romance Passion*

"*No Knight Needed* is contemporary romance at its best....There was not a moment that I wasn't completely engrossed in the novel, the story, the characters. I very audibly cheered for them and did not shed just one tear, nope, rather bucket fulls. My heart at times broke for them. The narrative and dialogue surrounding these 'tender' moments in particular were so beautifully crafted, poetic even; it was this that had me blubbering. And of course on the flip side of the heart-wrenching events, was the amazing, witty humour....If it's not obvious by now, then just to be clear, I love this book! I would most definitely and happily reread, which is an absolute first for me in this genre." ~*Becky Johnson, Bex 'N' Books*

"*No Knight Needed* is an amazing story of love and life...I literally laughed out loud, cried and cheered.... *No Knight Needed* is a must read and must re-read." ~*Jeanne Stone-Hunter, My Book Addiction Reviews*

❧ ❧ ❧

Praise for Not Quite Dead

"[Rowe] has penned a winner with *Not Quite Dead*, the first novel in her new NightHunter vampire series...an action-packed, sensual, paranormal romance that will captivate readers from the outset... Brimming with vampires, danger, resurrection, Louisiana bayou, humor, surprising plot twists, fantasy, romance and love, this story is a must-read!" ~ *Romance Junkies:*

Praise for Darkness Possessed

"A story that will keep you on the edge of your seat, and characters you won't soon forget!" - Paige Tyler, *USA Today* Bestselling Author of the X-OPS Series

"*Darkness Possessed*…is an action-packed, adrenaline pumping paranormal romance that will keep you on the edge of your seat… Suspense, danger, evil, life threatening situations, magic, hunky Calydons, humor, fantasy, mystery, scorching sensuality, romance, and love – what more could you ask for in a story? Readers – take my advice – do not miss this dark, sexy tale!" ~*Romance Junkie*s

Praise for Darkness Unleashed

"Once more, award winning author Stephanie Rowe pens a winner with *Darkness Unleashed*, the seventh book in her amazing Order of the Blade series…[an] action-packed, sensual story that will keep you perched on the edge of your seat, eagerly turning pages to discover the outcome…one of the best paranormal books I have read this year." ~*Dottie, Romancejunkies.com*

Praise for Forever in Darkness

"Stephanie Rowe has done it again. The Order Of The Blade series is one of the best urban fantasy/paranormal series I have read. Ian's story held me riveted from page one. It is sure to delight all her fans. Keep them coming!" ~ *Alexx Mom Cat's Gateway Book Blog*

Praise for Darkness Awakened

"A fast-paced plot with strong characters, blazing sexual tension and sprinkled with witty banter, Darkness Awakened sucked me in and kept me hooked until the very last page." ~ *Literary Escapism*

"Rarely do I find a book that so captivates my attention, that makes me laugh out loud, and cry when things look bad. And the sex, wow! It took my breath away... The pace kept me on the edge of my seat, and turning the pages. I did not want to put this book down... [Darkness Awakened] is a must read." ~ D. Alexx Miller, Alexx Mom Cat's Gateway Book Blog

⛨ ⛨ ⛨

Praise for Darkness Seduced

"[D]ark, edgy, sexy ... sizzles on the page...sex with soul shattering connections that leave the reader a little breathless!...Darkness Seduced delivers tight plot lines, well written, witty and lyrical - Rowe lays down some seriously dark and sexy tracks. There is no doubt that this series will have a cult following. " ~ *Guilty Indulgence Book Club*

"I was absolutely enthralled by this book...heart stopping action fueled by dangerous passions and hunky, primal men...If you're looking for a book that will grab hold of you and not let go until it has been totally devoured, look no further than Darkness Seduced."~*When Pen Met Paper Reviews*

⛨ ⛨ ⛨

Praise for Darkness Surrendered

"Book three of the Order of the Blades series is...superbly original and excellent, yet the passion, struggle and the depth of emotion that Ana and Elijah face is so brutal, yet is also pretty awe inspiring. I was swept away by Stephanie's depth of character detail and emotion. I absolutely loved the roller-coaster that Stephanie, Ana and Elijah took me on." ~ *Becky Johnson, Bex 'n' Books!*

"Darkness Surrendered drew me so deeply into the story that I felt

Ana and Elijah's emotions as if they were my own…they completely engulfed me in their story…Ingenious plot turns and edge of your seat suspense…make Darkness Surrendered one of the best novels I have read in years." ~*Tamara Hoffa, Sizzling Hot Book Reviews*

⁂ ⁂ ⁂

Praise for Ice

"*Ice*, by Stephanie Rowe, is a thrill ride!" ~ Lisa Jackson, #1 *New York Times* bestselling author

"Passion explodes even in the face of spiraling danger as Rowe offers a chilling thrill-ride through a vivid--and unforgiving--Alaskan wilderness." ~ Cheyenne McCray, *New York Times* bestselling author

"*Ice* delivers pulse-pounding chills and hot romance as it races toward its exciting climax!" ~ JoAnn Ross, *New York Times* bestselling author

"Stephanie Rowe explodes onto the romantic suspense scene with this edgy, sexy and gripping thriller. From the very first page, the suspense is chilling, and there's enough sizzling passion between the two main characters to melt the thickest arctic ice. Get ready for a tense and dangerous adventure." ~ *Fresh Fiction*

"Stephanie Rowe makes her entry into Romantic Suspense, and what an awesome entry! From the very first pages to the end, heart-stopping danger and passion grab the heart. ... sends shivers down the spine... magnificent... mind-chilling suspense... riveting... A wonderful romance through and through!" ~ *Merrimon Book Reviews*

"[a] thrilling entry into romantic suspense... Rowe comes through with crackling tension as the killer closes in." ~ *Publisher's Weekly*

⁂ ⁂ ⁂

Praise for Chill

"*Chill* is a riveting story of danger, betrayal, intrigue and the healing powers of love... *Chill* has everything a reader needs – death, threats, thefts, attraction and hot, sweet romance." ~ Jeanne Stone Hunter, *My Book Addiction Reviews*

"Once again Rowe has delivered a story with adrenalin-inducing action, suspense and a dark edged hero that will melt your heart and send a chill down your spine." ~ Sharon Stogner, *Love Romance Passion*

"*Chill* packs page turning suspense with tremendous emotional impact. Buy a box of Kleenex before you read *Chill*, because you will definitely need it! ...*Chill* had a wonderfully complicated plot, full of twist and turns. " ~ Tamara Hoffa, *Sizzling Hot Book Reviews*

A Real Cowboy Never Says No

ISBN 10: 1940968119

ISBN 13: 9781940968117

Copyright © 2015 by Stephanie Rowe.

Cover design ©2015 MJC Imageworks. For more info on the cover artist, please visit www.mjcimageworks.com.

Acknowledgements

Special thanks to my beta readers, who always work incredibly hard under tight deadlines to get my books read. I appreciate so much your willingness to tell me when something doesn't work! I treasure your help, and I couldn't do this without you. Hugs to you all! Thanks also to the Rockstars, the best buzz team ever!

There are so many to thank by name, more than I could count, but here are those who I want to called out specially for all they did to help this book come to life: Malinda Davis Diehl, Donna Bossert, Leslie Barnes, Kayla Bartley, Alencia Bates Salters, Alyssa Bird, Jean Bowden, Shell Bryce, Kelley Daley Curry, Ashley Cuesta, Denise Fluhr, Sandi Foss, Valerie Glass, Heidi Hoffman, Jeanne Stone, Rebecca Johnson, Dottie Jones, Janet Juengling-Snell, Deb Julienne, Bridget Koan, Felicia Low, Phyllis Marshall, Suzanne Mayer, Erin McRae, Jodi Moore, Ashlee Murphy, Judi Pflughoeft, Carol Pretorius, Kasey Richardson, Caryn Santee, Summer Steelman, Regina Thomas, and Linda Watson.

Thanks to Nawal M. Nour, M.D. for her advice on babies and pregnant moms, including polling her operating room on whether it was okay for Mira to jump off the rock into the pool, and for Kevin Raskin, M.D. and Sabeena Chacko, M.D., for their advice on prison hospital protocol and the best body part to stab someone in. You gotta love book research! Any mistakes and creative license should be blamed on me, however, and not my favorite doctor peeps, of course.

Special thanks to Michael James Canalas at MJC Imageworks for a wonderful cover. Mom, you're the best. It means so much that you believe in me. I love you. Special thanks also to my amazing, beautiful, special daughter, who I love more than words could ever express. You are my world, sweet girl, in all ways.

Dedication

To all the members of Rowe's Rockstars. I couldn't to do this without your help, support, advice, and laughter! I love you guys!

A Real Cowboy Never Says No

A *Wyoming Rebels* Novel

Stephanie Rowe

Chapter 1

Mira Cabot's first thought when she saw him was that cowboy hats didn't belong at this funeral.

Her second thought was that it was fantastic he was wearing one.

There was nothing like watching a genuine cowboy saunter boldly into a conservative southern church full of overpriced black suits and expensive leather shoes to remind her that life was not over just because someone she loved was dead.

She grinned, her first smile in what felt like years, knowing that AJ would have been thrilled to see the cowboy ignoring the rigid society rules at his funeral. He'd give the white cowboy hat two thumbs up, and he'd probably even toss in a bonus if the man didn't take it off when he met AJ's domineering father.

She knew AJ had always figured he'd wind up being fêted in a small service by the river, where they'd spent hours as kids. His funeral of choice would have been kids, dogs, bare feet, and a local band playing his favorite country music as a reminder to everyone to get off their butts and live life.

Instead, his father had taken over the largest church in town, and he'd booked the finest ballroom in five counties for everyone to retire to after the burial, because he was more concerned about status and money than he was about his dead son's desires.

The line inched forward, dragging her inexorably forward into the church where AJ's dad was presiding, but the cowboy didn't move from the doorway. Mira watched him standing in the doorway, surveying the church with methodical precision, as if he were taking stock of every person present. He was wearing jeans, but they looked sharp and crisp. His face was clean-shaven, but there were already hints of whiskered shadows caressing his jaw. His dark hair was barely visible beneath his hat, but it was clearly cut short. His blue eyes were shrewd and assessing as he scanned the occupants, apparently searching for someone. There was a life and energy exuding from him, as if he got up every morning and somehow managed to cram forty-eight hours of life into every single day.

He made her feel weary and bone-tired in comparison, but at the same time, it was energizing. She hadn't been around someone that alive in a long time, and it was a good reminder to get off her butt and get outside in the sunshine, just like AJ was probably shouting at her to do right at that very moment, stalking her from heaven.

The usher, one of AJ's cousins, took her arm. "First row, Mira? AJ always considered you his sister."

"You really think I'd be welcome in the family seats?" She almost snorted as she glanced at the front of the church. AJ's dad, Alan Joseph Wentworth, Sr., was flanked by his attorney and his only remaining son, Thurston Wentworth, the hard-drinking underachiever who would now inherit the business, much to the dismay of the clan's patriarch. Thurston looked presentable in a navy suit, and his hair was greased back to hide the unruly curls. Alan, however, was sheer, unassailable properness. His silver hair was precisely coiffed, and his crisp black suit fit him with the precision of a custom-made specialty.

Alan looked up, catching her gaze, and his face hardened.

She shot him a winning smile, the same "you don't bother me" grin she'd been giving him for years, which was a bald-faced lie because the man scared the hell out of her. He was a man who got what he wanted, and he was willing to hurt anyone to get it, including his own son or the family who had given him refuge.

Yeah, there was no chance she was going to sit with Alan today. "You know, that's a great idea to sit in the front, Todd, but I might have to leave early. I wouldn't want to disturb the service." And she didn't want her last tribute to AJ to be tainted by Alan. Instead, she gestured to the last pew. "I'll just slide in the back here."

Not waiting for assent, she ducked into the last row of benches, breaking protocol since the seats in front of her weren't full yet. Not that she cared, and neither would AJ. She wasn't here for his family. She was here for him.

She scooted into the far corner, letting the shadows of the balcony conceal her. She knew almost everyone who walked in, but very few of them would bother to notice her. Unlike Mira, the rest of the attendees were from the south end of town, the section of mansions and gated driveways that wished her end of town didn't actually exist. A few of her friends from high school were there, but they'd moved beyond their shared teenage angst.. Not a single one bothered to look over into her dark corner. There was a smattering of sharply dressed twenty-something men and women she didn't know, and she figured those had to be AJ's friends and co-workers from Boston, people from the part of his life she'd never known.

As she sank onto the thick, well-worn cushion, she glanced back again toward the entrance, but the cowboy was no longer in the doorway. Without his energizing presence galvanizing her, the enormity of what she was facing settled heavily onto her shoulders once again. Grim reality wrapped around her like a shadowy cloak trying to suck the last remnants of energy from her soul. She sighed and closed her eyes, trying to summon the inner strength that had gotten her through so much.

She needed a plan. She needed to take action. But what action? What was she going to do?

Sudden tears threatened, and she instinctively lifted her chin in defiance, willing them away.

She knew exactly what she had to do, and she'd known it for the last four hours. She was going to have to quit her job, pathetic as it was, and move away from the only place she'd ever lived, and the only place she'd ever wanted to live, to somewhere that AJ's dad would never, ever find her.

Chase Stockton knew he'd found the woman he'd come to meet.

There was no mistaking the depth of loathing in the gaze of AJ's dad when he'd glared at the woman in the pale blue sundress. There was only one woman Alan could despise that much, and it was Mira Cabot.

Chase grinned. After more than a decade, he was about to meet Mira Cabot in person. *Hot damn.*

Anticipation humming through him, Chase watched with appreciation as she ducked into the last row of pews, her pale shoulders erect and strong as she moved down the row. She was a little too thin, yeah, but there was a strength to her body that he liked. Her dark blond hair was curly, bouncing over her shoulders in stark contrast to the tight updos of the other women in the church. He'd noticed her flip-flops and hot pink toenails, a little bit of color in the chapel full of black and gloom.

Chase had hopped a plane to attend the funeral, but it hadn't been just to honor AJ. He could have done that from his ranch in Wyoming. Nope, he'd come here to meet Mira, because he'd had a feeling this was going to be his only chance.

He ignored the line of churchgoers waiting to be seated. Instead, he strode around the back of the last pew to the far side, where his quarry was tucked away in the shadows. As he approached, someone turned up the lights in the church, and the shadows slid away, casting her face in a warm glow, giving him his first view of the woman he'd been thinking about for more than a decade.

Chase was shocked by the raw need that flooded him. Her eyes were the same deep blue as in her photo. Her nose had that slight bump from when she and AJ had failed to successfully erect a tire swing in her front yard, resulting in her crashing to the ground and breaking her nose. Her lips were pale pink, swept with the faintest hint of gloss, and her eyelashes were as long and thick as he'd imagined. Her shoulders were bare and delicate in her sundress, and her ankles were crossed demurely, as if she were playing the role that was expected of her. Yet, around that same ankle was a chain of glittering gold with several blue stones. He knew that anklet. He'd helped AJ pick it out for her twenty-first birthday.

She was everything he'd imagined, and so much more. She was no longer an inanimate, two-dimensional image who lived only in his mind. She had become a real, live woman.

Mira was eyeing the crowd with the faintest scowl puckering her lips and lining her forehead, just as he would have expected. She didn't like this crowd any more than AJ had.

Chase grinned, relaxing. She was exactly what he'd imagined. "You don't approve?" he said as he approached her.

She let out a yelp of surprise and jumped, bolting sideways like a skittish foal. "What?"

Chase froze, startled by the sound of her voice. It was softer than he'd expected, reminding him of the rolling sound of sunshine across his back on a warm day. Damn, he liked her voice. Why hadn't AJ ever mentioned it? That wasn't the kind of thing a guy could overlook.

She was sitting sideways, her hand gripping the back of the pew, looking at him like he was about to pull out his rifle and aim it at her head.

He instinctively held up his hand, trying to soothe her. "Sorry. I didn't mean to startle you." He swept the hat off his head and bowed slightly. "Chase Stockton. You must be Mira Cabot."

"Chase Stockton?" Her frown deepened slightly, and then recognition dawned on her face. "AJ's best friend from college! Of course." She stood up immediately, a smile lighting up her features. "I can't believe I finally get to meet you."

He had only a split second to register how pretty her smile was before she threw her arms around him and hugged him.

For the second time in less than a minute, Chase was startled into immobility. Her body was so warm and soft against him that he forgot to breathe. He had not been expecting her to hug him, and he hadn't had time to steel himself. He flexed his hands by his sides, not sure how to react. It had been so long since anyone had hugged him, and it was an utterly foreign experience. It was weird as hell, but at the same time, there was something about it that felt incredible, as if the whole world had stopped spinning and settled into this moment.

When Mira didn't let go, he tentatively slipped his arms

around her, still unsure of proper protocol when being embraced by a woman he'd never met before. As his arms encircled her, however, a deep sense of rightness settled over him. He could feel her ribs protruding from her back, and he instinctively tightened his grip on her, pulling her into the shield of his embrace. In photographs, she'd always been athletic and solid, but now she was thin, thinner than he liked, thinner than he felt she should be.

She tucked her face in his neck and took a deep breath, and he became aware of the most tempting scent of flowers. It reminded him of a trail ride in the spring, when the wildflowers were beating back the last remnants of a stubborn winter.

The turbulence that constantly roiled through his body seemed to quiet as he focused on her. He became aware of the desperate nature of her embrace, reminding him that she was attending the funeral of her best friend, and she was no doubt being assaulted by the accompanying grief and loss.

He bent his head, his cheek brushing against her hair. "You okay?" he asked softly.

She took another deep breath, and then pulled back. Her blue eyes were full of turbulent emotion. "It's just that seeing you makes me feel like AJ's here again." She brushed an imaginary speck of dust off his shoulder. "You were his best friend, you know. You changed his life forever."

He wasn't used to anyone touching him with that kind of intimacy, especially not a woman. Women never got familiar with him. *Ever*. He simply didn't allow it. But with her, it felt okay. Good even. He shrugged, feeling completely out of his depth with her. "He changed mine," he said. "He did a hell of a lot more for me than I ever did for him." AJ had been a lifeline in an ugly existence that had been spiraling straight into hell. He knew exactly where he'd have been without AJ: dead, or in prison. It was a debt he could never repay.

She nodded, still not stepping away from his embrace. She lightly clasped his forearms, still holding onto him. "He was like that, wasn't he?"

"Yeah, he was." Unable to make himself release her, Chase studied her face, memorizing the curve of her nose, the flush of her cheeks, and the slope of her jaw. "You were his rock, you know. The only person in this world he truly trusted."

And that was it, the reason why he'd wanted to meet her. He was bitter, tired, and cynical, and he'd needed to see if the Mira Cabot his friend had always talked about actually existed. He needed to know whether there was someone in this world, anyone besides his brothers, who a man could actually believe in. Hearing that AJ had died had derailed Chase more than he'd expected, and he'd needed something to hold onto, something that connected him back to AJ and the hope that something good still existed in this world.

Her cheeks flushed, and she smiled. "Thanks for telling me that. We didn't keep in touch much over the last few years, but he's always been in my heart."

He stared at her, uncertain how to respond. Who talked about things in their heart? And with strangers? But he knew the answer to that. Mira did, and that was why he'd wanted to meet her.

She finally pulled back, and he reluctantly released her, his hands sliding over her hips. She moved further into the pew and eased onto the bench. "Sit with me," she said, patting the seat beside her.

"Yeah, okay." Instead of taking the aisle seat, he moved past her and sat on the other side of her, inserting himself between Mira and AJ's dad. The old man was across the church, but he hadn't stopped shooting lethal stares in her direction. AJ wasn't there to protect her, so it was now Chase's job.

He draped his arms across the back of the pew, aware that his position put one arm behind Mira's shoulders. Not touching, but present. A statement.

He looked across the church at AJ's dad, and this time, when the man looked over, he noticed Chase sitting beside her. The two men stared at each other for a brief moment, and then Alan looked away.

Satisfied, Chase shifted his position so he could stretch his legs out, trying to work out the cramps from the long flight. He was glad he'd come. It felt right to be there, and he'd sent the message to AJ's dad that Mira was under his protection.

He glanced sideways at her as she fiddled with her small purse. Her hair was tumbling around her face, obscuring his view of her eyes. Frustrated that he couldn't see her face, he started to move his hand to adjust her hair, and then froze. What the hell was he doing, thinking he could just reach out and touch her like that?

Swearing, he jerked his gaze away from her, a bead of sweat trickling down his brow as he realized the enormity of what was happening. *He was attracted to her.* For the last decade, Mira had simply been AJ's best friend, an angel of sorts who Chase had idealized from a distance, never thinking of Mira as anything more personal than simply a bright light in a shitty world.

But now?

He wanted her.

He wanted to brush her hair back from her face. He wanted to run his fingers over her collarbone. He wanted to feel her body crushed against his again. He wanted to sink his mouth onto hers, and taste her—

Hell. That spelled trouble, in a major way.

Suddenly, he couldn't wait to get on the plane and get out of there, and back to his carefully constructed world.

He hadn't come here for a woman. He'd come here for salvation, not to be sucked into the hell that had almost destroyed him once before. Mira Cabot might be the only woman on the planet worth trusting, but that wasn't reason enough for him to risk all that he'd managed to rebuild.

Nothing was worth that risk. *Nothing.*

※ ※ ※

Usually, Mira didn't mind being alone. She treasured her solitude, and had no problem standing on her own. Coming to the service by herself had been preferable to faking her way with acquaintances who didn't really care that AJ was dead.

But with Chase sitting next to her, his broad shoulders taking up half the pew, and his long legs stretched out to the side, she had to admit, it felt good to be beside him.

It was almost as if the sheer magnitude of his presence could keep the noise at bay, letting her settle into the shield he gave her, so that she could actually slow her mind long enough to think. His presence made it safe to take the time to *feel*.

She stole a glance at him as he watched the gathering congregation. He started to take his cowboy hat off, then he saw AJ's dad glaring at him. He immediately dropped his hand, leaving the hat in place as he shot a silent, unrelenting stare at AJ's dad. Her heart softened with the realization that Chase had gone against his instincts and left the hat on in a silent statement of solidarity with AJ, and his enduring battle to survive his controlling, abusive father. The hat would infuriate Alan, and it would make AJ's presence real at his funeral.

It was perfect, and she wanted to cheer at Chase's willingness to stand up for AJ in this church full of Alan's minions. His white shirt was unbuttoned at the collar, showing a gold chain against his tanned skin. He was rough and untamed, the antithesis of everyone in the church. It was weird to feel so comfortable with a complete stranger, but they weren't really strangers. AJ had connected them, and she knew that Chase was the only other person in the world that AJ had truly cared about. AJ's faith in Chase meant she could trust that he was a good guy.

He bent his head slightly toward her, but didn't look at her. "Is that Thurston? AJ's brother?"

She looked toward the front to where Alan and Thurston were talking with the minister. "Yes. They pulled him out of rehab to attend the service."

Chase laughed softly. "Alan must be angry as hell that AJ died before the old man could force him into the family business. Thurston will ruin the company if he ever takes over."

"I know." She shared his amusement. "AJ would appreciate that."

Chase glanced over at her, still smiling. Her heart skipped a beat at how handsome he was. She hadn't noticed a man for a very long time. The last thing she'd have expected was to be attracted to Chase Stockton, but she definitely was. It was a little unnerving, but her reaction also gave her hope that the part of her that was a woman was still alive inside her, and someday, she might even come back to life.

Chase leaned back against the pew, shifting his legs. The movement made his arm brush against her shoulder, and she stiffened, not sure whether she should pull away. A part of her didn't want to retreat, but the feel of his shoulder against hers was so distracting she couldn't focus on anything else. She pretended to cough, and used the movement as a way to reposition herself without making it look like she'd done it on purpose.

"Well, that's one thing that AJ can die knowing he did right," he said, apparently not noticing her strategic shift.

She raised her eyebrows. "What's that?"

"He never had kids that his father could get his claws into. Remember what AJ used to say? He'd never bring a child into this world so that Alan could destroy it. Alan's stuck without a decent heir, and his business is going to die because of it. Can you imagine if AJ had left behind a kid?" He whistled softly. "His widow would have had no chance of keeping the kid safe from Alan."

Mira felt the blood drain from her face, and she instinctively clutched her belly.

Chase's eyes sharpened, and his gaze shot to her hand, and then back to her face.

She froze, her heart pounding, as she frantically tried to think of a casual response.

Nothing came to her. Her mind was utterly blank.

"AJ lived in Boston," Chase said slowly, as if measuring every word. "Not here."

She nodded, her mouth bone dry as she forced herself to take her hand off her stomach. "Right."

"He never came home to visit," Chase continued with a casualness she didn't believe. "He despised everything in this place, except for you."

She managed a smile. "Yeah, I know."

Silence, but he didn't take his penetrating gaze off her. "Did you ever go there?" he finally asked. "Visit him in Boston? Recently, perhaps?"

"No," she said quickly. "My mom's been an invalid for the last eight years, as I'm sure you know. I was her caretaker until she died a few weeks ago. I couldn't ever leave town. She needed constant care." Her voice broke unexpectedly at the thought of her mother, and she turned away, clenching her hands in her lap. "The service is starting," she said, her voice snappier than she intended.

She focused intently on the minister, her lips pressed tightly together as she fought not to cry.

"Two funerals in a month? I didn't know your mom had died." Chase's voice was soft now, as were his eyes. "I'm so sorry, Mira. I know how much she meant to you."

She glared at him. "Don't be nice, unless you like it when a woman bursts into tears and sobs uncontrollably all over your crisp white shirt," she hissed.

His eyes widened in the moderate terror she'd expected, and he closed his mouth, cutting off his next question.

She folded her arms across her chest, her eyes blurring as she tried to listen to a bunch of strangers talk dispassionately about her best friend, and as she tried not to notice that Chase was intently watching *her*, and not paying any attention to the service at all.

Chapter 2

Chase had absolutely intended to leave town once the church service was over.

There had been no chance he was going to go to the highbrow after-funeral gala and socialize with the bastards who had driven AJ out of town. *No chance.* He had no time for people who were superficial, drank too much, and cared about nothing but themselves and their own agendas.

And yet, there he was, leaning moodily against one of the white pillars, watching Mira circulate through the lavishly decorated ballroom. Her chin was held high, and her curls were bouncing. She was animated and charming in her conversations with people, but he wasn't buying it.

Whenever she had a moment to breathe, her shoulders slumped, and her face became lined with exhaustion and grief. She'd kept careful track of Alan, and had made sure not to run into him.

Chase had been watching the old man as well, and he knew that Alan was not going to let Mira leave without cornering her. He'd been watching her with dangerous hostility all night, a predator stalking his prey, waiting for the chance to isolate her.

Mira excused herself from her latest conversation, and started working her way toward the restroom. As Chase watched, she put her hand on her stomach.

That was the twenty-seventh time she'd done it in the last ninety minutes.

Shit.

He suddenly realized that Alan was striding across the floor toward her, his face determined. Chase jumped forward, almost sprinting through the crowd to get to Mira before Alan did.

They arrived at the same moment, but Alan didn't notice Chase's approach. He grabbed Mira's upper arm and jerked her to him. "I know my son came to town for your mother's funeral, and I know he stayed at your place. Two days later, he changed his will to give all his money to charity." He jerked her closer, ignoring her yelp of pain. "If I find out that you convinced him to change his will, I promise you will suffer—"

"Hey." Chase stepped between them, using his body to force the older man back. "Let go of her."

Alan stared at him, and his fingers tightened around Mira's arm. "Who the hell are you?"

Chase's hand balled into a fist instinctively. "Let her go," he repeated, his voice lethally soft. All the lessons he'd learned about violence from his piece-of-shit dad came rushing back, and his knuckles tingled, anticipating the impact before he even moved to strike.

The old man glared at him. For a long moment, they simply stared at each other, and then Alan's eyes widened, apparently seeing in Chase's eyes exactly the kind of no-good, bastard genes that ran through him.

With a low swear, Alan released Mira, shoving her back hard enough to make her stumble.

Chase caught her before she could fall, pulling her against him as she rubbed her upper arm. He could feel her trembling against him, and it made more anger roll through him. "Mira Cabot is under my protection," he said, an unspoken threat lacing his words. "Remember that."

Alan gave him a thin smile. "I own this town, cowboy. You remember that." He shot another vicious glare at Mira, and then spun on his heel. A woman draped in diamonds accosted him, and he graced her with a smile charming enough to win over the most bitter of old women.

"Bastard," Chase muttered.

"Thanks," Mira said, leaning into him for a brief moment.

He nodded, not taking his gaze off Alan, daring the old man to come back. "No problem. Glad I was here."

"Me, too." She paused, drawing his attention to her. There were circles beneath her eyes, and she looked exhausted.

He frowned. "Are you okay?"

"Fine. I just need to get out of here." She managed a smile that didn't reach her eyes. "Thanks again. It was good to meet you. Have a good flight back to Wyoming." Dismissing him, Mira ducked past him, no longer heading for the bathroom, but for the exit. She was walking fast, not even noticing the people who tried to engage her in conversation.

Chase hesitated. He could let her go. He could allow her to walk out the door, and she wouldn't be his problem. He didn't trust women. Ever. He couldn't afford to take on her problems. He had rules that he hadn't strayed from for fifteen years. He'd made a promise, and he couldn't risk being derailed from it. Following Mira out that door was the wrong choice on every damn level... except for the fact that she was in trouble, she was AJ's best friend, and he owed AJ his life.

Shit. He had only one choice, didn't he?

Swearing, he jammed his hand into his pocket for his car keys, and followed her out the door.

🐾 🐾 🐾

Twenty minutes later, Mira slammed her car door shut, the sound reverberating in the dark night. She kicked off her high heels, and then broke into a run, her bare feet sinking into the damp grass. She didn't slow down until she got to the edge of the river.

The water was rushing, churning violently after the recent rainstorm. The familiar sound wrapped around her like a blanket, easing the tightness gripping her so ruthlessly. She slowed to a jog and then finally stopped beneath the huge willow tree on the edge of the river.

Her initials were carved into the trunk just below AJ's, and she traced her fingers over them, remembering how many times they'd hid by the river when his father was looking for them. The old pieces of wood they'd used for a ladder were still there, crookedly nailed to the tree trunk. AJ had been three years older than she, so she'd climbed that tree by herself many times after he left for college. It had always made her feel closer to him, despite the fact he was gone. Maybe it would work today as well.

She grabbed one of them, testing it. The wood was cracked and rotting a bit, but it seemed strong enough. Besides, what was the worst that could happen? That she'd fall a few feet to the muddy ground? Not exactly a mind-numbing tragedy.

Almost hoping for the distraction of a fall, she quickly pulled herself up the ladder they'd built for themselves so long ago.

A few seconds later, she was perched in the crook of the tree, her knees pulled to her chest. She took a deep breath, letting the damp air fill her lungs. She hadn't come here in so long, but suddenly, tonight, she'd had to return. She looked up into the starry sky, barely visible through the thick branches. How many nights had she sat in that tree, making wishes about a future that had never unfolded to match her dreams? "AJ," she whispered. "I don't know what to do. This was really bad timing for you to die, you know that, don't you?"

Of course he didn't answer. It was just a lonely, empty silence.

Headlights swept across the riverbank, and she glanced over her shoulder as a black pickup truck swung in beside her battered sedan. Stiffening, she sat up, watching as the driver's door opened. The broad-shouldered silhouette that emerged from the car was immediately recognizable, and it wasn't simply because of the cowboy hat. There was a lithe grace and rugged strength that emanated from Chase, as if he were a man who could barely contain his true self long enough to survive in polite society for an evening.

She nestled deeper into the crook of the tree as he scanned the area, then grimaced as he stepped into the grass and headed right for her. She watched with growing dread as he walked straight to the tree, and peered up at her. "Got space up there?"

His deep voice rumbled through her just as it had at the church. There was something so warm in his voice. It seemed to wrap around her like a blanket, at the same time it rolled through her belly like a searing kiss designed to make her insides burn. "Not really," she said. Between the shadows and the brim of his hat, she couldn't really see his face. "I'm not feeling sociable right now."

"Yeah, me either. I hate crowds of superficial bastards. They always make me cranky."

To her surprise, she found herself laughing, despite her cranky mood. "Okay, fine, you can come up, but I can't promise I'll be good company."

"No problem. I'm rarely good company myself." He swung up the ladder with the practiced ease of a man who was used to a physical life. He settled in beside her in the crevice that had always had plenty of room for her and AJ. Now, however, it felt cramped and tiny. Chase's shoulder was against hers, and there wasn't enough space for her to move away.

Then he leaned back against the tree trunk, adjusting so they weren't touching. Although she was grateful for the space, at the same time, a part of her wanted to inch just close enough to him to feel the heat of his body against hers, penetrating the cold that seemed to be buried so deeply inside her.

Chase clasped his hands behind his head and propped his feet up on another branch. He tipped his hat over his eyes, as if he were stretching out in a hammock for a nap instead of invading her personal space in a tree fifteen feet in the air.

He said nothing, and after a few moments, she began to relax. The night sounds returned to her. She listened to the roar of the river, the chirp of birds, and the rustling of the leaves in the tree. With Chase beside her, the moment felt complete. This place had been meant for two people, and she was used to a comforting male presence beside her.

Chase wasn't AJ, but in a way he was, and that made him safe enough for her to relax around. She rested her chin on her knees and thought about the last few weeks, trying to figure out what she was going to do. Somehow, with Chase beside her, her life didn't feel so overwhelming. She still didn't have any answers, but at least she felt composed enough to think clearly.

"He'll figure it out, you know," Chase said after a while.

She jumped, startled by the sound of his voice, and his hand shot out to steady her, settling around her elbow with effortless ease. "Sorry. I was in my own world," she said, her heart hammering at the sensation of his fingers grasping her arm.

"I noticed."

"You did?" She realized that although his hat was tipped forward, it didn't obscure his eyes. He was watching her intently.

Awareness tingled over her skin. "Who will figure what out?" She didn't actually care what he was talking about. She just wanted a distraction from how she was reacting to him.

"Alan."

She frowned. "AJ's dad? He'll figure out what?"

Chase's eyes bore into her, and with sudden dread, she knew what he was going to say before he said it. *Oh, no.* She definitely didn't want to get into that discussion with him. "I'm getting tired," she said quickly, faking a yawn. "I think I'll be heading home." She pushed lightly at his legs, urging him to move out of the way.

He didn't. Instead he sat up, moving with a slow, relaxed ease that was in direct contrast to the sudden pounding of her heart. He leaned forward, his gaze boring into her relentlessly. "Alan's going to figure out that you and AJ slept together when he was here for your mom's funeral. He's going to realize you're pregnant with AJ's kid, who happens to be Alan's grandchild, and his best chance for an heir to his throne."

Mira felt like her entire world had congealed into horror. "I'm not—" She stopped herself before she'd even completed the lie. What was the point? Chase would never believe her. Instead, she sagged back against the tree, too exhausted to fight the battle she'd already lost. "How did you figure it out?"

He shrugged. "I'm a master of observation." His words were light, but his eyes were still boring into hers. "Alan's a bastard. He'll have legal custody of that kid before it's even born."

Mira bit her lip. "I know he'll try." She managed a smile. "It's okay. I've already figured it out. I'll leave town. He won't bother to track me." But even as she said it, she remembered Alan's accusation at the hotel ballroom. If he thought she'd influenced AJ's will, he *would* pursue her relentlessly, no matter where she went.

No, no, no. She couldn't worry about that. She and AJ had never discussed his will, and she had to believe Alan would realize that and let her disappear.

Chase said nothing for a long moment, and she began to relax. Then, he said. "What are you going to do for money? Last I heard, you had to quit even your part-time admin job to take care of your mom. You've been moonlighting as in the office of the middle school, but with school budget cuts, there hasn't been much work. Do you even have savings?"

"I'll find something." She lifted her chin, annoyed that AJ seemed to have shared so much about her situation. "There's no reason for me to stay in town, now that my mom and dad are both gone." Well, there was no reason except for her one, dear friend, Taylor Shaw. New tears threatened. Taylor had been her rock over the last few years. How could she leave her behind? How on earth would she ever start over by herself? She managed a perky grin. "It'll be an adventure."

Again, Chase was silent, and she wondered if he believed her. Even she didn't believe it, but she had to.

"And if Alan finds you in six months with a swollen belly? Or in a year with an infant on your hip? What happens then?"

Mira swallowed. There was no good answer to that. They both knew what Alan was like.

Chase finally tipped his hat back, so she could see his face more clearly. His jaw was angular, and the moon was casting his face into shadows. He looked dangerous and lethal, the kind of man who would walk beside her with a machete if that was what it took to keep her safe.

"I owe AJ my life," he said quietly. "You're the only person in this world who really mattered to him, and now, he has a kid on the way. You're both in danger, and he's not around to protect you. So it's my job."

"Danger?" She managed to laugh. "I think you're being a little melodramatic."

He unfastened the cuff of his shirt and jerked the sleeve up. His muscular forearm was covered with dozens of small round scars, just like the ones that had covered AJ's back. Her heart clenched, and she put her hand over the marks. His muscle flexed beneath her touch, but neither of them pulled away. "Cigarette burns?" she asked softly.

He nodded. "I know what AJ's dad is like, because mine wasn't that different."

Sadness bore down on her, and she wanted to hug this man she'd just met. She knew the kind of pain a man like Alan could inflict on his son, and it made her sad to think Chase had endured the same things as AJ. "I didn't know. He never told me that about you."

Chase shrugged, dismissing her sympathy as he pulled his sleeve back down. "There's no chance in hell I'm leaving you unprotected," he said. This time, there was no hesitation. He just looked right at her. "Tonight, I'll spend the night at your place, and leave my truck in your driveway for the whole town to see."

She gaped at him. "If you do that, everyone will think that I picked you up, and we had sex the night of my best friend's funeral."

He nodded. "I'm a couple weeks late, but the timing should work okay for the baby."

Tears filled her eyes as she realized what he was offering. "You want the world to think you're the biological father of AJ's baby?" Then she could stay in town. She didn't have to leave.

He looked at her, and her words died in her throat at the expression on his face. There was something else he hadn't said. "What?"

"It's not enough," he said. "You know that won't be sufficient against Alan. It's a start, but it needs more. He'll know damn well that there's an equal chance it could be AJ's baby, and he won't stop until he's certain. A DNA test is going to tell him what he wants to know."

Mira bit her lip, the fleeting hope abandoning her. "You're right."

"There's only one way." He brushed his fingers through her hair, ever so slightly. His face was dark and intense, his eyes turbulent with emotions she couldn't begin to decipher. "After we set the stage tonight, you're going to have to move to Wyoming and marry me."

Chapter 3

Chase almost laughed at the expression of absolute horror on Mira's face. It wasn't that different from what he'd felt the moment he'd proposed to her. Shock, surprise, and yeah, maybe a little horror. He hadn't intended to offer to marry her. He hadn't intended to ever offer to marry *anyone*, but now that he'd done it, it felt right. He knew in his gut that it was his duty to be there for both of them.

She, however, didn't appear to agree with him. "Oh, no. *No.*" She shook her head, scrambling backward so fast she almost fell out of the tree.

Chase caught her arm just as she started to slide backwards. "Why not? I'm a great guy. You know I am."

Her mouth dropped open. "Marry you? Seriously? No." She twisted her arm free, and scrambled over his legs. Her breasts brushed over his arm, and desire clenched through him. For a brief moment, her body was pretzeled up with his, and then she was over him and flying down the makeshift ladder.

For a brief moment, he considered not following her. He really didn't want to get married any more than she did. He never had. But he thought of the cigarette burns on AJ's back, and he knew there was no way he was going to leave AJ's kid to face that future.

Swearing, he swung down from the tree, not even bothering with the ladder. He sprinted after Mira, who was running toward her car. He caught up to her just before she got her door open.

He leaned against the door and folded his arms across his chest, blocking her access to the car. Her face was pale in the moonlight, and something tugged inside him at the vulnerability of her expression. "I didn't mean to scare you," he said softly, using the same tone he reserved for frightened horses.

Mira backed up, then set her hands on her hips, visibly summoning her strength. One strap of her dress had slid off her shoulder and down her arm, a visceral reminder of both her femininity and her vulnerability. "I am not going to marry you," she said.

"Why not? It seems like a logical choice." He wanted to slide his fingers beneath that strap and coax it back in place. He could imagine how soft her skin was…shit. He dragged his gaze off her shoulder and pinned it to her face.

"It's not just you," she explained. "I'm not going to marry anyone."

He frowned at her blanket statement, which sounded way too much like something he'd say. "Why not?"

"Don't you know?" She cocked her head, apparently confused. "You seem to know everything about me."

"I have no idea what you're talking about." He shrugged, and held out his hands in a gesture intended to make him appear harmless, despite the fact he was still firmly blocking her car door. "Tell me."

She sighed, and pulled the strap back up over her shoulder. "When I went to college, I fell in love freshman year. I got engaged. We were going to get married the summer after my sophomore year."

Sudden jealousy surged through Chase. She'd been engaged? Why the hell hadn't he known about that? "What happened?"

"What happened?" Her voice became slightly high-pitched, revealing emotion he could tell she was struggling to contain. "I got a call that my parents had been in a car accident. My dad was dead, and my mom was paralyzed."

Chase swore under his breath. He remembered that call. AJ had been absolutely devastated. Mira's parents had been the only source of love and family AJ had ever had, especially Mira's dad. As sheriff, he'd been the one man in town with the power to stand up to Alan and protect AJ from him, and he'd done it repeatedly. The tragedy had derailed AJ. Maybe that was why AJ had never mentioned Mira's romantic entanglements at the time. During that period, AJ hadn't cared about anything other than the loss of Mira's dad.

"I decided to drop out of school to take care of my mom," Mira continued, her voice becoming calmer now, as if she'd somehow managed to separate herself from the memories. "My fiancé refused to even come to the funeral, because it was too close to exams and he needed to study. After two months, he called and announced he didn't want to marry someone who was stuck caring for an invalid. He said I had to come back to school and live a real life, or he was calling off the engagement." Tears filled her eyes. "I loved him, and my family had been taken away from me. I had no one to lean on except him. How could I let him go? I told him I would come back to school, but I needed more time to get things settled with my mom. For two weeks, I tried frantically to find a way to secure care for her, but I was really struggling to find someone I trusted. I wasn't fast enough, and he broke up with me. He married my roommate three months later."

Shit. Chase shook his head in empathy. He knew what it felt like to be hit when he was down. It sucked. "Bastard."

A strangled laugh choked out, a breath of humor breaking through the pain in her blue eyes. "I won't do that again."

"Get engaged?"

She shook her head. "No, count on a man like that and commit to him. I was actually willing to give up taking care of my mom for him. What if I'd done it? What if I'd left my mom to wither and die in some nursing home so I could marry some jerk?"

He touched her arm. "You didn't do that. It's okay, Mira."

"But I *would have* if he hadn't dumped me." She sighed, searching his face for understanding. "I'm so scared of how close I came to marrying someone who would have taken me away from what was important to me. I won't ever give someone that kind of power again. My parents loved each other unconditionally. It was so beautiful, and I thought I had that with Brian, but I was wrong. I was stupid and desperate, and willing to marry a jerk just to have the fairy tale." She ran her fingers through her hair, her hands shaking. "I realized that it's better to never be married than to settle for less than what my parents had." She met his gaze, and he saw the depth of torment in her eyes. He realized then how deeply she'd been traumatized. "I know you're AJ's best friend, but how on earth can I trust you with my life and my child's? Because it's not just AJ's baby. It's mine, too."

Chase was stunned by her story. AJ had told him how she'd stepped up to take care of her mom, but Chase had never comprehended how much she'd had to endure. He had always thought of her as the rock, the steady balance in life, and yet she'd suffered greatly. He felt her pain, the betrayal she'd endured, and her genuine fear of being married to someone who would betray her. "I get it," he said. And he did. She'd been burned badly, and she was smart enough not to want to risk it again.

She blinked. "What do you mean?"

He sighed at the question, realizing that she'd read more into his statement than he'd meant to share. But she'd been honest with him, and she deserved the same thing in return. "My mother died when I was born," he explained. "I never knew her. But my dad married three more times, and all three of my stepmothers were brutal, on many different levels, not to mention some assorted girlfriends that he mixed in." He didn't want to go into the details, because he'd long ago stopped wasting energy on them, but he needed Mira to understand. "I watched them tear my father apart, and destroy what was left of my family. I watched my brothers suffer as each one was born, and I fought so hard to protect them all from the women my dad had chosen. As bad as my dad was, the women he married made him worse. I don't trust women. I don't trust marriage. And I'd never give a woman any power over me."

He couldn't keep the coldness out of his voice, and she cocked her head, listening intently. "Then why would you ever offer to marry me?" She didn't sound scared. She actually sounded relieved, as if his antipathy toward marriage eased some of her fear.

"Because you're Mira Cabot." He walked over to her and took her hands. Her fingers were cold, but her hands weren't trembling anymore. "I've known you vicariously through AJ for over a decade, and I know what kind of person you are. You're the one person in the world he trusted, and that means you're the one person in the world that I know I can trust as well."

Her eyes glistened with sudden moisture. "I'm not an angel, Chase."

"No. I know that. I know you get cranky as hell when you're hungry or tired. I know you stole a gun from your dad's squad car when you were fourteen because you were going to shoot Alan with it. I also know you cheated on your seventh grade geography test."

Her eyes widened. "You know all that, but you didn't know I was engaged?"

He paused at her question. Why hadn't AJ told him that? Had it just been because AJ had been distracted, or had it been something else? And what else didn't he know about her? Suddenly, he wanted to know. He wanted to sit her down and grill her with a thousand questions, discovering everything about this woman who had existed only in his imagination for the last ten years.

Mira pulled her hands out of his. "Listen, Chase, it's very heroic of you to sweep in and rescue me, but we both know it won't work—"

"I'll have my lawyer draw up a contract. Child support, alimony, and everything you'll need. We'll live together at my ranch for a year. Once the baby is born, and we've solidified my fatherhood, we'll get 'divorced.' This won't be a real marriage, Mira. Just a business partnership designed to protect you and the baby."

She cocked her head, studying him. For the first time, she looked thoughtful. "A business partnership?"

"To protect you and the baby," he repeated. Alan was lethal, and his tentacles were strong and powerful. Chase knew he'd have to address every possible eventuality to ensure Alan could never take the child. "I owe AJ a life debt. You can trust that, if nothing else. AJ was a distrustful loner, and you know he wouldn't have trusted me unless I deserved it."

She studied him for a long moment, then she reached into her purse. She pulled out a cell phone encased in a cracked, black case. Silently, she scrolled through it, and then held it out to him. He looked down and saw his name, cell phone, and current address listed in her contacts. He frowned. "How did you get this information?"

"AJ always believed he would die young. He knew his time on this earth would be short, and he worked hard to make his imprint in the time he had." Her voice trembled slightly, and she cleared her throat. "After my dad died, AJ was concerned that there was no one to protect me. He told me that if I ever ran into trouble and he wasn't around to help, then I should go to you. He made sure I always had your updated contact information. Every time you moved, I knew how to find you at any hour of the day."

Son of a bitch. Chase closed his fingers around the phone. "He didn't tell me he gave you my info."

"He said you didn't need to know. He said you'd just say yes." She managed a smile. "What he didn't say was that you would come riding up gallantly on your white horse and throw yourself at my feet in a desperate attempt to save me when I didn't even ask for help."

"My horse isn't white. He's a bay, and he'd be highly insulted to know you called him white." Chase knew why AJ hadn't told him that he was first in line as Mira's savior.

If he had, Chase would have found a way to talk him out of it. He wasn't a protector, and he didn't have time to do anything but focus on repairing the damage his father had done to him and his brothers. And yet, Chase had decided to rescue her anyway, all on his own. "You would never have come to me for help, would you?"

She shook her head. "Never." She shrugged. "I'm kind of an independent girl. I like to save the world on my own."

"Yeah, I suspect you do." He cocked his head thoughtfully. "AJ knew you'd never ask, didn't he?"

She nodded slowly. "Yes, he probably did." She looked at him. "So why did he give me your information?"

Chase rubbed his jaw. "He knew that I'd offer. By telling you that I was the guy to ask for help, he was setting the stage for you to trust me, so that when I offered to help, you'd let me. He had it planned all along, didn't he? Manipulative bastard." He couldn't keep the affection out of his voice. AJ had known them both too well.

She laughed then, her fingers brushing against his as she retrieved her phone from him. "You're much more stubborn than I'd have expected you to be, getting all insistent on marrying me."

He grinned. "You're a hell of a lot more difficult to convince than I'd have anticipated. AJ led me to believe you had the ability to think logically. I had no idea you would get all emotional on me. I'm not really into the emotional thing, just so you know."

"Well, you'll have to learn to deal with it," she said, poking the phone into his chest. "I'm highly emotional. I find it cathartic. Suppressing emotions will never get you anywhere."

Her words made something leap through him. "I'll have to learn to deal with it? Is that your way of saying, 'Yes, Chase, I am willing to sully my pristine reputation by getting knocked up by you and then running off to Wyoming to be your shotgun bride?'"

She laughed out loud then, a sound that made him chuckle. Damn, she had an engaging laugh. "A shotgun bride sounds so romantic," she remarked with a deadpan expression. "I've always dreamed of it."

He stiffened at her words, knowing full well how women fantasized about their weddings. He didn't want her to have expectations that he would inevitably fail to meet. "I'm busy on the ranch," he warned her. "I can't be the husband type, so don't expect it. One year of cohabitation while you get big and fat with my kid."

"Well, I have no interest in turning my loyalties over to a husband, so we're even." She cocked her head, and he saw her eyes soften. "*Your* kid? You said that like it was already true, like you mean it."

He nodded, possessiveness surging through him. "There's no halfway in my book. Yeah, I'm claiming that baby that's in your belly. Obviously, I have sperm of steel to knock you up long distance, but hey, I've always been an overachiever."

He reached out and put his hand on her stomach, feeling the softness of her flesh beneath his touch. "That's my kid in there, Mira. From this moment onward, there is no other truth."

"I believe you," she said softly as she put her hand over his, not to pull him off her belly, but to hold his hand there. It was an intimate moment, one he'd never thought he'd experience, but it felt right. "You truly will stand beside AJ's child as your own, no matter what."

"Of course."

She bit her lip. "One year?"

Hope surged through him, and fear, but also something else. A feeling of anticipation that he hadn't experienced in a long time. A year of Mira living in his house sounded good. Really, really good. "One year. Then you're free, but even after we divorce, I'll always, *always*, be Dad. I won't fail either of you."

She stood on her tiptoes and pressed a kiss to his cheek. Her lips were warm and soft, and the kiss far too fleeting. "Well then, cowboy, you better get your shotgun, because you just got yourself a bride."

Chapter 4

Mira was sitting on her living room couch, grimly studying the stack of moving boxes in the corner, ready to be put into storage. Prior to Chase's proposal, she'd already had almost the entire house packed up to be sold. The house was going on the market in three days, regardless of whether she left town or not.

She had no choice but to let go of the house she'd grown up in. She needed the money from the sale of the house to pay off her mother's remaining medical expenses. It was the right thing to do. But sitting there, surrounded by the things that reflected her past, including the last remnants of her parents' belongings, it suddenly felt clinical and cold to be packing up and moving out, to be leaving so she could marry a man she didn't even know.

It had been bad enough selling the house when she was at least going to stay in town and do something heroic like try to get a job filing permits at the town office. But to be leaving behind every last memory of her family to marry a stranger and possibly raise a child in the barren, friendless world of the untamed west? It felt a little barbaric.

She looked around the living room. The walls were empty now, but the outlines of the picture frames had left marks on the formerly white paint that had since turned yellow and stained. Thirty-two years of sunlight had left their mark.

She knew every photograph that had once hung on the walls. Her parents' wedding picture. Her baby picture. Her dad's first day on the job as sheriff. A photo of her and AJ at their high school graduation, bedecked in their black gowns and huge smiles.

Every memory of a lifetime was now packed away. She was taking only one photograph, the one taken of her and her parents the day they'd dropped her off at college. It was the last time she'd seen them both alive and healthy. Her mother's clothes were already bagged up to be donated to charity. Her life, her world, stripped away—

The front door slammed open, making Mira jump as her best friend, Taylor Shaw, strode in. "You slept with him? After all these years, you finally met Chase Stockton, and then slept with him? Why didn't you tell me?"

Mira grinned at Taylor's energetic, unapologetic entrance. The mere appearance of her friend made her feel better. "You were on a transcontinental flight at the time," she said. "I figured it could wait."

"Sex can never wait, especially for you, my celibate friend." Taylor was wearing jeans, her favorite pink sweatshirt, and a pair of old flip-flops, indicating that she'd just arrived home from her trip to Indonesia. Taylor always went for her comfy clothes after spending an eternity on a plane. Her curly mop of blond hair was somewhat bouncing irreverently around her face, but the three-inch gold hoops dangling from her ears added that hint of femininity she never seemed to lack. "I had to hear about it from Octavia, who accosted me before I even pulled into my driveway. Apparently, the whole town saw his truck in front of your house all night after the funeral. You're a complete slut, and I mean that in the most affectionate, supportive way." She flopped down on the couch, then glanced around at the boxes. "Did you find a place yet? Clock's ticking."

Mira grinned at the change in subject. Taylor never worried about societal proprieties. She just dealt with life straight on, and she loved that about her friend. "I sort of found a place," she said, hesitating before explaining further. She still hadn't decided whether to tell Taylor the truth about the pregnancy. Chase had been adamant that no one could know AJ was the biological father, because Alan was just that good. But Taylor was her best friend, the one who had stood by her all the years while she'd been taking care of her mom. "I'm moving to Wyoming to live with Chase," she said carefully, testing the waters. "To marry him, actually." The words tasted thick and muddy on her tongue, and for a moment, she felt like she was going to throw up. What had seemed like a solid, logical solution two nights ago now sounded...less than sane, pretty much.

Taylor's blue eyes widened. "*What?*" Then she sighed. "Oh, man, I know you're devastated by AJ's death, but marrying his best friend isn't going to bring him back, not for either of you. One night of sex doesn't create that kind of bond. Just because AJ loved Chase doesn't mean that you would automatically love him. You've hated every boyfriend I've ever had, right? Love doesn't translate across third parties."

"Yeah, true, but that's because you have singularly bad taste in men."

Taylor wrinkled her nose. "This is about you, not me, and the fact you're having a thinly disguised emotional collapse. To be expected, of course, but marrying a hot cowboy is a bit of a permanent solution, you know? Although, as bad decisions go, I guess it could be worse, like throwing yourself off a cliff, for example. "

Mira picked up a tape gun and dragged it across one of the few remaining boxes, locking away more of her past. "It's kind of a trial thing. For a year." She sliced the tape off, then grabbed a marker to jot a note about the contents on the side of it.

"A year? What?" Taylor stood up, her hands on her hips. "This is completely unaccceptable. I'm going to kidnap you. We're going to have a crazy girls' weekend and you'll realize that you can handle your life just fine, even though it kind of feels overwhelming right now." She held out her hand, and wiggled her fingers for Mira to take them. "Come on. Let's leave now. We'll be back in two days, enough time to finish clearing out the boxes before it goes on the market."

"I'm pregnant." The words burst out of her mouth before she'd even decided to say them.

Well, so much for not telling Taylor the truth. But just saying it felt like a thousand burdens had fallen off her shoulders.

"What?" Taylor's mouth dropped open, and her hand

fell limply to her side. "How could you possibly know already? It's been twenty-four hours since he left."

God, here it came. Was she really going to tell her? Mira dragged another box over to her to tape it, avoiding Taylor's gaze. "Yeah, well, when my mom died last month, AJ came to town to see me. He stayed over."

Taylor sank back onto the couch beside her. "You slept with *AJ*? But you guys are completely platonic. Like siblings, though not actually siblings, for which I think we're both eternally grateful given the fact that he *knocked you up.* Dear God. How is this possible? There's no connection between you guys."

"Was," Mira corrected. "And I know there was no romance between us. It was a one-night thing. We were both in bad shape, because you know how much he loved my mom. She was more his mom than his own mother was. We cried, we held each other, and then it just happened."

"Oh, God." Taylor leaned forward, searching her face. "Was it good? Was it worth a ten-year dry spell?"

"Eight years, and it was perfect, in the way that it was, but no, nothing really sexy about it." She still couldn't believe she'd been naked with him, but being held in his arms when the grief had been so overwhelming was a gift she'd never forget. Neither of them would have made it through that night alone.

"Wow." Taylor rubbed her forehead. "It's AJ's baby, for sure? Did he know before he died?"

"No. I just found out Wednesday morning."

"Oh, *God.* On the morning of his *funeral?*" Taylor shook her head. "You know, AJ would probably have loved that timing. He'd want you to be looking toward the future instead of wallowing in the past. Can't you see him in heaven, cheering you on as you pee a stick right before his funeral?"

Mira managed a smile. "This is true. He would have enjoyed that."

"Knowing AJ, he probably did it on purpose. He decided to leave behind a legacy, and figured you were the one woman with enough cojones to kick his dad's ass if he came after the kid. So, yay, girl power, I guess? Maybe you could get like an award or something?"

This time, the laughter bubbled out. "You're insane, Taylor."

"I know. It's my gift. But I'm guessing that since you discovered your MTB status after his skydiving accident, you weren't able to scrape any money from him? All to charity?"

"Yep. And what's MTB status?"

"Mother-to-be, of course. Hello, get with the times." Taylor eyed her belly. "Is it kicking yet?"

"Talking actually. Asked me for cash yesterday. I told it to get a job. I feel like I need to set some standards early on, you know? My dad would never approve of being soft with the kid."

"Amen, sistah. Sheriff Cabot will be watching you." Taylor leaned back and propped her feet up on a cardboard box. "So, what's the old bastard's status?"

"Alan? He knows AJ spent the night after the funeral. He thinks I used my body to convince AJ to change his will. I suspect he's going to try to use me to invalidate the will."

Taylor nodded. "Rock on. So he's after you for money, but in the process of trying to expose you for the deceitful fraud we all know you are, he'll get the delightful surprise of figuring out that when you croon to your uterus, you're actually talking to his grandchild. How fun is that? It's like a cat and mouse game, but he's this shape-shifting, immortally deadly panther, and you're like, a stuffed mouse, staked out in the yard, waiting to be munched."

Mira blinked. "I think my odds are a little better than that."

"Sweetie, no one's odds are better than that when it comes to Alan. Your dad was the only one who could stop Alan. The only reason Alan respected your dad was because he knew that your dad would shoot him if necessary, all in the name of duty, of course, but still. Once your dad died, there was no one to stop Alan. AJ had to forget to open his parachute in order to escape him. You think you can dodge that bullet?"

Mira frowned. "AJ didn't forget to open his parachute. It was faulty." But even as she said it, she remembered all too clearly the Christmas Eve she'd found him on the South Bridge, ready to jump into the freezing water when he was thirteen. If she'd been five minutes later, she would have lost him that night, instead of a few days ago. Deflated, she sank down. "You think AJ killed himself?" She hadn't thought of that, but it was possible.

Taylor shrugged. "I don't know, Mira, but it wouldn't surprise me. You know perfectly well that Alan was trying to buy AJ's company so he could steal it from him and force AJ home. He almost did it too. His reach is incredible. AJ believed in life after death, so, yeah, I think it's very possible he figured the next life was better than this one." She cocked her head. "And now you have to take on Alan yourself. You'll lose, you know. You'll lose the battle, and you'll lose the kid."

Well, there was nothing like stark honesty from a best friend to make a girl more convinced that marrying a total stranger might actually be the least insane choice at the moment. "That's why Chase and I set it up to make it look like I slept with him. He's claiming to be the dad."

"Seriously? You didn't sleep with Chase?" Taylor looked at her thoughtfully. "That's sort of heroic of him."

"Isn't it? After I stopped freaking out at the sound of the words, 'marry me,' I came to the same conclusion."

"It may be control-freak, hero-complex, overcompensating-male 'heroic,' but it also could be simple super-nice-guy 'heroic.'" Taylor settled more deeply into the couch. "Girl, I think you need to tell me everything."

Mira did. Forty minutes and a pint of ice cream later, the entire sordid story had been replayed. Just retelling the facts had reinforced the enormity of the situation she was facing, and the magnitude of the decision she'd made with Chase. "So, I'm heading off to Wyoming to enter into a one-year business contract involving illusionary sex and marriage vows that are total lies. I think it's the perfect foundation for a relationship, don't you?"

"Absolutely. We need more marriages based on lies, abstinence, and the exchange of money." Taylor folded her arms across her chest. "But I have to admit, I'm going to have to veto it. You can't marry him."

Mira's heart fell. "What are you saying? I needed your support. I thought you were on board with it. I'm a little freaked out about moving to Wyoming to marry a guy I barely know. I need a kick in the pants, not someone telling me I can't do it. AJ trusted him, so—"

"I know, I know." Taylor waved her hand dismissively. "I'm sure Chase is a great guy, and he'll fulfill his part of the bargain. I trust AJ's judgment. And you do need help dealing with Alan, or you're never going to see your child again. I'm on board with all that."

Mira frowned. "Then why did you say I can't go?"

"Because, my dear friend, of how you look when you talk about him."

Something clenched in Mira's belly, and heat suffused her cheeks. "How I look?"

"Yes. You got a little starry-eyed, girl."

"What? I so did not. I don't even have that gene anymore when it comes to guys."

"You do, and you did." Taylor pried herself off the couch and knelt in front of Mira, putting her hands on Mira's knees, searching Mira's face with the earnestness of a best friend. "You believe in him, Mira. You don't know him, but a little part of you is a little bit in love with him."

"*What?*" She gaped at her friend. "You're insane—"

Taylor rolled her eyes. "Yes, we already covered that, and I concur. However, I'm also right. Insane people can be correct a large percentage of the time. And you, my dear friend, are looking at Chase like he's going to swoop in and whisk you off to the land of magic and fairy tales, just like you did with Brian."

Mira snorted, laughing at her friend's description, refusing to give credence to it. "Seriously with that, Taylor? I'm not like that anymore. I don't get dreamy about guys, and I am very clear on the fact that I do *not* want to be rescued by any man, ever again. I'm using Chase to rescue myself. There's a difference. He's like a hammer. Or a roll of duct tape. Things you can use in an emergency to save your life."

Taylor's eyebrows shot up. "Chase is duct tape? Really?"

"Yeah. Not the boring gray kind. He's like that crazy kind with the cool colors. He's pretty duct tape that smells good." She shrugged, recalling his scent when he'd climbed into the tree with her. "Duct tape with a nice voice, too. And shoulders. Great shoulders. He's like designer duct tape—you appreciate how fantastic it looks, but in the end, you use it to tape the fender on your car just the way you'd use any other duct tape. I'm marrying duct tape for the sake of my unborn child. It's pretty basic. No love involved."

Taylor snorted. "You're pregnant, broke, and alone. Your mom just died. Your best friend and the father of your baby just died. You've spent all your money taking care of your mom, and selling the house will barely even cover medical expenses. You are incredibly resourceful and practical, and yes, Chase is definitely duct tape of the highest quality, but you're *seeing* him with your hopeful little heart instead of your practical Girl Scout hands." She sighed. "Besides, what woman wouldn't want to be rescued by a handsome cowboy? Because I heard he was devastatingly handsome, and his rental car wasn't exactly cheap."

Mira bit her lower lip. "I did notice that he's handsome," she admitted. "And nice. I definitely noticed both of those things." Crud. Was Taylor right? Was she really being stupid again, like she'd been with Brian? She was too smart to get emotionally invested in another man, especially when something this important was at stake.

Taylor tucked Mira's hair behind her ear. "You don't need to tie yourself down forever to a man just to get out of this current situation. Marriage is forever, babe. Even if you get divorced, he'll be on record as that baby's father, which gives him rights. Trust me, you don't want that with the wrong guy."

"Parental rights?" Wow. She'd forgotten about that. Weight settled on Mira's shoulders, dragging her down. "I can't fight Alan on my own. You know that." Her hand settled protectively over her belly.

"We'll think of something." Taylor squeezed her hand. "You have several months before you'll start to show. Rushing off to marry Chase is the wrong choice. You're panicking, and you're seeing him through rose-colored glasses because you're desperate."

Mira closed her eyes, trying to quell the rising sense of panic. "I'm not wrong about him. I can trust him."

"Just like you could trust Brian?"

"Dammit, Taylor!" Mira pulled away and stood up. She walked across the room and braced her hands on the window frame, staring out at the tiny, weed-filled yard that her parents had once tended so lovingly. Was Taylor right? Was she being stupid again? Was she overreacting to her situation? She'd always managed to pull herself through every situation. Why would this one be different?

But it was different, because it wasn't only her own life that she had in her hands. It was her baby's. AJ's baby. A child with a horrible, horrible enemy who was stronger than she was.

"I'll help," Taylor said. "You're not alone."

Mira laughed softly, and turned to face her. "Taylor, you travel almost all the time for your job. I love you, but your life is on the road, in every country but this one. You couldn't even get your boss to let you off to come home for the funeral. I'm the one living here, who has to face my life."

Taylor didn't give up. "I have money. I'll give you some."

"Even if you gave me every last cent you had, it wouldn't be enough to fight Alan, and we both know it."

Taylor bit her lip, and gave a slight nod. "He is a pretty rich bastard," she acknowledged with a grimace.

Mira looked around the room. This time, instead of lost memories, she saw only the faded paint on the walls and the tattered carpet. The air was tinged with the scent of hospitals and sick people, and the odor of mold that could never quite be cleansed. "I don't want to be here anymore, Taylor. I almost got out and started a life when my parents got in the accident, and now I am not only free to go, but I have motivation to leave." She met her friend's gaze. "I want to get out. I want to do this. Chase is giving me the chance to start a new life, and I want to do it."

Taylor studied her, then sighed. "Okay, then. Go to Wyoming, but put off the wedding. Get your freedom, get your feet under you again, but don't trap yourself or that baby. Escaping Alan is worth nothing if you get yourself in a trap that will haunt you forever." Involuntarily, Taylor rubbed her ring finger on her left hand. It was empty now, but it hadn't always been.

A chill crept over Mira, remembering what Taylor had endured at the hands of a man that the entire town had loved. "You have a point," she conceded.

"Of course I do. We've both made terrible, terrible mistakes when it comes to men. They were both men we had every reason to believe in, and we were wrong. You don't even know Chase, other than what AJ has said about him." She gave Mira a steely look. "Protect yourself, Mira. Don't fantasize that he's some fairy tale hero. Chase is a man, and by definition, that means he's flawed. Never forget that." She sighed wistfully. "Your dad's not around with his gun anymore to rescue us."

She laughed softly. "I know. He was handy for that, wasn't he?"

Taylor smiled. "He was. Your dad was awesome. That's what your baby deserves, a man with a gun who isn't afraid to use it. Hang on until you find that guy, okay? Don't marry Chase tomorrow."

"Chase is a cowboy," Mira felt compelled to point out. "I'm sure he has guns. He didn't seem the type to resist using them."

Taylor raised her brows. "Fine, he has guns. Will you at least do me the favor of stalling the wedding until you make sure you like what he aims them at? Two months."

Two months felt like an interminable time to acquire the protective shield of marriage to Chase. "Two weeks."

"One month. You won't even be showing by then. It will be more believable if you wait long enough to find out that you got pregnant from your night with him. If you get married *after* you 'find out' you're pregnant with his child, then it makes sense you guys would get married in a hurry. Otherwise, it doesn't ring true."

Mira considered this. "That idea has some validity, from a strategic perspective."

"At last!" Taylor clapped her hands in mock celebration. "The girl finally sees the light!"

"I can't lie to Chase, though. I'm not going to go out there under false pretenses." She walked over to the table and pulled out her phone. "I'm going to tell him that I'm not going to marry him right away."

Taylor stayed her hand. "Maybe you should wait until you're out there. You don't want him to change his mind—"

"I'm not going to lie to him," Mira insisted. "If he

decides not to help, then I'll think of something else." She started to dial his number, when a movement outside caught her eye. She glanced up in time to see a long, black limousine pause in front of the house. Her heart started to pound as she watched Alan roll down the back window and peer at the house.

She caught her breath, her heart pounding as his gaze met hers. He gave her a small salute, and then rolled up the window and the car drove off.

Sweat broke out down her back and slithered down her spine. "He's not going to give up," she said, softly. "He hates me for taking AJ away from him, and now it's his chance for payback. He wants to invalidate AJ's will and get his money, and he's going to use me to do it." She looked back at Taylor, who was standing up now, concern etched on her face. "He'll dig deep enough that he'll find out I bought the pregnancy test in town, won't he? He'll know I bought it before Chase ever came to town." Suddenly, she felt sick, sick all the way to the depth of her soul.

"Dammit, girl." Taylor walked over to the window and put her arm around Mira's shoulder. "You better get on that plane to Wyoming, and because I love you dearly, I'm going to hope like hell that Chase is the man you think he is, because if he's not, you might be out of your league."

Mira looked at Taylor. "You think I should marry him? Right away?"

"Right away sounds like an awfully risky step, but so is leaving yourself exposed to Alan." Taylor bit her lip. "I don't know, Mira. I just don't know."

"Yeah, me either." She put her arm around Taylor's waist and leaned her head on her shoulder, watching Alan's car disappear down the decrepit road.

"He's hot, right? Chase?"

Mira smiled. "Very."

"Good kisser?"

"Apparently. He managed to seduce me the night I met him, right?"

"Powerful?"

"He exudes power. He stood up to Alan at the reception, and Alan backed down."

"Really?" Taylor grinned. "I'd have loved to see that."

Mira smiled. "It was a good moment." She had been so shocked when Alan had grabbed her that she hadn't had time to prepare herself. When Chase had stepped in, it had been an amazing respite from the crush of emotions flooding her.

"Well, then, maybe this time, you're supposed to leap without a net." Taylor glanced at her. "You've been to hell and back, and you're going to be a mom. At some point you need to trust your gut."

"My gut says he's a good man." She didn't even hesitate.

"Then, my friend, just maybe it's time for you to get married." Taylor grimaced. "Or just buy a big gun. One or the other. I'm not sure which is the best choice."

Mira sighed. "Me either."

Taylor raised her brows. "So what are you going to do?"

Mira looked down at the phone still clutched in her hands, the one that AJ had programmed Chase's phone number into. "I'm going to call him," she said.

"And say what?"

She started to dial. "I don't know." But she did. She knew in her gut exactly what she needed to say to him. The shadow from Alan's drive-by still lurked, reminding her exactly how bad a wrong choice could be. Could she really bind herself to a stranger just to hide from Alan?

She couldn't. It wasn't worth the risk.

She knew what she had to do...but as she dialed the phone, she felt her stomach sinking, telling her that the choice she was about to make was wrong. Dead wrong. But she knew she had to do it anyway.

Chapter 5

What the hell had he done?

Wearily, Chase drove up the long driveway to his ranch, his mind still spinning. When he'd left Mira's house that morning, he'd been feeling like a gallant hero doing the right thing. But the further he'd gotten from that small southern town, the more the doubt had set in.

What the hell was he doing? Marrying a woman and offering himself up as a father? He had no business doing either one. He didn't want to get tangled up with a woman, and he had no damned idea how to be a dad.

Swearing, he slammed his truck door shut and strode across the dirt toward his front door, his boots crunching into the rock. He vaulted up the front steps, then paused when he saw a familiar motorcycle parked in the shadows by the door.

Irritation flooded him at the sight of the motorcycle that belonged to one of his brothers.

He wasn't in the right frame of mind to deal with Zane tonight...shit. Had he really just thought that? He'd been working on his brothers since he'd bought the place, trying to get them to move to the ranch. Zane's appearance was a rarity, something Chase had been trying to cultivate for years. He should be fired up that Zane was at his place waiting for him, but he just felt *annoyed?* It was because of his preoccupation with Mira. Was he really going to let the distraction of a woman interfere with his relationship with his brothers? His reaction to Zane's motorcycle made it obvious that he couldn't go through with the deal with Mira.

He couldn't marry her or claim fatherhood of the kid. He'd give her money, set her up in a different town, but he was not going to bring her into his life. He couldn't afford it.

In an even worse mood now, he flung open the front door and strode into the foyer. He didn't bother to call out. He just walked straight into the family room. Sure enough, Zane was stretched out on the couch like he owned it, except for the fact that his boots were still on, as was his thick leather jacket, always ready to leave on a moment's notice. His jeans and his plaid shirt were the only cowboy left in him, but he'd been one of the best bull riders in the region at one time. He'd traded the bulls for a bike, and claimed to never think about his old life at all.

Chase didn't believe him. He'd seen Zane watching the horses in the corral when he'd thought Chase wasn't around. What he didn't know was why Zane had walked away from that life, and refused to ever look back.

"I poured you a drink." Zane nodded toward the tonic water sitting on the coffee table. "I brought you the hard stuff. Raspberry flavored, I think."

Chase sat down on the black leather couch and studied his brother, ignoring the water. He didn't drink alcohol, thanks to the lessons he'd learned from his father. "Where have you been? It's been six months. I thought you'd cracked up your bike for the last time. You good?"

"Always." Zane swung his feet to the floor, his motorcycle boots thudding on the polished wood. His dark brown hair was cut short for once, but the diamond earring glittered in his left ear. Where the hell was the guy who used to wear a cowboy hat and well-worn boots? "You look like shit," Zane commented. "What happened?"

Chase sighed, the weight of his recent decision returning with no mercy at the question. "A good friend died. He knocked up his best friend before he bit it. She's got no money, and his dad is like ours, only with serious leverage and power."

Zane whistled softly as he took a swig of the cold beer he'd helped himself to. Chase always kept his favorite brand in the fridge, for the occasions when he stopped by. "Brings back memories, doesn't it?"

"Yeah, it does." Chase watched his brother swig the beer, and suddenly, he wanted one as well. He wanted to feel that bitter taste coat his tongue and burn down his throat. Shit. He hadn't wanted a drink in years. Scowling, he tossed his hat on the table, and then bent his head, running his hands through his hair as he tried to pull himself together. "I told her I'd marry her and claim the kid. I gave her a plane ticket for tomorrow to move out here."

Zane didn't answer, and after a long moment, Chase looked up. His brother was spinning the bottle between his fingers, leaving prints on the condensation. He was studying the bottle intently, as if he hadn't even heard what Chase had said.

But Chase knew he had. That was Zane's way. Silence until he had something to say.

Zane finally looked up. "You heard from anyone else lately?"

Chase knew Zane was asking about their seven half-brothers, the legacy of their bastard father. "No." Chase had bought the ranch five years ago with the goal of bringing his family back together. He had enough acreage for every Stockton man to have his own ranch, but so far, no one had come. Granted, Steen was in prison, so he had a valid reason, but no one else had come back to the town they'd grown up in. Chase wasn't giving up, though. The bond between the brothers was intense and unshakeable, and he knew that every single one of them would drop everything for each other, if one of them needed help. The connection was there, and someday he was going to bring them back together. "You going to move into the ranch?" he asked Zane, knowing the answer, but unwilling to let his brother off the hook.

"No. I like the road." Zane raised his eyebrows. "At some point, you have to stop trying to fix what's broken, bro. Broken's okay."

"Yeah, I know broken is okay, but fixed can be better."

"You so sure about that?" Zane leaned forward, his beefy forearms resting on his muscular quads. There was a tattoo on his arm of his favorite bull, the one that had dumped every single cowboy, except for Zane, who'd ridden him three times.

"You want to bring a woman into this house? You want to marry one?" He raised his hand. "Blood oath, bro, remember? Never let a woman come between us? Or did you forget that?"

Chase rubbed the mark on his palm that all the brothers carried. "I remember."

Zane studied him for a long moment. "So, you think she's different, then? You think she doesn't make you violate the oath?"

The oath had been a promise to never allow a woman to bring negative energy between the brothers or to take a position of power in any of their lives, which basically banned marriage or a significant relationship. All the Stockton men knew how badly women could screw things up, but none of them were willing to go celibate. Hence, the creatively worded oath that basically translated to "brothers first, women last, every single time."

"I'm not sure. I barely know her." But he felt like he did know her. She *was* different. This was the woman he'd known for a decade, and yet, at the same time, he'd known her only for a few hours. Shit. He stood up, restless. "I'm going to go for a ride."

Zane didn't move. "Sit down. It's almost midnight, and your pony is napping."

Slowly, Chase sat down, surprised by Zane's command. His brother never wanted to talk about anything. "What's up?"

"How bad's the dad?" Zane asked.

"Bad."

Zane was quiet for another moment. "How about her?"

"I trust her."

Zane looked sharply at him. "No shit?"

He shrugged.

"They won't come if there's a woman here," Zane said. "None of them will come."

He was referring to their brothers, the ones Chase had been working so hard to bring home. Chase ground his jaw, not answering, but he knew Zane had a valid point. His ranch offered a respite from women, a place for the brothers to bond. Although none of them had moved back, they all stopped in from time to time, just as Zane had done tonight. They were linked by a brutal childhood that had required them to fight for each other and protect each other. Nothing came between their commitment to each other, especially a woman. "I—" His phone rang suddenly, and he looked down. His pulse quickened when he saw it was Mira. "It's her." He answered it immediately. "You okay?"

"I can't marry you." She spoke without preamble, direct and to the point.

Something plunged through his gut like a knife, and he tightened his grip on the phone. "What?"

"I don't know you. I can't bind myself to you for life, or give you parental rights to my child. Forever is a long time." There was a panicky edge to her voice, and she was talking so fast that he knew she was on the verge of falling apart. "I'm running from one nightmare. How do I know I'm not running into another one? I can't risk it, Chase. I mean, I know you through AJ, but what does that mean? We don't know each other. This is my life, my baby, my everything. I just...I just can't."

Based on his conversation with his brother, her backing out should have relieved him, but it hadn't. It felt completely wrong, edging him toward panic. He felt like he was sinking into quicksand and it was closing over his head. "Mira, just get on the plane. Come out here. We'll give it four weeks. If you feel like you can't trust me by that point, then we'll call it off."

There was a moment of silence, then she took a deep breath. "Really? We don't have to get married right away? You're okay with that?"

"Of course I am." There it was. Such an easy solution. Bring her out there, but not tie himself down. It gave him time to see if he could find a way to repay his debt to AJ without sacrificing what mattered to him. If not, the marriage was off. "We won't even tell anyone you're pregnant. We'll just do a test run and see if it can work."

She laughed softly, her voice filled with relief. "Okay, then. I wanted to come, but I sort of panicked. I didn't want to come under false pretenses and not marry you once I got there. I feel better now. We'll just see how it goes, then."

He smiled at the sound of her laugh. The fact that she'd been panicking as well made his own tension abate, replaced by a need to step up and protect her. "It'll be okay. We'll get it right."

"Okay." She was smiling now. He could hear it in her voice. "I'll see you tomorrow, then, okay?"

"I'll meet you at the airport...unless you want me to fly down there and get you?"

She laughed again. "I'm very capable of navigating an airport by myself, but that's a very nice offer. I appreciate it, but I'm fine. See you tomorrow night. And...Chase?"

"Yeah?"

"Thanks. For all of it."

He smiled. "My pleasure." He was still grinning when he hung up the phone, then his smile faded when he saw his brother studying him. "What?"

"The mighty has fallen."

❦ ❦ ❦

Mira saw him the moment she walked through the gates into the luggage area.

Chase was leaning against the far wall, his hands jammed into his pockets as he carefully scanned the faces pouring through the gate. He was wearing a brown cowboy hat this time, and his faded jeans sat low on his lean hips. His plaid shirt was open at the collar, revealing tanned skin and the same gold chain she'd noticed before. He looked like a real life, untamed cowboy, and a ripple of anticipation pulsed through her. This man was here for *her*.

He finally saw her, and his gaze stopped, pinned to her. Heat flushed her body, and she lifted her chin, trying to quell the thudding of her heart. He levered himself off the wall and strode toward her, the languid, easy gait of a man who could saunter across a thousand miles of barren country and never break a sweat. He never took his gaze off hers as he neared, but his expression was unreadable.

He came to a stop in front of her, still studying her face.

She pulled back her shoulders, craning her neck to look up at him. "You're taller than I remembered."

"Am I?" He slid his hand behind her neck, his touch warm and seductive. "My dear Mira," he whispered. "I know everyone in this town, and this is a small airport. If we decide to go through with it, it needs to be set up from the start, or there will be holes for Alan to find."

Her heart started to pound even harder. "What are you saying?"

"We slept together two nights ago, and now you're moving out here to live with me." His fingers tightened on the nape of her neck, drawing her closer. "I have to greet you the right way. You on board?"

Oh, God. *He was going to kiss her.* Why hadn't she thought of that before? But he was right. "Okay," she managed, her voice no more than a nervous squeak. "Lay it on me, cowboy."

He grinned. "Be careful what you ask for, sweetheart. A cowboy has a lot of talents, and kissing just happens to be one of them." Then he lowered his head and kissed her.

Her heart leapt the moment his lips touched hers. The kiss was tender and tantalizing, his lips so warm and soft against hers that she melted into him. His fingers tightened on the back of her neck, and she felt his other arm wrap around her waist, tugging her against him.

The well-muscled hardness of his body was in sharp contrast to hers, and he seemed to tower over her, wrapping her up in an embrace that was so delicious she never wanted to leave it.

He angled his head and deepened the kiss, sending spirals of electricity running through her. Instinctively, she slid her arms around his neck, leaning into him. His tongue slipped through her parted lips, and for a split second, she almost melted right there. Dear God. Was this what a real kiss was supposed to be like? It had been so long she'd completely forgotten what it felt like to be thoroughly kissed by a man. She wanted more, more kisses, more of him, more touching, more—

"Who in the hell's this?" A deep, raspy male voice blasted in her left ear, and she jumped back, completely embarrassed to be caught nearly climbing into Chase's skin in the middle of an airport next to a baggage claim.

Chase, however, pulled her right back against him, tucking her under his arm before he swung around to face whoever had interrupted them.

A weathered cowboy in well-worn jeans and scuffed boots was standing beside them. His salt-and-pepper hair was just visible beneath his black cowboy hat, and his denim shirt looked like it had been through a thousand washings. There was a sparkle in his blue eyes, and his grin was engaging as he surveyed them.

Chase tightened his arm around her shoulders. "Evening, Gary. This is my cousin, Mira Cabot. Mira, this is Gary Keller."

Cousin? She blanched. Was Chase *that* kind of guy, the kind who lived in a world where people made out with their cousins on a regular basis?

Gary burst out laughing, and he slammed his hand onto Chase's shoulder. "Always think you're funny, don't you, Stockton? Cousin, my ass." He swept off his hat and bowed low to Mira. "Welcome to Wyoming, my lady. If Chase gives you a hard time, you feel free to ring me up. He's never too old to get his hide tanned."

She grinned with relief, realizing it had all been a joke. "Thank you. I appreciate it."

Gary set his hat back on his head, gazing at her more intently now. "Haven't seen Chase around women much," he said thoughtfully. "You must be somethin' special."

She felt her cheeks turn red. "I, um—"

"She is." Chase pressed a kiss to the top of her head. "It took me ten years to get her to come out here, but she finally made it. The right bribe makes all the difference."

Gary guffawed again, and she smiled, relaxing against Chase. It had been a long time since she'd had much to laugh about, and it felt good to be around a man who wasn't going to get weighed down by what they were embarking upon.

"Ten years, eh?" Gary eyed her. "Why'd you keep him waiting ten years?"

She grinned. "My mom always told me that the right guy will wait. So, I had to test him. I figured ten years was about long enough."

"Shoot, I married my lady two weeks after I met her. I'd never have waited ten years for her." He flexed his arms. "She knew she had to grab me while the grabbing was good, or I'd have been gone forever."

Chase laughed. "It took you nine years to get her to say yes, you old liar. Don't mess with Mira, or I'll have to hunt you down."

Gary feigned fear, clasping his heart. "Oh, I'm scared now. Watch out, Mira, the man's a force to be reckoned with." The older man winked. "Sunday dinner? The little lady would love to meet the woman who finally got Chase's attention."

Dinner? Mira started to panic. How could she go to dinner and keep up a façade with such a nice man. "Oh, I don't—"

"You bet," Chase said. "I'll bring the pie."

"Excellent." Gary winked at Mira again. "I invite Chase only because he makes the best apple pie in the county. It's the only reason anyone invites him anywhere." He tipped his hat, his affection for Chase evident. He was so warm and engaging that Mira knew he was the real deal, a genuinely nice cowboy who lived by the code of loyalty. "Welcome again, Mira. If you're good for Chase, then you have my vote. See you guys on Sunday."

Sunday? As she watched him walk away, the enormity of what she'd just stepped into suddenly seemed to loom up. This wasn't a simple façade between the two of them. This was an intention to deceive an entire world, one by one, laying the seeds for a deception that had to be strong enough to last the lifetime of her child.

Good God, what had she done?

Chapter 6

Chase leaned moodily on his kitchen counter, watching Mira inspect his kitchen. He'd spent a lot of time refinishing the cabinets and installing the granite countertops. He was proud of how the kitchen had come out, but right now, he didn't even care what she thought of it. All he could do was focus on her. Her hair was loose, tumbling around her shoulders. She was wearing old jeans that fit her with enough sensual perfection to make his gut clench every time she turned around. He'd noticed her bright pink toenail polish, and her bare ankles made it clear she was still wearing the anklet she'd had on when he'd first met her.

At the funeral, she'd been gorgeous, all fancied up in her dress, but now that she was casual and walking through his house, it was different. It was real now. She was real, and accessible.

He hadn't meant to kiss her when she'd arrived, but when he'd seen her standing there looking both terrified and brave as hell, kissing her had made sense. He'd wanted to claim her, right there, in front of everyone. Kissing her had set her up as being under his protection, and he'd wanted to do that.

Ah, hell, who was he trying to kid? It hadn't been a conscious, strategic decision. It had been a raw, visceral need to imprint himself on her before anyone else could do the same.

The kiss had been incredible. Amazing. Best moment of his life...and then Gary had interfered. After Gary had left, Mira had withdrawn. She'd been careful not to even brush against him as they walked, and her smile had been taut and distant.

The warm, open woman he'd met at the funeral was gone, and he didn't like it.

He wanted the Mira he knew back, but as he watched her walk through *his* house, he had no idea what to do to make it happen. "I'm not used to having a woman in my house," he said finally, hoping that she might take pity on him and help him figure out what to say.

She glanced over at him, and for the first time since the kiss, he saw a small smile curve her mouth. "I'm not used to being in a man's house, so we're even." She turned to face him, her eyes finally meeting his. "I'm not comfortable going to Gary's, Chase. I feel like we're spiraling too fast into a situation that's out of my control."

Ah...so that was it. He considered her concerns for a moment, but it took him less than a split second to dismiss them. He didn't know what it was, but something was burning in him that he hadn't expected. Going to Gary's would cement their connection in the public eye, and he wanted that to happen. Yeah, it wasn't real, and it was, as he'd said, a business partnership only, but he wasn't going to leave her high and dry. His need to protect her and the baby was growing stronger every minute he was with her. "You don't turn down an invite from Gary," he said simply.

She blinked. "Why not?"

He shrugged. "He's a good guy." He didn't want to explain any more than that. To explain what Gary meant to him was to go places he didn't go with people, especially not a woman he barely knew.

Awkward silence settled between them, and he shifted. He had no idea what the hell to do with her. He hadn't been lying when he'd said that he didn't know what to do with a woman in his house. He was so out of his league. "How are you feeling?"

"Fine." She sighed, and he suddenly noticed how tired she looked. There were shadows under her eyes, and her shoulders were slumped.

"You're tired." He walked over to the front hall where he'd dropped her luggage. "Sorry for being an insensitive ass. I'll take you to your room." He swung her bags off the floor and headed down the hall toward the bedrooms. His suite was at the far end, taking up one entire end of the house. "This way."

There were two guest bedrooms. One in the basement, and one right next to his room. The basement would give her privacy and space. It even had a kitchenette so she could make her own meals, and its own bathroom. He'd never even have to see her if he put her down there. They could both live their lives and do their own thing. It would be like not even having her in the house.

He glanced over at her as she walked beside him. His gaze fell on her mouth, and he remembered what it had been like to kiss her. She seemed to sense his perusal, and she caught his eye. Neither of them spoke, but a sensual awareness slithered down his spine and wrapped itself around his gut.

This wasn't simply a woman. It was Mira Cabot, the woman who'd been a part of his consciousness for over a decade.

She wasn't going in the basement.

She was going in the room next to his.

※ ※ ※

Mira awoke at midnight, her heart hammering.

The moonlight was streaming across her bed, casting an eerie glow across the rustic furnishings. A light breeze was making ripples flutter across the surface of the navy bedspread. For a moment, she forgot where she was, and then the events of the last two days came flooding back over her. How could she forget? She was in cowboy country now, shacking up with the father of her child...potentially. Possibly about to embark on the façade of her life...

Not something that happened to a girl every day.

Sighing, she rolled over onto her side, staring out the window. What had awakened her? The utter silence of the night? The lack of fluorescent lights outdoors? Or the sense of sheer isolation descending upon her like a great weight suffocating her? Was she running away like a wimp? Or taking the brave plunge of a woman who would fight for those she loved? Or was she simply just a confused sod wandering cluelessly through life?

Yeah, any of those could have been enough to drag her out of a well-needed sleep. She'd never been a good sleeper through stress—

An eerie haunting howl drifted through the night. She bolted upright in bed, her heart hammering as the creepy sound sent chills racing down her spine. What in heaven's name was that?

Another howl filled the night, and she listened intently, trying to discern what it was. Wolves? Or was it the tortured ghost of an old west outlaw who had met his demise on the gallows and then committed his eternity to haunting the progeny of all those who had betrayed them?

Wolves would probably be better.

There was another echoing howl, and then another, until the night was filled with the mournful wail of the wild animals.

Definitely wolves. Beautiful, but also chilling.

She climbed out of bed, and padded over to the window in her bare feet. She peered outside, searching the night for four-legged shadows. It had been dark when she'd arrived, and she'd been too tired to look around, but now that the moon was full, it was casting the ranch into silvery, glistening shadows.

There was a massive barn several hundred yards away, and numerous corrals, some with grass and others with soft-looking dirt for riding. Beyond the barns stretched dark hills with rocky outcroppings, the perfect place for wolves...or rattlesnakes...or mountain lions.

A loud thud sounded from the barn, jerking her attention back there.

The door slid open. She gripped the windowsill in sudden nervousness, but quickly realized it wasn't a jet-black panther intent on making her his midnight snack. It was a huge dark horse, trotting easily out the massive barn doors. Chase was silhouetted on his back, a figure so imposing that she shivered in awareness. He spun the horse deftly around to close the barn door behind him, his cowboy hat and broad shoulders creating a breathtaking silhouette. He moved in perfect unison with the animal, as if they were one.

After shutting the door, he swung the horse toward the hills, and she caught her breath, leaning forward to get a better look. The pair went still, poised in suspended animation as they prepared for flight. The moment was pure, unbridled freedom, a man and his horse, unlike anything she'd experienced in her life.

She was used to a life of service, never being away from home for more than an hour, in case her mother needed her. And yet, this was Chase's life, climbing onto his horse for a midnight ride, just because he wanted to.

Yearning coursed through her, an almost painful craving for a life beyond what she'd lived. She wanted to be more than she was, to live more than she'd done, to be brave enough to step out over an abyss just to see what would happen when she went airborne. Suddenly, the night didn't feel like the oppressing constraint of isolation. It felt like a fresh start, a chance to live again.

Chase turned his head suddenly, looking directly at her window. She stiffened. Could he see her? She knew she should probably duck inside and pretend she hadn't been playing the part of a voyeur, but she didn't move.

A part of her wanted to be caught by him, to be swept into this surreal moment of magic and moonlight, of cowboy and horse.

He swung his horse toward her, and urged the animal into a lope. Anticipation pulsed through her as he neared. He reined the animal into a sliding halt just outside her window. Since it was a ranch house, she was almost exactly level with him. He was so close, she could almost touch him if she reached out.

"Can't sleep?" he asked, his voice somehow deeper and sexier in the shadows of the moon.

"The wolves woke me up." She was in awe of his mount. The horse stood quietly, intently focused on his rider, awaiting the next command. He had a white blaze on his face, and a sock on his left hind leg. Other than that, he appeared to be a deep, rich, beautiful brown. "What's your horse's name?"

"Red Devil, but he lets his friends call him Red." Chase's face was shadowed beneath his hat, hiding him from her. "Did the wolves scare you?"

She shook her head. "It was beautiful."

"Want to go see them?"

She caught her breath, jerking her gaze from his horse to him. "Now?"

"Yep."

Her instinct was to refuse, and retreat responsibly into her bed, so she would be rested and capable of handling life in the morning, as she'd been doing for the last eight years. But instead, she smiled, unable to keep the anticipation off her face. "I'd love to." Somehow, in the darkness of the night, immersed in the vastness of his ranch, real life didn't seem to matter. The only thing that mattered was embracing this moment.

He grinned, his teeth glistening white against his shadowed face as he held out his hand. "Hop on, then." He edged his horse closer, clearly intending to have her ride with him.

Excitement rippled through her. Ride double with him into the moonlight to look at wolves? This was so not her life, was it? "Okay." She started to reach for him, and then suddenly remembered that she was wearing only a light camisole, no bra, and a pair of thin, cotton sleep pants. Embarrassment flooded her cheeks "I'm not dressed. I should put on jeans—"

"You look perfect to me. It's unseasonably warm for this time of year. You don't need anything else." There was a sensual undertone to his voice that made her belly tighten, but before she could dive back into her room in search of a sweatshirt, he held out his hand. "Come on. The wolves don't stay put for long, and they don't care what you're wearing. I'll catch you."

I'll catch you.

Rightness rippled through her, and she knew, in that moment, she wanted to be caught by him. "Okay, but if you drop me, I'll shoot you." She climbed up on the windowsill and swung her legs over the side, gripping the windowsill as she perched precariously, her bare feet dangling above assorted bushes that, for all she knew, could be thick with thorns. "Are you sure about this?"

"Never doubt a cowboy. It offends us and forces us to overcompensate, which is never a good thing." He leaned over, grabbed her around the waist, swept her off the windowsill, and settled her in front of him in the saddle. "This okay?"

"Um...yeah. Sure." Her back was flush against his chest, and her bottom was wedged up against his crotch. The thin material of her pants gave her little protection from the heat of his body cascading through her, and the sensation of so much physical contact was almost overwhelming. His arm was wrapped securely around her waist, anchoring her against him. Any hope she had of being proper and leaning forward so she wasn't using him as a lounge chair was completely eliminated by how securely he had her tucked against him. She had a feeling his horse could fling them to Georgia and Chase still wouldn't lose his grip on her. "It's been a long time since I've ridden a horse."

"Well, lucky for you, I've got that angle covered." He swung his horse around toward the hills. "If you get scared or need a break, let me know, okay?"

She nodded, looking ahead toward the rocky hills. Was she really going to do this? Ride into the night with a man she didn't know? He could abduct her, and no one would ever find her body in the vastness of this land.

Then he nudged his horse into a lope, and the time to retreat was gone.

※ ※ ※

By the time they reached the southern ridge, Chase knew he had a problem on his hands.

Or, more accurately, in his lap.

It had taken exactly twenty-five yards of riding double with Mira for his cock to get hard, and it hadn't chilled out in the hour they'd been riding. He hadn't had a never-ending hard-on since he was a hormonal teenager, but the feeling of Mira's body snuggled against his had stirred up a need in him that wasn't going to stand down.

Even though she said she hadn't ridden in years, she moved naturally with the movement of the horse, relaxing into Chase and letting her body follow his. It was seductive as hell, and tempting beyond words.

The fact that her shirt was so thin it felt as if his hand was on her bare stomach didn't help. Nor did the fact that her hair was whipping against his cheek, and he couldn't stop breathing in the smell of lilacs that seemed to be clinging faintly to her.

In her white pajamas and bare feet, she was so feminine

he didn't even know how to respond. As they got further and further from the ranch, and the terrain got rougher, he realized she was completely dependent on him to keep her safe. She didn't even have shoes on. What the hell had he been thinking, taking her out on the range at night, while she was wearing something so thin and sexy that even the buzzards would have a hard time not noticing?

Protectiveness surged over him, and he locked his arm more tightly around her waist. She'd trusted him enough to let him bring her out here. He wasn't going to let her down.

"What's that one called?" She pointed to a three-pointed outcropping to the north. "It's so beautiful."

The awe in her voice was genuine, and intense satisfaction settled more deeply through him. She'd been peppering him with questions about the ranch the entire ride, noticing things about his land he hadn't noted in years. Mira appreciated his ranch the way he did, and that got him right in his gut.

"It's called Triple Threat. It's a really steep drop off on the other side. If you went over, it'd be a bad day for you." Again, his arm tightened reflexively around her, in a gesture that was fast becoming habit.

He reined in his horse and paused. "Listen. We're almost there."

They sat quietly together as Red went still, the three of them in total sync. The night was pregnant with silence, and then he heard the howl directly off to his right.

Mira tensed and turned sharply, scanning the night. "It sounds like it's right next to us," she whispered.

"It almost is." He kept his mouth right by her ear, a whisper meant for her alone. "Stay quiet." He urged Red ahead, and the horse deftly navigated the rocky terrain, his bare hooves almost silent on the boulders.

They rounded the corner, and he felt Mira suck in her breath as he reined in Red. Less than twenty yards away, on the butte aptly called Wolf Hill, were six wolves. Two of them had their noses turned toward the sky, and their low, echoing howl filled the night.

Red stood absolutely still, trained to perfection, and Mira was immobile against Chase. The only sign that she'd seen the wolves was the reflexive tightening of her hand around his forearm.

He grinned, leaning forward to rest his cheek against hers. "See the one with the white chest?" he whispered against her ear, keeping his voice so low he could barely hear the words himself.

She nodded.

"I call her Sheera. She's the alpha female of the pack. Jam, the alpha male, isn't up there right now. Gorgeous, aren't they?"

"Incredible." She squeezed his hand. "Thank you for bringing me here, Chase. It's unbelievable." The genuine awe in her voice made him grin.

Even his brothers had never seen Sheera or Jam. The wolves had never paid a visit when his brothers had been in town, and it felt good to share them with someone. With her, specifically.

"What are the names of the others?"

He rested his chin on her shoulder, pointing out each one. She nodded, relaxing against his chest as he explained the personalities of each wolf. He couldn't believe how interested she was, and how appreciative. He loved the solitude of his midnight rides, and never in his life would he have wanted to share them with anyone, but having Mira with him had cast the night into another light, one that was unexpected, but not so bad.

This woman as his wife?

Maybe she'd fit in okay. Maybe it wouldn't be so bad. Maybe his brothers would learn to accept her. But even as Chase thought it, he knew that his brothers would never get on board. Their scars ran too deep, and survival had taught them lessons they would never unlearn.

His phone rang, blasting out into the silence. The wolves scattered, Mira jumped, and even Red flicked an ear.

Swearing, he dug the phone out of his pocket, instinctively responding to the ring that he'd assigned only to his brothers. He looked down and saw it was Travis, one of his brothers. "Hey." He took the call, as he always did when it was one of his brothers.

Travis didn't waste time on pleasantries. "Is she there?"

He frowned. "Who?"

"Mira. The wife. Is she there already?"

Chase realized that Zane must have already talked to Travis. "Yeah. What's up? Something wrong?"

Travis swore. "You realize you have money, bro, don't you? Lots of it. Enough that women will want it. You're a target, just like dad was."

Mira leaned back against him, resting her head on his chest. Instinctively, Chase tightened his grip on her, breathing in that lilac scent. He turned Red toward home, the idyllic moment shattered. "She's not like that."

"I'm coming out there," Travis said. "I'll be there tomorrow night. Don't get married tomorrow."

Chase frowned. "You're coming here?" Travis hadn't been to the ranch in two years.

"Yeah. I'll see ya." The phone clicked, and Travis was gone, leaving Chase staring at his phone. What the hell had just happened?

Chapter 7

The weight settled more deeply in Mira's chest the further they got from the wolves. The magic of the night had vanished, replaced with the reality of life. "Who was on the phone?" she asked.

"My brother." Chase had been quiet since the call, but his hold on her was still secure.

"I didn't mean to eavesdrop, but I could hear the whole conversation. Should I buy a gun before tomorrow night?"

She felt him chuckle at her words, and a tiny bit of the tension eased from his body. "You know how to shoot a gun?"

"My dad was a sheriff. I can shoot anything."

He whistled softly. "You can borrow one of my guns if Travis gets out of line. He'd appreciate a woman with a gun." He was silent for a moment, and she closed her eyes, lulled by the smooth gait of the horse and the warmth of Chase's body.

She didn't want to think about choices, the future, or a hostile brother coming to the ranch to drive her away. She just wanted to be in this moment, enjoying the sensation of being held in Chase's arms, and breathing in air so fresh it seemed to make her lungs twenty pounds lighter each time she inhaled.

"I have eight brothers," he said finally.

"Eight? I don't have any. Well, I had an older brother, but he died when he was six months old." Nine kids growing up in the same house. She couldn't imagine what that would be like. "Are you close?"

"Yeah. Hell forges unbreakable bonds."

His words brought back the memory of the cigarette burns on his forearms. Instinctively, she rubbed her hand over the marks that were hidden by his shirt, as if she could erase them simply with her touch. Eight boys trapped in a life of abuse? "Where's your dad now?"

"Dead."

"Good." Even as she said it, she felt a wave of sadness that anyone could be in a situation where their dad's death made life better. When her dad had died, it had been devastating. As terrible as the grief had been, it had also meant that she'd had an amazing father who had meant everything to her, and she'd never trade that for less grief. If her dad were around, he could show Chase what a dad could be like, just as he'd done for AJ.

"Yeah."

Again, they fell into silence, but there was an edge to it now, a darkness of the past hovering over them. A chill began to creep through her bones, and she wasn't sure if it was because of the turn in the conversation, or the temperature of the night.

"I killed him," Chase said finally.

The chill turned into a knife. "What?" She twisted in his arms, turning so she could see him. His face was hard and chiseled, still shadowed by the brim of his hat in the moonlight.

"When I was twenty-two, my youngest brother called me. My dad had beat the hell out of him, and locked him in the garage. Travis's ribs were broken, and he couldn't breathe. He called me to tell me what happened and ask me to send the cops. My dad's wife at the time wouldn't let the cops in, and he sat there in that garage until I got there the next night from New York. He was almost dead." Chase's voice was so hard that she was almost afraid of him. "I had to break the door down to get to him, and my dad came after me. He was drunk off his ass, and he had a gun. He shot me. I got the gun, he wound up dead, and the shit was over."

His voice was so even, as if he were telling a story about picking up a can of beans at the store, but she didn't believe it. She'd heard similar stories from AJ too much, and she knew the depths of suffering that made a man become so impenetrable. "I'm sorry," she said softly.

His gaze flicked to hers, and for a moment, she

saw anguish in those blue eyes, but he shuttered it almost immediately. "My dad married three times, and had countless other women. He used his fists and belts, sometimes cigarettes. They used cigarettes, too, but also irons, and other shit that caused damage no one could see, the kind that eats away inside until there's nothing left."

Tears filled her eyes. "Oh, Chase—"

"I didn't have it as bad because I was older by the time things got really ugly. I wasn't home much, and I was big enough to defend myself. But some of my brothers were pretty young, products of assorted women. Sometimes, the women took them when they left. Other times, they left them behind, but they were all my brothers, no matter what." He shook his head once, silencing her when she started to respond. "With each woman, my dad became worse. They took his money, they fucked him over, and they twisted him deeper into the pit he was falling into. The day I left for college, my brothers and I took a blood oath that we would never let a woman destroy us, and we would always protect each other from any enemy, but especially women." He held out his hand, and she saw a small scar on his palm.

She traced the mark silently, his palm roughened from all his ranch work. "He's coming here to protect you from me, isn't he? Your brother? The one who called you?"

"Yeah."

She looked up at him. "Will he hurt me?" It wasn't a question based on fear. It was a question designed to help her understand exactly what she was about to face. She'd been the daughter of a sheriff for too long not to know the questions to ask.

Anger flashed in Chase's eyes, and he flipped his hand over, trapping hers against his thigh. "No one will hurt you, Mira. I swear it on my life. Do you understand? *No one will ever hurt you.*"

The vehemence in his voice sent chills down her spine, and she knew that the abused child had become the protector of the innocent at any cost. His brothers were his posse, but somehow, because of AJ and the baby, she had come into his circle of protection.

But at the same time, the bond between the Stockton men was obvious, and she had inadvertently stepped right between them. She had a feeling it wasn't a good place to be. "Chase," she said slowly. "I think maybe getting married isn't the right thing to do. I won't come between you and your brothers. They mean too much to you. Maybe I should just go into town or something." She managed a shrug. "Now that I'm in Wyoming, I'm probably safe."

Probably? That might be a little strong. Possibly safe? Still too much. Not likely. Hardly at all. But being in Wyoming bought her time to figure out a more permanent solution.

For a long moment, Chase stared at her, his face inscrutable. She could almost hear the thoughts roaring through his head as he tried to reconcile his loyalty to both his brothers and to AJ, trying to find a way to balance it.

She sighed. "If it takes that long to decide, then we know the answer. I'll leave in the morning." She managed a smile. "At least I didn't unpack." She turned back toward the front of the horse, leaning forward slightly so she didn't lean against Chase. Suddenly, she felt hugely embarrassed that she'd hopped on a plane to come live with him. She felt even more embarrassed by how she'd responded to his kiss, and how she'd snuggled into him on the ride.

She realized that Taylor had been right. She'd let it get personal with him already. If she hadn't, she wouldn't feel so empty inside just because she was going to leave in the morning, and start a new life, her real life, without him.

※ ※ ※

Mira smelled good.

Really, *really* good.

Way better than any of his brothers ever had.

Chase gritted his teeth as they rode in silence back to his ranch. Mira was stiff, holding herself away from him, even though he still had his arm around her waist. Her hair was drifting against his face, tickling his skin. He missed the feel of her body against his. Somehow, even though she was a woman and she was in his space, she'd given him a sense of peace tonight that he didn't usually have.

He wanted her around.

But his brothers had suffered enough. How could he take away their safe haven?

He swore under his breath, urging his horse into a faster lope. The easy rhythm rocked Mira back against him, and he took advantage, leaning into her. She slid back into him, her bottom nestled against his crotch, just as it had been on the ride out. Rightness settled through him, an absolute sense of everything being in equilibrium. It was the feeling he'd been striving for ever since he'd bought the ranch, but it had eluded him at every turn.

Mira had given it to him.

Suddenly, it was no longer about AJ or the baby. It was about Mira, and what he wanted. He wanted her for himself. No, he *needed* her. His entire body craved every inch of physical contact he could steal from her.

He had no idea how he could make this fly, but he knew with absolute certainty, that he had to find a way.

He reined Red in as they neared the ranch. "Want to come to the barn, or be dropped off at your window?"

She leaned forward again, trying to put space between them, but he didn't let her. "Window, please."

"I've never dropped a woman off at her bedroom window before," he mused as he navigated Red across the rustic landscaping. "As a cowboy, that's probably a big failure on my part. Seems like something I should have done before."

He was rewarded with a small laugh. "Yes, well, now you can say you've done it."

He paused Red a few feet away from the window, too far for her to jump. "Okay."

She was still for a moment, then twisted around to look at him. Her hair was tousled and sexy, tangled over her shoulders from the ride. "I know I look really athletic, but I'm not actually capable of leaping from a horse's back, over a row of bushes, into an open window, without causing severe damage to myself."

The moonlight was dancing across her features, showcasing her long, thick lashes, the cute upturn of her lips, and the weary shadows beneath her eyes, indicating a woman who had pushed herself to the edge. Slowly, he slid his hand around her neck, just as he'd done at the airport.

She stiffened, but didn't pull away as he stroked his fingers over the nape of her neck, almost unable to believe how soft the strands were. "Like silk," he said softly. "The most delicate spun silk."

"What are you doing?" She didn't sound mad. Confused. And something else he couldn't quite decipher. Intrigued? Interested? Burning with need for him? God, he hoped so.

"Cowboys survive on instinct," he said, sliding his fingers deeper into her hair. Soft, and thick, and so sexy. "It's all I know. I'm not a thinker. I just listen to my gut, and I do."

She swallowed, and her hand went to his chest, her fingers digging in ever so slightly. "Stop," she said. "I need to stay focused. You aren't a knight in shining armor, and you're not going to rescue me."

"I'm no knight," he agreed, spreading his fingers over the back of her head, lightly, ever so lightly, drawing her closer to him. "And you're much too strong to need to be rescued. But even your dad would say it's always good to have a backup plan." And with that, he bent his head and kissed her.

Her lips were so soft, a sensation utterly foreign to him. In the airport, the kiss had been hot and fiery, but it had been in the midst of the frenetic bustle of crowds and travelers. Now, in the silence of the night, there was nothing but the two of them. There was no assault on his senses to distract him from the utter perfection of her mouth beneath his.

He kissed her again, silently urging her to kiss him back. The need for a response from her was hammering through him. He didn't just need physical contact. He needed to know that she wasn't immune to him, despite her independent ways. He *needed* that connection.

He nibbled at her lower lip, and pressed a kiss to each corner of her mouth. She started to tremble, but still didn't kiss him back, though her fingers were digging more fiercely into his chest, and she wasn't pulling away.

"Don't leave tomorrow," he whispered against her mouth.

"You're trying to seduce me into staying?" she whispered.

"That's a little unethical."

He kissed her jawbone, then her earlobe. She tasted fresh and untainted, like the mountains after a spring rain. He trailed kisses down the side of her neck. "Seduction and staying are completely unrelated," he said between kisses. Her shoulder was bare, and he brushed his kiss over her collarbone. The strap of her camisole was thin, so delicate, it would snap with the slightest tug. It was pure femininity, and his gut literally clenched at the sight of it. "You're such a woman," he said as he thumbed the strap off her shoulder, watching it drift down her bare arm. "Incredible."

"Incredible that I'm a woman?" Her eyes were closed, and she was utterly still, not fighting him, but still not responding, as if she was doing everything she could to hold herself aloof.

"No. Just incredible." He pressed a kiss to the curve of her shoulder where the strap had been. Her skin was so soft, and he grinned when he felt the goose bumps pop up. "Are those from me?"

"No. I'm cold." Her voice was throaty and breathless, making him smile wider.

"I'm not doing my job if you're cold." He reached around her, and slid his hand around her thigh as he pressed a kiss to the side of her neck. He grasped her leg and lifted it across Red's neck, turning her sideways in his lap.

From this angle, he could see her nipples through the thin fabric, tight and visible. Raw desire hit him, a need so deep he felt like the axis of his world was shifting. "Come here," he said, unable to keep the gruffness out of his voice. "Face me."

He grasped her other calf, and she moved her leg between them across to Red's other side, so she was facing him. Her legs were over his thighs, a seduction of heat and warmth that was sheer perfection. They were close to each other now, too close in the saddle, and there was nowhere for her legs to go except where they were, draped over his thighs. Her eyes were wide, and he could see both fear and anticipation in them.

He had no words to reassure her. He was in a place he was pretty sure he'd never been in before, and he had no tools to manage it. All he knew was that he wanted her. He needed her. He burned for her. He dropped the reins, and set his palms on either side of her face. "This isn't about the baby," he said. "Or AJ. This is just us, here, right now."

She swallowed. "Okay," she whispered.

Okay. Raw desire coursed through him, and he bent his head, unable to stop himself, unwilling to deny himself this moment. He took her lips in his, and was nearly stunned by the sensation of her mouth against his once again. "So incredibly soft," he whispered against her mouth. He felt huge and awkward in comparison to her delicate frame. "I'm afraid I'll break you just by breathing on you."

She smiled then, a flash of warmth in those gorgeous eyes. "Such a sweet man," she said softly.

It was the tenderness in her voice that broke him. He couldn't remember anyone ever using that tone with him in his life. With a low groan, he swept his arm behind her back, pulling her against him, and kissed her like his very survival depended on it.

And this time, she kissed him back.

❧ ❧ ❧

Chase's kiss was amazing. Mira couldn't believe how incredible it felt to be in his arms. His kiss poured fire and heat into her, igniting a need deep inside her, a need she didn't even know was a part of her…until he'd awoken it.

There was no way for her to resist what he offered her: strength, passion, and a sense of connection that had eluded her for so long. She slid her arms around his neck, and sighed when he locked his arms around her lower back, crushing her against him. His chest was rock hard against her breasts, and her nipples were burning at the feel of his rough shirt against her. His hands were hot against her back, searing her skin through her thin fabric of her top.

Her pulse was hammering so fast she couldn't even feel the separate beats. She was nervous, sort of terrified, by her reaction to him, but the fear wasn't enough to supersede how his kiss made her feel. Sexy, desirable, protected. *Feminine.*

He lightly nipped her lower lip, and then his tongue slid over hers, a sensual caress that made her belly tighten.

Tentatively, she responded, and he let out a low groan, deepening the kiss. Within moments, the kiss seemed to turn to fire. His mouth seemed to burn her everywhere he kissed: her mouth, her neck, her collarbone. Her entire body was humming with desire, a need for him that trumped almost a decade of fear and hesitation.

He grabbed her hips and pulled her further onto his lap. She could feel his erection pressing through the thin material of her pants, and the zipper on his jeans was digging into her sensitive flesh. His hands flanked her hips, trapping her against him. His grip was strong and unyielding, but she didn't feel like she was trapped, just protected.

He kissed her throat, and she leaned her head back, giving him full access. She closed her eyes, all her senses riveted on his mouth as he kissed down her throat, and then lower, moving down between her breasts.

She started to tremble again, and he palmed his hand between her shoulder blades, holding her up as he pressed a kiss to the swell of her breasts. *Oh, God. Really?* Every inch of her skin was tingling in anticipation, as he swirled his tongue across her skin, lower, and lower, until it brushed over her nipple.

Her entire body clenched in response as he pulled the taut bud into his mouth, lightly biting the sensitive tip.

"Feels good?" He swept his tongue across her nipple, a damp seduction of incredible softness.

"Of course not. Why would you say that— Oh!" She let out an involuntary yelp as he bit her nipple again.

"Don't lie to me, woman. A cowboy has ways of extracting the truth." He pulled her up again, and caught her mouth in a searing kiss that obliterated the last of her defenses. She kissed him back, desperate now, pouring herself into the kiss. The kiss grew harder, deeper, so urgent that it was almost violent, but not quite, never quite crossing that line to someplace that scared her.

He swept his hand under the loose waistband of her pants, sliding his hand over her bare bottom, never letting up his relentless assault on her mouth as he gripped her hips again, this time, skin against skin in a dazzling seduction of sensation and strength.

Red stomped his foot once, the sound jerking her back to the present. She was on a horse! "Chase, we have to stop—" He cut off her protest with another kiss, sliding his hands under her bottom and lifting her so tightly against him that his clothes seemed to merge with her own skin.

Sensation flooded her senses, and all she could do was cling to him as he continued his sensual, delicious assault on every level. She was vaguely aware of a rocking motion, and realized that Red was walking, but Chase gave her no time to think about it. He wrapped his arms around her, and then swung her off his lap in an effortless move that made her feel like she weighed about five pounds. He swept her through her window, depositing her inside the room. For a brief moment, she felt the cool night air sweeping over her now, filling with regret and loneliness. Why had he ended the kiss so quickly? Even as she thought it, however, she took a deep breath, steeling herself against the turbulence of emotions as she turned away from the window.

It was better this way. She needed space from him to think, to figure out, what she needed to do—

Suddenly, she heard the thud behind her, a thud that sounded suspiciously like Chase coming through her window after her. Her heart leapt in anticipation, and she spun around, but she didn't have time to fully turn before his arms wrapped around her, sending heat rushing through her. Before she could decide whether to protest, he scooped her in his arms and carried her toward the bed.

Chapter 8

Oh, God, was she going to do this? They were just going to leave his horse in the middle of the ranch? "Red—"

"He's well-trained. He's fine. I took off his tack before I followed you in. He'll head to the barn and settle down for the night." He set her on the bed, and pulled back, his blue eyes gleaming at her. "But I appreciate the fact you were concerned about him."

It was such a small thing for her to have done, but she could see from the intensity of his gaze that he meant it. By thinking about his horse's well-being, she'd somehow passed some test she doubted he even knew he had. Her heart tightened for him. This wasn't simply a man whose kisses ignited a passion in her. It was a man who'd suffered greatly as a child, and dedicated his life toward keeping his family together, a man who was touched by the fact she'd cared about his horse...a man who was afraid he'd break her if he breathed on her.

She smiled, her heart softening as she ran her fingers over his cheek. "You're a good man," she said softly. "Your brothers are lucky to have you."

He went still, and for a moment, she thought she'd said the wrong thing by bringing up his brothers. Of course it had been a mistake. His brothers were his reality, the meaning of his life, the rock that had held him together for so long...and she was not a welcome part of it. "Listen, I don't want to interfere—"

He cut her off with a kiss, a kiss that was almost desperate with need. The fierceness of the kiss broke through her walls, and she wanted to cry with the intensity of her response. She understood the loneliness that drove him, because she'd lived it with AJ, and because she'd experienced it in the years since her parents' car accident.

Chase was so alive, so passionate, a survivor who had transcended his past and become an indomitable force. Still kissing her, he eased her backward, until he was on her, his weight pressing into the bed. It felt so good to be beneath him, to feel his warmth and strength enveloping her. Her entire body practically vibrated with a need for him, a need that was nothing like what had driven her into AJ's arms.

AJ had been about finding comfort with a friend in the midst of devastating grief. This moment with Chase was about her own need as a woman. It was about Chase as a man. It was lust and desire, and something more, an attraction and a source of strength greater than she was. She tugged at his shirt, pulling it out of his jeans, needing to feel the man beneath the rugged exterior.

He eased off her and dragged his shirt over his head, showing a lean body cut with the muscles of a man accustomed to a physical life. Scars crisscrossed his flesh, and her heart tightened at the reminder of all he'd suffered. She instinctively sat up and pressed a kiss to the one over his heart, a jagged line that looked like a knife had torn his flesh apart. "I'm so sorry," she whispered.

His fingers tangled in her hair, and he went still as she kissed another mark on his ribs. "It's okay," he said softly. "It was a long time ago."

"Never long enough," she said, as she kissed a scar on the front of his shoulder. "It's always too raw," she said. "I know it is."

Chase felt his entire body shudder as Mira kissed each of his scars. He didn't even think about them anymore, but having her isolate them one by one brought them all roaring back to life. But it felt different now. Instead of flashbacks of the pain and fear he felt as a kid, his muscles relaxed, releasing the tension that he'd been holding for so long. His muscles trembled as they let go, as if they didn't even remember how to be normal.

Then, she rose to her knees, as if to go around him

and see his back. He stopped her, pulling her against him. "My turn," he said.

She smiled as he bent his head, the intoxicating smile of a woman who had stopped his world on its axis. He kissed her, this time a slow seduction. He tasted her lips with careful purposefulness, taking the time to slide his tongue across every inch of her mouth, memorizing the feel and taste of her.

He started to lower her to the bed again, and she pushed at his chest. "Boots?"

"Boots?" He nibbled his way down her neck. "What about them?" He had no idea what she was talking about. All he could focus on was *her.*

"I think they're super sexy and everything, but I don't want to be the woman who isn't even worth taking boots off for."

"What?" He pulled back, then grinned when he saw the twinkle in her eyes. "You know you're completely worthy of ditching the boots." He swung off the bed, and yanked off his cowboy boots. He didn't waste time, sliding his jeans off as well, leaving behind only his boxer briefs.

She was propped up on her elbows, watching him, her face shadowed by the moonlight as if she were an ethereal goddess who had come to earth just to ease his pain.

"You are one fine woman," he said as he eased onto the bed, crawling across the navy comforter until he was above her, suspending himself, not quite touching, but almost, a temptation so great his muscles were actually shaking with the effort he was exerting to restrain himself.

Mira placed her palms on his chest, a sensual, incredibly delicate touch that made his abs tighten. "Kiss me, Chase."

"A cowboy never says no to his woman," he said, lowering himself on top of her. This time, it was pure heat between them, the thin fabric of her top and pants no more than a tease. Her skin was hot, a sinful temptation. Her breasts were straining against her camisole, her nipples hard and ready.

"I'm not your woman," she whispered.

Yes, you are. He didn't say it aloud. He just kissed her, a kiss that staked his claim on the woman he'd coveted since the first time he'd seen her picture on AJ's desk during orientation week their freshman year.

She sighed in capitulation, and wrapped her hands around his neck, pulling him closer. Her kiss was as fervent as his, stoking the embers already burning within him. This time, when he slid his palm beneath the hem of her silky top, he moved his hand upward, sliding her top aside. Her breasts spilled free, and he pulled the shirt over her head, tossing it to the floor.

He cupped her breasts softly, stunned by the sight of them. Petite and soft, they filled his palms as if they were meant for him. "Perfection," he whispered, as he bent his head to place a reverent kiss on each nipple.

Mira stiffened beneath him, a soft gasp slipping from her lips as he kissed her breasts. Satisfaction poured through him as he drew her nipple into his mouth and bit lightly.

"Oh, wow." She gripped his shoulders, twisting beneath him. "I can't believe how good that feels."

He grinned. It felt right to have her responding to him so completely. She was entirely accessible to him, allowing herself to feel every sensation he stirred up. He wanted her to feel amazing, to drift to the heavens in ecstasy. He wanted to give her everything he had to offer.

New furor surging through him, he kissed his way down her belly to the waistband of her pants. Her skin was so soft and smooth, her muscles trembling as he moved lower. He thumbed the waistband of her pajama bottoms, and ever so slowly began to slide them downward as he kissed her.

The soft tuft of hair tickled his chin, and then he pressed a kiss to the swollen nub between her legs. Mira's body jerked, and she let out a soft cry, and tried to pull away, even while her fingers dug into his hair, holding him right where he was.

He grinned, and wrapped his arms around her thighs, holding her still as he kissed her, sweeping his tongue across her folds. She tasted like the sweetest honey, one that was created just for him. It was intoxicating perfection, stirring up a sense of possession inside him. He wanted to claim her as his own, forever and ever, locking her down against him. His muscles were taut with need, as he continued to kiss her, intense satisfaction roaring through him as she responded to him, giving herself over to him completely. Her trust in him settled in his gut, and it felt so right. This was his woman, the one he'd been waiting for his entire life. *Mine.*

Her body started to tremble, and she gripped his shoulders. He took advantage, upping his assault, driving her relentlessly, tightening his grip on her hips as she bucked against him. Anticipation roared through him and he bit lightly, just enough, just right, exactly how he knew it should be. "Chase!" She gasped his name, and then her body shuddered under the sudden, ruthless, orgasm.

Red-hot desire roared through him as she came apart in his arms, and raw need pulsed at him. He needed more. He needed to be inside her, to make her his in the only way he knew how.

He ditched his underwear, and then moved up her body, kissing as he went. She opened her eyes, and smiled. Her cheeks were flushed, and her eyes were half-lidded as she held out her arms to him. "Make love to me, Chase."

"God, yes." He slid his knee between her thighs, parting them.

She immediately wrapped her legs over his hips, and his heart seemed to stutter at her complete trust of him.

His cock pressed against her damp entrance, but he didn't enter her. Instead, he took her face in his hands and kissed her, the gentlest kiss he knew how to deliver. It wasn't a kiss of untamed lust. It was a kiss that was for her, and her alone. He didn't have words to describe it. He didn't know how to articulate the promise he was making, because he wasn't even sure what it was.

He poured it all into the kiss, and she responded with equal passion, until the world seemed to vanish, and all that remained was the woman in his arms. Need coiled within him, escalating with each moment until his muscles ached and screamed for release.

He shifted his hips and slid right into her, their bodies coming together in the perfect synthesis of desire, lust, and partnership. She gasped, her legs tightening around him as he sank deeper inside her.

The feeling of being so connected with her was almost surreal. It was so incredible, as if this were the moment his entire life had been building toward. She was the one he'd been waiting for, the one who could somehow strip him of all the hell that haunted him. She was the one who could make him whole again.

He thrust again, pulling out, then driving even deeper, again and again, until he couldn't think of anything but her. She seemed to fill his entire existence, a great flash of sunlight burning up all the crap searing into him. He needed more. He needed everything. He needed this moment. He needed *her*.

She gasped his name, and her body went rigid as the second orgasm flooded her. The moment she found her release, he released his ironclad control over his own lust. His orgasm hit him so hard that her name tore from his throat. He bucked against her, holding her tight in his arms as he rode the wave that seemed endless and merciless, dragging him into her spell until there was nothing left but the two of them, and the fire that had marked him forever.

🙋 🙋 🙋

Mira awoke to a heavy weight wrapped around her, suffocating her. Her eyes snapped open, and she saw rustic wooden walls, and a masculine room she didn't recognize. Where was she? Panic rushed through her, and she tried to sit up, but the weight tightened around her.

"It's okay," Chase muttered, sleepily. "Just me."

Chase? She turned her head to see him beside her. He was on his side, facing her, his leg draped across her hips, and his arm tucked around her torso. His eyes were closed, and thick whiskers lined his jaw.

Relief rushed through her and she sank back onto the sheets. She became aware of the fact they were both naked. The heat from his body was burning through her, and the hair on his legs was prickling her thigh. She could even feel his erection pressing against her hip. Desire and awareness licked through her as she recalled the previous night. What had she done, sleeping with him like that?

Embarrassment flooded her cheeks, and she rested her arm across her eyes, half-wishing she could sink into the mattress and disappear. She didn't even know him. Her grand plan had been to come out to Wyoming and start her own life, not fall into his arms less than five hours after arriving.

What would he think of her? He already knew she'd slept with AJ less than a month ago, and now she'd jumped him like a dog in heat? Granted, AJ had been her first in years, but still, how would he know that? Her chest tightened, and she fisted her hand in frustration. What kind of standard had she set? How could she possibly protect herself from him now? Would he want her to jump into bed with him every night? Because it would be really difficult to maintain a "business partnership" marriage if she was getting naked with him every night. Not that it would be bad, because sex with him was amazing, but she couldn't do this.

Chase moved his hand, spreading his palm over her left breast.

She tensed, hating the way her nipple tightened at the contact. She wouldn't have sex with him again right now. She couldn't. She needed her space—

"Your heart is racing," he mumbled, his voice still heavy with sleep. "What's wrong?"

Her heart was racing? That was why he'd spread his hand over her breast? To check on her, not seduce her? Tears suddenly filled her eyes, and exhaustion overwhelmed her. "Don't be nice."

He grunted, and shifted. Before she could react, he pulled her onto his chest, so she was looking right at him. His eyes were at half-mast, and he looked so sinfully sexy that she wanted nothing more than to scoot up his body and kiss him until he made love to her again.

He reached up, gently moving her hair off her face. He sifted through her curls, his fingers deftly untangling the knots. As sleep wore off, his eyes were becoming more alert, roaming her face carefully. "Why are you panicking?"

She cleared her throat. "I'm not panicking."

He smiled, a half-smile that showcased the dimple in his left cheek. "Sweetheart, I make a living by knowing how to read the physical cues of my horses. I'm really good at it." His fingers were comforting as they worked through her hair, and she couldn't help but begin to relax. "I wake up after the best sex of my life, to find that your entire body has gone rigid, your heart is racing like a filly in flight, and you don't even want to look at me. So, yeah, panicking. It's my job to make that go away. It's what I do."

She immediately dragged her eyes off his chin and met his gaze. "The best sex of your life?"

"Hell, yeah." His gaze was thoughtful, still roaming over her face and her hair, as if he were trying to imprint her on his memory. "This complicates things," he said.

"I know." She bit her lip, trying desperately not to lose herself in the magic he was weaving in her hair. "I'm not ready for this."

His fingers stilled. "You loved AJ," he said quietly. "Shit. Sorry. I rushed you into this."

"Well, of course I loved him..." She saw his face become shuttered, and realized what he was thinking. "Not like that. He was my best friend, but I didn't love him romantically." She suddenly saw a chance to try to explain. "We'd never even kissed before a month 'ago. We were both so devastated by my mother's death. It was like we were trying to hold onto her through each other. It's weird to say, but it wasn't sex. It was more like... survival, trying not to drown in the grief. I don't know if that makes sense." She felt her cheeks redden. "I don't sleep around. AJ was the first guy I'd been with since Brian, and then you. I mean, that's it. I—"

She stopped when he brushed a kiss over her knuckles, her belly clenching.

"Mira."

She swallowed. "What?"

He pressed another kiss to her knuckles. "I know who you are. You don't need to try to explain it. I've seen you through the eyes of a man who respected and trusted you more than anyone else on the planet. There's no chance that I'd be judging you."

For a moment, she started to relax, and then his words sank in, the truth behind his beautiful speech. "You know me through AJ," she said.

"Of course. I've known you for more than ten years." He brushed a tendril of hair back from her face. "You're the one who saved him. You brought him back home to your family and you welcomed him. You never cared about his deformed foot, and you taught him to look past it." He frowned, searching her face. "I've been waiting for you for ten years, Mira. I didn't know it, until I saw you in that church two days ago."

"Ten years?" She frowned.

He nodded. "Since the first week of college, when AJ first mentioned you. I was bitter, and I hated women. You seemed to be an exception, though, a woman worth trusting. AJ didn't believe in anyone except you, and I soon realized you were someone I had to meet." He grinned. "It took ten years, but at least we finally met."

Betrayal seemed to wrap around her heart, and she bit her lip, reality finally sinking in. She now, finally, understood why he'd brought her back to Wyoming. It wasn't simply because of AJ, which she had been able to accept. It was also because he saw her as some magical fantasy woman who would save his world. He wanted her to rescue him, the way she'd rescued AJ.

The hurt bit deep, as deeply as it had when Brian had betrayed her. Her college love had wanted her to be a fun-loving co-ed, and he'd tossed her aside when he'd realized she wasn't always the carefree socialite she'd been in college. Now, Chase was the opposite. He saw her only as a salvation who could soothe the scars he still carried from his terrible childhood. He wanted her to save him, like he thought she'd done for AJ, like she'd tried to do for her mother.

She had nothing left to give him, nothing left to give anyone else. She wanted him, someone, *anyone*, to see her as she really was. She wanted someone to see that the woman who put on a brave front was terrified. She wanted someone to realize that the woman who took care of other people wanted someone to hold her up. She needed someone to realize that even though she cried, sometimes she just wanted to forget life and be a little irresponsible and fun.

"I'm not a goddess," she said, rolling off him. "I'm just me. I get angry. I cry. I yell. I break promises. I'm not perfect, Chase. Not at all. I'll make terrible mistakes as a mother, and I'm sure I'll make my kid cry. I can't save anyone. I can't save you. I'm not this fantasy woman that you have created in your mind. I'm real, and I'm a mess."

She sat up, grabbed the nearest item of clothing, which was his plaid, button-down shirt. She yanked it on and held it closed over her breasts.

Chase frowned as he watched Mira withdraw from him. What had just happened? He leaned over the bed and grabbed her wrist as she tried to climb out of the bed. "Mira," he said gently, trying not to spook her any more than she already was. "Come back here."

She looked down at his fingers wrapped around her arm. "Please let me go."

"What happened? What's going on?" A rising sense of urgency pulsed through him. She was slipping through his fingers. After all these years, he'd finally found her, and he was already losing her. "Mira. Talk to me."

She looked over at him. "For ten years, you've had this vision in your head about who I am. You don't see me."

He frowned. "Of course I see you—"

"No." She touched his lips, silencing him. "You don't. You had a terrible childhood, which I understand, and my heart breaks for you. You see me through the eyes of AJ, not for who I am." She sighed, realizing the truth of the words before she even spoke them. "I see you the same way. I never would have slept with you last night or even come out here if it wasn't for everything AJ had said about you."

He nodded. "Yeah, of course. He connects us more deeply than we would have been able to do on our own this quickly. But that's okay. It means we know who we really are, and we don't have to do that stupid dance while we figure each other out."

"That's my point! Don't you get it?" She pulled her wrist free of his grasp, and he reluctantly let her go. "I'm not the woman you've created in your head. I can't save you. I didn't save AJ. He saved himself, and I was just his friend." She touched his face. "And you can't save me, either. I have to go figure out who I am, Chase. I can't live in the shadow of who I once was, which is who you want me to be."

Swearing, he rolled out of bed, catching her arm as she walked toward the door. "I don't want you to be anyone but yourself," he said. "What are you talking about? It's you that I made love to last night, not some figment of my imagination."

She turned to face him, and he went cold at the resolution he saw in her eyes. "No, you didn't. And I didn't make love to you. I made love to a sense of safety and trust created by AJ. And I'll be honest, all I want to do is fall into your arms right now and let you make love to me a thousand more times, until the rest of the world disappears and all that's left is you."

Something twisted in his gut at her words. He would have expected it to be fear, maybe even terror at the thought of getting irrevocably entwined with a woman, but fear wasn't what he felt. It just felt...right. The most intense feeling of satisfaction. "That's a problem?"

"Yes. I need it to be real, Chase. I need you to be with *me*, not a fantasy, and it needs to be the same for you." With a sigh, she laid her hand on his cheek. Her fingers were so soft that it was almost surreal. "I think I fell a little bit in love with you the moment you said your name at the church, and that's how I know it's not real. It's too soon for how strongly I feel about you, which means I've fallen in love with a fantasy who isn't real, and it's the same for you." She dropped her hand and stepped back. "I'll leave today, Chase. I have to. I can't live under false pretenses anymore."

Before he could respond, she grabbed some clothes from her luggage, and ducked out into the hall. He heard the bathroom door shut, and the shower began to run.

With a deep sigh, he sank down on the bed, and ran his fingers through his hair. Was she right? Was he making shit up because of ten years of idealization? He wasn't a fool. He knew that she was flawed. She had to be. So what would he do the first time she did something that triggered a memory, one of those hot spots that made him shut women out? Would he still believe she was different from all the other women? Or would he react instinctively to protect himself and his brothers from a perceived threat, and boot her to the curb without giving her a chance, like he'd done with every other woman he'd ever been with? She deserved more than that, so much more. But could he give her more? Could he give her the trust she deserved and was worthy of, when the shit got difficult, which he knew it would?

He turned his head to look at the picture on the

nightstand. It was a photograph of him and two of his brothers from when they were kids. They were on the Johnson ranch, standing around Killer, the dead-mean old bull that ran the place. All three of them were grinning their heads off, each of them with a hand on the bull that they'd once been too scared of to go near. He picked up the photograph and looked at it, running his finger over the faces of his brothers.

Without the Johnson ranch, he would be dead now, and so would his brothers. Old Skip Johnson had chosen to put him to work on the ranch instead of turning him over to the cops when he'd found him drunk and trying to steal his booze. That ranch had been Chase's salvation, and that was the ranch he now had his home on. He'd bought it from Skip five years ago, giving his former mentor one year to live his fantasies out as a retiree in Florida before he'd died.

Was Chase really willing to risk the dream of rebuilding his family just for a chance at a fantasy with a woman, a fantasy that was so lofty that he knew it wasn't based on reality? Mira was right. There was no way she was the flawless woman he'd created in his mind, and there was no way she, or any woman, was worth risking his relationship with his brothers for. Silently, he set the picture back down.

The answer had to be no.

It wasn't only his life. It was his brothers' as well. He couldn't do this thing with her. He would have to let her leave. It had all been a mistake.

Regret pouring through him, he stood up and strode across the room to retrieve his jeans, which were in a pile on top of her suitcase.

He grabbed his pants off it, but the belt buckle caught on the suitcase, jerking it off the table. It landed with a thump, dumping the contents across the pine flooring.

Swearing, he scooped everything up, trying to shove it all back inside before she returned to the room. He tried not to notice the black lace bra or silk underwear. He ignored the bottle of nail polish that was in the exact shade of his favorite wild flower in the spring. And he refused to contemplate how that crazy-soft light cream sweater would hug her curves.

But when he picked up a pair of light blue baby socks,

he couldn't toss them aside. He just stared at them, shocked by how tiny they were. How in the hell could a kid be small enough to fit in them? Then he noticed another pair. Pink. Slowly, he reached down and pulled those free of the pile.

He held both pairs in the palm of his hand, two tiny pairs of socks. They were so small, it was as if they were for dolls. He instinctively cupped his hand around them, already prepared to protect the tiny being who would wear socks that small. She'd bought one of each, ready for whatever gender she was carrying. Even though she was facing hell, she was set to take on the challenge.

Those socks would be on the feet of the kid she carried, the one who had no dad, and was saddled with a true bastard of a grandfather. Chase looked at the burn marks on his forearm. He looked back at the socks, then back at his arm. He was going to sentence a kid to that? AJ's child? The baby of the first woman he'd trusted enough to allow into his house and his bed? Yeah, technically, it was the guest bedroom, but it was the same thing. His world. His sanctuary.

He wasn't a fool. He was a bitter, cynical bastard who didn't trust anyone. If there was *any* reason for him not to trust Mira, he would have seen it. But instead, he'd brought her into his world.

Yeah, maybe he saw her through his fantasies, but he knew he was right about her being worth trusting. She was willing to walk away from his help and face AJ's dad herself, rather than lose her freedom to a man.

He gently laid the socks on top of her clothes, and he knew what he had to do.

He'd won over a lot of battered horses, and gained their trust. It was time to do the same with Mira. He could make this work.

Chapter 9

Mira leaned against the wall in the shower, letting the hot water wash Chase's scent off her skin. She felt surprisingly, achingly alone. She knew she had to leave the house, but last night in Chase's arms had been amazing. It was the first time she'd felt alive in a long while.

She hadn't been lying when she'd said a part of her wanted to lose herself in the moment with him, but Taylor's words kept ringing in her ears. She was falling too hard and too fast for him, and there was so much at stake. Her own life, and her baby's.

The truth was, she was a complete mess right now, from her mom's death, and then AJ's, and then the baby thing. Of course she was latching onto Chase. What woman wouldn't? But that could only lead to bad things. She couldn't even find her own feet right now. How could she trust her judgment?

She wanted to be saved, and the last time that had happened, she'd wound up pregnant. The time before that? She'd wound up engaged to a man who'd wanted her to abandon her paralyzed mother to go party with him at college. So, what would it be with Chase? What more did she have to lose?

Her baby. He'd already said he'd go on record as the baby's father. That would give him all the power in the world when it came to her life.

There was a light knock at the bathroom door, making her jump. "Who is it?" Dumb question. There was only one person in the house besides her.

"It's me." Chase's deep voice rumbled through her, making goose bumps pop up on her skin.

Why did the blasted man have to affect her like that? "What do you want?" The glass door to the shower was fogged up, but not enough for privacy.

"We need to talk."

She almost laughed at his timing. "I'm in the shower."

"I know. Can I come in?" The door opened as he asked it, and she instinctively covered her breasts as she saw him step into the room. He was blurred from the steam on the shower door, but she could tell he was wearing only his jeans. His chest was bare, and she could see the shadows of his muscles and the breadth of his shoulders, even through the distortion of the fogged glass.

"Can't you wait until I get out?"

He leaned against the sink and folded his arms over his chest, facing the shower. "No."

"I'm naked."

"I know. I'm not blind." He held up something pink and blue. "You bought these?"

She couldn't tell what they were. "Chase, seriously, I'm not comfortable with you in here. Can you wait outside?"

"I spent half the night kissing every inch of your body. I made love to you three times, and I know what every part of you tastes like. I know every curve on your body. I know you have a scar on your left breast, and a freckle on the inside of your right thigh. I know you have a birthmark on your left butt cheek in the shape of a butterfly, and I know the sound you make when you have an orgasm, and how it changes depending on whether it's an orgasm from oral sex or making love. The feel of your naked body entwined with mine while we slept will be imprinted upon my mind forever, as will the color of your skin in the moonlight. Having me wait outside won't change any of that, no matter how much you wish it could, so yeah, I want to talk, and I want to talk now."

By the time he finished his little speech, her cheeks were hot, her skin was tingling, and her lower belly was clenched in memory of all the sensations he'd evoked in her last night. "Yes, we were naked last night, but this is different. You've never seen me in the shower—"

The shower door slid open before she could finish her sentence, and she found herself face-to-face with him. His blue gaze was intense, drilling into hers so deeply she felt like ducking behind a tree. He wasn't even looking at her body. Just her face. "Now I've seen you in the shower," he said. "We need to talk, Mira."

She wrinkled her nose at him. "You have no sense of personal space."

He didn't even acknowledge her point. "You can't leave."

She blinked, startled by his change in topic. "Leave where?"

"My house. You said you were moving out." He frowned. "You're not?"

"Oh, that, right." She cleared her throat, and gave up arguing with him about the shower. He was right. There wasn't any part of her left that he hadn't claimed last night, and he was clearly a man on a mission. "Go away." She grabbed the door and slid it shut.

He opened the door back up and held up what she now recognized as the baby socks she'd spontaneously picked up at the gift shop at the airport on her way to Wyoming.

Embarrassment flooded her cheeks. "It was just a whim."

"It's a baby." His gaze finally left her face and went to her belly. "You're carrying a baby, Mira."

Her hand instinctively went to her stomach, which was still in its ordinary, "a little too much chocolate" rounded state. "I know."

"Sex last night was great," he said. "I'm not going to deny that I'd move you into my bedroom in a split second if you'd do it."

Something inside her twisted, and she couldn't tell if it was stark, raving terror, or the deepest, most beautiful desire. "Chase—"

He held up his hand. "I know the arguments. I was just saying it like it is." He folded his arms over his chest and leaned back against the sink, giving her the illusion of a little bit of personal space. "Here's the truth. I'm not going to lie and try to claim that I'm not attracted to you. I never let myself get a hard-on for a woman. I make sure it doesn't happen. But it's going on with you, and that's the way it is. But—" He again held his hand to silence her when she opened her mouth to protest. "I get that there are issues here. I've been obsessed with you for a decade. I'm not going to lie about that either, but I get your point that we've both been living in a fantasy land about each other."

Something tightened in her chest. A decade? He'd really thought about her for a decade? She didn't know what AJ had said about her, but she knew it wasn't glamorous. He'd seen her with dirt under her toenails and sweat stains under her arms hundreds of times. "Okay, so—"

He flipped the baby socks in his hand. "But what's reality is this kid, and the fact that he's got a grandfather who will abuse him if he gets his hands on him. You can't stop Alan alone. I can't stop him alone. But together, we have a chance."

She sighed. "So, we're back to where we started."

"No, we're not." He caught the socks, snatching them out of the air. "I spent the night making love to you. We're not back to where we started. We'll never be back there, and I don't want to be."

Suddenly, the water seemed too hard against her skin. Too hot. Her skin felt sensitive and on fire. "I do."

"No, you don't." He levered himself off the sink and walked over to her, stopping on the threshold to the shower. This time, his eyes burned over her body, searing her with the raw desire in his gaze. "It's complicated, but it's good."

She lifted her chin, letting the water run over her body, refusing to cower before him. "It's not good." At his raised eyebrows, she sighed. "Okay, it *was* good. Great. But—"

"They're two different things," he said. "Us, and the baby. For the baby, you need to stay here. For us..." He shrugged, his gaze boring into her. "We need to figure that out, but I'll never let what happens between us affect my commitment to making sure that kid wakes up every morning of his or her life feeling safe."

Her throat tightened at the passion in his voice. He meant every word. "Does that mean safe from you?"

He blinked, his brow furrowing. "What?"

She couldn't help blurting out the fear that had been

gnawing at her since her conversation with Taylor. "What if you wind up being the bad guy, too? What if you're the baby's father on paper, and you wind up being the bad guy? Who protects us from you?"

He stared at her, and a cold, cold mask settled over his face. "You think that just because my father was an abusive drunk that I'll be that kind of father? You think I'd actually do something to hurt another living being? A *child*?"

At his words, a deep feeling of foreboding settled over her. "I didn't mean it like that—"

"No?" His voice was cool. "What did you mean, exactly?"

"I just meant that I've judged people incorrectly before. I believe in you, but how do I know I'm right? To give you parental rights to my child when I don't even know you is terrifying on any level. It has nothing to do with what kind of father you had, and everything to do with the fact that I don't know you."

He stared at her, and said nothing, and she began to realize that she'd just touched upon a nerve that was buried deep inside him.

"Chase." She shut off the water and stepped out of the shower, not even caring that she was naked anymore. "I grew up with AJ. His father is a terrible man, but AJ inherited none of his anger, his violent tendencies, or his lack of humanity. I know from personal experience that a person's parents don't define who they are. I *know* that, so please don't ever think I'm judging you based on that."

Again, he said nothing, but she felt the wall that was building between them.

Fear rippled through her, and she realized that he was slipping out of her grasp. Too late, she realized that she'd already begun to count on his support and his loyalty. Without him as backup, she was in a really precarious position. "Chase." She set her hands on his chest, and his muscles flexed beneath her palms. "Don't judge me based on your own past. I'm really scared right now, and struggling to make choices with my head, and not with my heart. My heart wants to trust you, but I don't know you that well. Please understand that."

He closed his eyes for a moment and inhaled deeply. His skin was damp from the steam of the shower, making her fingers want to slide off his chest.

"Chase?"

He opened his eyes, and his gaze bore into her. "I'll have my lawyer draw up a contract that protects you from me. I'll pay for you to have another lawyer look it over. In the meantime, we need to get you a doctor in town. I'll ask around, and find out who's the best. We'll hold off on getting married until you're far enough along. That would be what, the third month? That's when things are usually pretty confirmed? In the meantime, you need to stay here and make the world believe that we're in love, having sex all the time, and I knocked you up. Sound good? Safe enough?"

Gone was his warmth and affection. She could practically see his shields going up between them. It was what she wanted, right? His protection but not risking her heart? But it felt terrible. She hated it. "I'm not the women who betrayed you so many times, Chase," she said softly. "I'm just me."

Something flickered in his eyes, and for a moment, she thought she saw the old Chase, the one who made her feel like the most cherished woman in the world. Then it was gone. "I know." He reached out and brushed his finger across her cheek. She went utterly still, her heart pounding in anticipation.

When he'd first walked into the bathroom, she wanted nothing more than for him to leave. Now, all she could think about was how much she wanted him to kiss her.

His gaze dropped to her lips, and she went still. Tension rose between them, thick and steamy, and her pulse quickened. *Kiss me, Chase. Don't give up on me.*

She couldn't ask him to do it. She couldn't reach out. She was too scared. He needed to make the first move and bridge the gap between them, to hold them together while they battled through the scars they both carried.

His gaze met hers, and she saw decades of abuse in his eyes. Hurt, pain, suffering, and a fierce, indomitable will to survive and protect. "Chase?"

He sighed. "What the hell am I going to do with you?" His fingers slipped under her chin, and he bent his head to kiss her.

His lips were like velvety magic against hers, his kiss a seduction that swept through her like a sensual caress. She instinctively melted against him, needing the physical connection with him. She clasped her hands behind his neck as his arms locked around her, pulling her against him. Her breasts were flush against his bare chest, and her nipples hardened instantly at the sensation of his body against hers. They were both damp from the shower, and the wetness made her breasts slide over his chest as he backed her against the sink, deepening the kiss.

He lifted her onto the counter, cupping her buttocks as she wrapped her legs around his hips. Last night, making love to him had felt like a fantasy drifting through her life for one moment. This time, it felt different. This time, in the light of day, it was real. She felt almost desperate, as if she were trying to hang onto the first good thing that life had given her in such a long time.

His kiss was equally desperate, almost rough, as if he were driven by a need beyond what he could control. He cupped her breasts, pinching her nipple. Desire leapt through her, and she fumbled for the fly of his jeans. She didn't want foreplay. She didn't want to think that much. She just wanted him inside her, as if that would bind him to her.

He helped her with his zipper, and then freed himself. His jeans were still around his thighs as he pulled her onto his cock and thrust inside her. She gasped at the invasion, her whole body clenching at the feel of him inside her, filling her so completely. He drove deep and hard, holding her tightly to keep her from sliding on the granite counter. His kisses were relentless, intermixing with his thrusts to spiral her out of control, until she could barely even think. She was overwhelmed by the enormity of his being, and the strength of his body.

He moved one hand between her thighs, sweeping over her folds. "Come with me, Mira. Let it go."

The orgasm leapt through her so fast she screamed.

"That's my girl." He kept his hand between them, driving deeper and faster, taking her further and further over the edge, not letting up his assault, until her whole body was on fire with the orgasm that sucked her into its endless cycle of ecstasy.

She screamed again, digging her fingers into his shoulder, and then he came as well. He bucked against her, locking her tight against him as he drove so deep inside her that she felt like he would be a part of her forever. He buried his face in her hair, whispering her name over and over again as he came, his orgasm lasting as long as the ones that had taken her.

It felt like an eternity of heaven before the final aftershocks faded. His arms were still around her, his hands palming her butt. He rested his forehead against hers, and she closed her eyes, stunned by the impact of their lovemaking.

She ran her hands over his chest. The bumps from his scars mingled with the sweat rivulets trailing over his skin, and her fingers tangled in the dark hair accenting his chest. She didn't even know what to say. Making love hadn't changed what they were facing, but at the same time, she felt better, as if the wall that had grown between them had been torn down by their lovemaking.

Chase pressed a kiss to her forehead, and slipped one hand through her hair, lifting the curls off the back of her neck. He lightly massaged the nape of her neck, releasing tension from her muscles that she hadn't even realized she was carrying.

"Chase?"

"Yeah."

"I'm really not judging you based on your dad." She pulled back to look at him. "I'm just scared."

He said nothing for a moment, seemingly distracted by untangling her hair with his fingers. "Your point was valid."

She frowned. "What?"

He finally stopped playing with her hair and stepped back, his cock sliding out of her body in an agonizing sensation of loss. "When I was sixteen, I was already drinking heavily. I'd slept with six girls by then, and I couldn't remember half of them because I'd been drunk. My friends and I snuck onto this ranch to steal alcohol and joyride his tractor. I was the one who volunteered to go through the kitchen window, and I wound up with the rancher's shotgun wedged in my chest."

Her heart ached for the expression on his face. There was so much torment and guilt. "What happened?"

"He gave me the choice of going to jail, or working for

him twenty hours a week for two years, until I graduated from high school." Chase pulled his jeans back up over his hips. He didn't fasten them, but they rested low on his waist. "Old Skip had strict rules, and I followed them, because I'd seen my dad go to jail and I knew what it was like. I didn't want to be my dad, so I shaped up. I never would have done it without being forced to. I'll never forget the day Old Skip handed me my first pair of cowboy boots, telling me to earn them." He looked at Mira. "I had never thought I was capable of earning anything, but I'd wanted to be worthy of those damned boots, so I started working my ass off for him." He ran his hand through his hair, remembering. "Gary was Old Skip's buddy, and he used to keep us in line when Old Skip wasn't around. He's a good man." He gestured to the walls. "I bought the place five years ago. This is the ranch that saved me, but without AJ, I never would have taken it this far. I never would have believed I could buy it and make it mine."

She smiled, accepting a towel when he handed it to her. "So, you should feel proud. You broke free from your past."

"No." He leaned forward and planted his hands on either side of her hips, staring intently at her. "Don't you get it? I *was* my dad for a while, and then I cleaned myself up. But my dad was okay too, until my mother died. He loved her, and she died when I was born. That's what put him over the edge and started the spiral that he never came out of." His fingers dug into the sink. "I'm one bad choice away from being my dad, Mira. One sliver of a breath." He ran his finger over her jaw. "A woman broke him, and I never understood how that could happen, until now."

Her heart tightened, and for a moment, she couldn't seem to breathe. "Chase, it's been a long time since you were that boy. You're not your dad—"

"No?" He traced a circle above her breast. "Then why, when I thought you saw me as a monster a few minutes ago, did something inside me simply snap?" He cupped her breast, a tender, possessive touch that made her belly tighten. "I don't think I'm capable of handling how I'm beginning to feel about you, because you're right. You're human, and I'm not sure I can handle anything except the fantasy."

His words were like cold water being dumped over her naked body. So, he didn't want her, the woman she was? That felt fantastic to hear after having sex with him four times in the last twelve hours. "I see."

"Do you?" His voice was urgent, almost desperate. "Do you understand the depths of how far I could fall? Do you know how bad I could be? Because I do. I have the scars to prove it, and so do all my brothers." He picked up the blue baby socks from the floor where they'd fallen, and he set them in her hand. "I never thought about it until now, until I realized the impact I could have on those that I've sworn to protect if I screw up." He closed her fingers over the socks. "One mistake, Mira. That's all it would take for me to fall into the pit that consumed my dad."

She crushed the socks in her hand. "You really think you'd make that mistake? After all you've endured?"

He looked at her. "When I was a freshman in college, I met a girl. I fell in love. She cheated on me with one of my teammates. When I found out, I was devastated. I went straight to a party and started drinking. It was the first time I'd touched alcohol since I was sixteen, and I didn't even pause. AJ found me and dragged me out of there before I finished my first drink. Without him, I'd have been down that path again. So, yeah. I think I have that potential." He looked down at the socks. "And now there's going to be a child," he said softly.

The cotton was rough and damp in her hand, no longer soft and pristine. They were wrinkled and wet. "Yes, there is," she said quietly.

A door slammed somewhere in the house, making them both look toward the door. "Chase!" A man's voice echoed. "You around?"

Chase swore under his breath. "That's Travis."

She stiffened. "Your brother? The one who has come to drive me away and save you from me?"

"Yeah." He raised his voice. "I'm in the bathroom," he called out. "I'll be out in a second." He turned back toward Mira. "Promise me you won't leave the house, that you won't move out."

She hesitated, confused. "But you just said—"

"We'll keep it professional. I'll keep my distance." His

gaze swept over her nakedness one more time. "I don't know how the hell I'm going to keep my hands off you, Mira, but I won't risk you or the child. I'll find a way to be the man my father never was."

Her chest tightened at his promise, and suddenly she wanted to cry for the past that haunted him so ruthlessly. He was such a good man. Was it really possible he could betray himself and her and cross that line?

The door suddenly opened, and she yelped, jerking the towel over her breasts as Chase leapt in front of her, using his body to shield her as a man walked into the bathroom. He was even taller than Chase, and his hair was rough and unkempt. His visage was harder than Chase's, but he had the same blue eyes and straight nose. He was wearing crisp blue jeans and cowboy boots, with a white hat that was tipped low over his face. His gaze swept right past Chase and bore into her.

She stiffened and raised her chin. "You must be Travis. I'm Mira Cabot."

Travis's eyes narrowed, and he looked from her to Chase, swiftly noting her nakedness and Chase's low slung, unfastened jeans and shirtless torso. "Zane said this was a business arrangement," he said. His voice was rough, lazy with a cowboy drawl that didn't conceal his burning intelligence. "This looks like a hell of a lot more than a business partnership."

"Get out of here, Travis." Chase's voice was mild, but it carried a steely edge that made her shiver in appreciation that he was on her side. "I'll be out in a minute."

Travis looked at her again, and she saw a promise in his eyes, a promise to do whatever it took to protect his brother. "I'll be in the kitchen." He stepped backward, his boots thudding on the floor as he pulled the door shut behind him, just hard enough to make a point.

As his footsteps echoed down the hall, Chase ran his hand through his hair. "Tell me you'll stay, Mira."

She sighed. "I don't want to get in the middle—"

He wrapped his hands around her upper arms, pulling her against him. "Tell me you'll stay." His voice was edged with desperation, and she saw something in his eyes that drained the last of her resistance.

"I'll stay for now," she said, finally. "I won't leave without telling you."

He held her for a moment longer, then finally acknowledged her comment with a brief nod. "Okay. We'll talk more later, but I have to go see Travis." There was an edge of excitement to his voice that made her smile.

"How long has it been since you've seen him?" she asked as Chase reached for the doorknob.

He looked back at her. "Five years," he said. "He's only here because of you, so thank you for bringing him back." He gave her a brief smile, then ducked out of the bathroom, pulling the door shut behind him with a soft click.

Mira leaned back against the sink with a sigh. Two Stockton brothers in one house? Because one hadn't been more than she could deal with, right?

She looked up at the ceiling. "AJ, you brought him into my life, so what am I supposed to do now?"

Of course, he didn't answer, but she could almost hear him chuckling. He'd always claimed life was meant to be lived, but what exactly did that mean?

She wasn't entirely sure, but at least one thing was certain: there could be no more sex with Chase. That much she was sure of. But then what?

The low murmur of male voices drifting down the hall told her that she was about to find out.

Chapter 10

Travis was leaning against the counter, his arms folded across his chest, waiting, when Chase walked into the kitchen. He wasn't eating, or doing anything. Just waiting.

Something tightened in Chase's chest at the sight of his younger brother. "Good to see you." He walked over to him, and dragged him into a rough hug.

Travis stiffened, then hugged him back, gripping tightly.

After a moment, Travis pounded him on the back and the brothers released each other. "You're getting old, bro," Travis said. He touched his temple. "Got some gray going on there?"

"Not as much as you. You look like you've got some miles on you." Chase released his brother and stepped back, scanning him. The last time he'd seen Travis, his kid brother been nineteen years old, with a backpack and a guitar, heading off to Nashville. Travis was carrying another thirty pounds of muscle on his once lanky frame, but his face had some lines on it now. In fact, there were shadows beneath his brother's eyes, and his face was thin, almost too thin. He didn't simply look older. He looked worn. "What's the scar on your jaw from?"

Travis touched the mark. "Bar room brawl."

Chase tensed, and then Travis laughed. "Shit, bro, you need to chill. You really think I'd be in a bar room brawl? I'm not that guy. You know I'm not a drinker."

"Yeah, but it's been a while. People change." Chase turned away and started the coffee machine. "Want something to eat?"

"I won't change that way," Travis said. "That's a line I don't cross. And are you offering one of your famous omelets? I'll never turn that down. You got any jalapeños in that fridge of yours?"

"Always." Chase opened the fridge and pulled out the ingredients. He started mixing the eggs, and then decided to add some more for Mira. After cooking for himself for so long, it looked like the biggest batch of eggs he'd made in years. It wasn't a fraction of what he used to whip up for his brothers, but it was a start. It was good. "How's the yodeling going?"

Travis shrugged. "I'm on tour through the end of October." He sat down on one of the bar stools that lined the granite bar. "Fifty-two cities, ninety-six shows in the last four months."

Chase didn't miss the bitterness in his brother's tone, and he cocked an eyebrow at him. "Not going well?" Travis had busted his butt in Nashville for years before signing a deal. It was all he'd ever wanted, and he'd gotten it, and a whole lot more.

"It's fine. I sell out everywhere. Got a couple nominations this year." Travis shrugged. "Living the dream, bro, right?" He looked around. "Place looks good," he commented, changing the subject. "Better than I remembered."

Chase didn't push the topic, but he wondered what was going on. "I've been fixing it up." Even though Travis was a few years younger than Chase, he'd still followed the path of the Stockton boys and started working on the ranch as soon as he was old enough. Old Skip had taken every one of the boys on as help, and they'd all had more than a few hot meals in that kitchen. Some weeks, Skip's chili had been the only decent thing they'd eaten. "Skip hadn't done much to it over the years. He was sick for a while before he passed away." The coffee ready, he poured a cup for Travis and slid it across the counter to him. "Can you stay for a while?"

Travis shook his head. "Have to be in Millingham, Alabama tomorrow night. I blew off tonight. Said I had food poisoning." He inhaled the coffee, and closed his eyes. "You still make the best damn coffee on the entire planet, bro. There's no place in this country that's better than your kitchen in the morning."

"Yeah, thanks." Chase pulled out a mug for Mira, then started chopping onions. "She's okay, you know."

Travis didn't bother to pretend he didn't know what Chase was talking about. Neither of them bothered with small talk anymore. Life didn't slow down enough to waste time dancing around when things had to be covered. "You can't bring her here," Travis said, without preamble.

"I can."

"Shit, man." Travis put down his mug, and gestured around the kitchen. "Look at this place. You've sunk every dime you have into it. You've got a viable business going on with the horses. You've got everything to lose. If you marry her and claim that kid, she's got a knife aimed at your back for the rest of your life."

Chase ground his jaw. "She's not like that—"

"How the hell do you know? This place is *our* history. What if she takes it? It's all we've got."

"The ranch matters to you?" Chase looked up, surprised by his brother's comment. "You've never come by even once since I bought it."

"I know, but it's always *here*." Travis leaned forward, his expensive watch glistening on his wrist. "I talk to Zane. I talk to some of the others. We all know this place is here. If the shit blows up, we got this. If we lose the ranch, the thin, fragile tie that binds us together will break, and we'll all scatter for good."

Chase stared at his brother. "When did you become so poetic?"

Travis shrugged. "I write songs. It's what I do. It's not that hard." He thumped his chest. "You have to feel it to write it. You know my song, *Fence Sittin'*?"

"Your first number one? Yeah, I know it." Chase would never forget the first time he heard Travis's song on the radio. He'd been driving to the train station to head into the city, and they'd said his little brother's name and played that song. He'd pulled over and sat in his car, listening to every single word of it. That moment had been one of the best experiences of his life. Travis had gotten out, and he'd made it.

"That song is about this place. It's what it means to me." Travis stood up and walked over to the window. He braced his hands on the sill and looked out over the front porch. "I still remember sitting on that porch with Old Skip the day he brought out his old guitar and put it into my hands. He said I had talent and I was a stupid bastard for sitting on my ass and chasing girls." He looked back at Chase. "If you marry Mira, she has rights to this place, no matter what you put in the contract. With the right lawyer, she could get it."

Chase put down his knife. "I'm not going to lose the ranch, Travis."

"How do you know?" Travis turned back toward him. "Those women took everything from Dad. Every last thing he had. They can do that."

"Shit, Travis, this isn't like that." Anger rushed through him, and he grabbed the knife and started slicing tomatoes. "Mira's not like that. Hell, she doesn't even want to marry me. I'm the one trying to force her."

"Really?" Travis's eyes narrowed. "Then what the hell are you doing? If she doesn't want to marry you, then take that gift and get out while you can." Travis's voice was hard.

"Really? You think I should just walk away?" Chase slammed down the knife. "That baby she's carrying is the child of my best friend, who I owe my life and this ranch to. You think I should walk away and let that kid live the same life we did? You think that's what I should do?"

"You can save the kid in other ways than marrying her! Hell, Chase, you don't even like women. What the hell has she got on you?"

"Nothing!"

"Then why don't you use your damned head and think of a solution that doesn't put any of this place at risk?"

"Because I don't want to!" The words burst out before he could stop it, and then hung in the air, suspended between them.

Travis whistled softly, understanding dawning on his face. "You've fallen for her. Completely and totally. It's not about the baby. It's about *her*."

"Shut the hell up." Chase jammed the knife through the bell pepper, chopping it up into jagged pieces.

"You don't even *know* her." Travis walked over and

leaned on the counter next to Chase. "Talk to me, bro. What's going on?"

Chase kept chopping. "Just doing my civic duty." Even as he said the words, his conversation with Mira came tumbling back. He set down the knife yet again, looking at his brother. "Do you think we'll all end up like him? You ever hit a woman? Or a kid?"

Travis was silent for a long moment, then shook his head. "No. I never have." He met Chase's gaze. "But I get pissed. A lot. I have a punching bag in my tour bus. I use that."

"You think a kid would be okay with you as a dad?"

Again, a long silence, then Travis shrugged. "I hadn't thought about it, but I don't know. What do we know about being good for anyone, let alone a kid?"

"Nothing." Chase picked up the knife again, and started slicing the jalapeño. "Not a damn thing."

Travis sighed, and leaned against the counter, his arms folded loosely over his chest. "This thing with Mira is wrong on a thousand different levels, bro. You know that. It's wrong for the ranch, for us, for you, for her, and for that kid."

Chase said nothing as he dumped the vegetables into the bowl of beaten eggs. Travis's words made sense, but he couldn't own them. The thought of walking away from Mira felt wrong all the way to his gut. Was it just because he'd had her in his head as a fantasy for so long? Or was it a real response to the woman he'd made love to all night? He added his signature spices, stirring the mixture until it was well-blended.

"Some of us aren't meant to get married and be a dad," Travis said. "Some of us are meant to live a different life."

Chase poured his concoction into the frying pan. "Yeah, maybe." He'd always thought that of himself, but Mira had made him think differently. Now he was thinking about things he had no business contemplating, but he couldn't stop himself.

"That's us," Travis said. "The nine Stockton fuck-ups. We're meant to be solo, and to come back here and recharge and make sure our roots are secure. You're the anchor, and so is this place. It's just how life is." He reached across the counter and snagged his mug. "We're meant to drink good coffee and try not to fuck up the world we live in, and you know it."

Chase grabbed a spatula, watching the omelet begin to sizzle and bubble around the sides. Travis was simply repeating the truth they'd all come to accept as they'd gotten older and realized how close to the edge they all treaded. Only Steen had realized it too late, winding up in prison due to a battle over a woman. The poor bastard was still there, but the clock was ticking down on his release. What did a man become after four years in prison? "I know."

"Let Mira go, Chase. Give her a wad of cash if you want, but let her go. She deserves more than what you can give her, and we all deserve more than what a woman will bring into our lives—" He stopped suddenly, cutting himself off, staring past Chase toward the hallway.

Chase looked over his shoulder, and his gut sank when he saw Mira standing in the doorway. She was wearing jeans and a tank top. Her hair was still wet, and her feet were bare. Without makeup or any adornments, she looked so young and vulnerable that his heart tightened.

She was staring at Travis, and he knew that she'd heard at least the end of the conversation. He quickly replayed it in his mind, trying to recall what they'd said.

Slowly, she pulled her gaze off his brother and looked right at him. He saw the question in her eyes, asking him what he wanted her to do.

He didn't need to ask what she felt. She was prepared to walk out and leave him to the life he'd worked so hard to accomplish. Travis's comments had made him realize that his efforts to create a homestead for his brothers was working. It would be a slow process to get them all back there and reconnected, but it was already working. He had what he wanted. He had *everything* he wanted.

Would he really risk it for a woman he barely knew? A woman who wasn't even ready to trust him, or even trust her own feelings for him? A woman who was so tightly entwined through his soul that he didn't even know which parts were his fantasy and which were real? For a child who could embroil him in a legal battle that could decimate his finances if he fought it all the way through? Alan was a formidable opponent, far more than his own father had ever been, but just as rotten to the core.

Mira raised her eyebrows, and he knew she was waiting for his answer. She wanted it now. She needed it, because she had a life she had to figure out, and the clock was ticking. All he had to do was nod, and she would walk away without a single look back.

Travis looked over at him, and he saw his brother's dark expression, already retreating from the presence of a woman in their sanctuary. "Tell her, Chase."

Mira pressed her lips together and raised her chin. "Tell me what?"

He looked back and forth between them, and he knew that the only two things in the world that made him feel alive were standing there, and he had to choose between them.

※ ※ ※

"I've made a decision," Mira cut Chase off just as he opened his mouth to answer.

Travis raised his eyebrows. "Did you?"

"No." Chase interrupted. "Mira—"

"There's no need to get married." She blurted out the words before Chase could speak. She'd heard enough of the conversation between the brothers, and she'd seen the look of torment on Chase's face when she'd walked in. She didn't know what he would choose, but either one was unacceptable. If he'd stood up for her against Travis, he would lose his brother. If he'd told her to leave... God, the mere thought of it made something inside her want to cry with loss. There was no way she could handle him cutting her out, but there was no way that she'd be responsible for coming between the brothers. Which meant she had to take herself out of the equation before Chase could be forced to make a choice.

Chase shot an angry look at Travis, whose relief was obvious. "Don't listen to my brother," Chase said. "He's—"

"He cares about you," she interrupted. She stepped into the kitchen, knowing what she had to say. She'd realized the moment Travis had cut himself off and looked at her. Everything had become clear when she'd seen the bond between the brothers. She'd been touched by the depth of their fear of how broken they both were, and she now understood how important the ranch was to all of them. It had been beautiful seeing their connection, but at the same time, she'd felt like an intruder into their space.

She deserved more than to live life as an outsider, and so did her child.

"The issue with the baby is not whether I'm married to Chase. It's whether we can convince Alan that Chase is the biological father. If I stay here for a few months, it sets up our relationship sufficiently." She didn't look at Chase as she talked. She couldn't. It was harder than she thought to pull away from him, even after this short time. "I don't need to marry him." She looked at Travis. "And I don't need his money."

Chase swore under his breath. "You do need money."

"Just a roof over my head and food until I can get a job. Selling my parents' house should cover most of the medical bills." Her throat suddenly tightened, and she felt a wave of sadness at her mother's death, but she lifted her chin. "It's clear that I can't put AJ's name on the birth certificate, and I feel that leaving it blank is too dangerous." She met Chase's gaze. "The only thing I think I really need from you is your name on the birth certificate. With any luck, nothing more will ever happen, but it gives us the ammunition if we need it."

She knew the risk of giving him parental rights over the child, but she couldn't think of any other way. Chase's name had to be on there, or the child would always be vulnerable to Alan.

Chase's eyes narrowed. "It might not be enough, if Alan comes after him."

"Marriage doesn't change whether you're the baby's biological father or not. If we make our relationship clear and visible, and your name is on the birth certificate, then it's just as good as if we were married. The only issue will be that the baby will be born 'early,' so we need to lay low until then. Alan has to forget about me." She shrugged. "If he forces a DNA test, then it doesn't matter whether you're married to me or not."

"It might help." Chase was gripping the spatula so hard that his knuckles were white.

"The omelet's burning," Travis said. "Needs to be flipped."

Chase glared at him, then turned back to the stove. He

flipped the omelet deftly, making it apparent that he didn't lack kitchen skills, which was a little surprising. It made him seem softer, and more human, which she really didn't need.

Travis walked past her, poured a cup of coffee, and then held it out to her. "You want cream or sugar?"

She was so surprised by his offer that for a moment, all she could do was stare blankly at him. "What?"

"You drink coffee? Chase makes the best."

She glanced at Chase, then accepted the mug. "Black is fine."

Travis inclined his head, then returned to his place at the counter. "The omelet is worth hanging around for, too."

Chase frowned at his brother, as if he were as confused as she was by Travis's sudden congeniality. "I made enough for you," he said, glancing back at Mira.

Okay, she was completely confused. She'd been in the middle of a great speech, and now the guys were talking about food? "Great. I love omelets." Were omelets and coffee actually part of a secret code she knew nothing about? Had she just agreed to a midnight bloodletting ceremony in the hayloft? She looked at Travis. "Are you trying to poison me, or do you suddenly not think I'm a curse cast upon this place and your brother?"

Travis grinned, and tapped the brim of his hat in a salute. "It was a good speech, Ms. Cabot. I believed it. You don't want my brother, his money, or his ranch, so yeah, I'm good."

She blinked. "Just like that? You believe me?"

"Yeah." He picked up his coffee. "People don't impress me much, but I know good stock when I see it." He raised the mug in a toast. "To bastard fathers who bring people together."

Mira glanced at Chase. He didn't look nearly as pleased as Travis did. "I think you should stay until the baby is born," he said tersely. "No point in risking it."

Relief rushed through her at his words, and she felt herself relax. She'd meant every word of her speech, but the truth was that a part of her wanted nothing more than to stay on his ranch in his protective circle. Staying until the baby was born, without getting married, gave her time to get her feet under her and set up her life. "I can live with that." Instinctively, she looked over at Travis and raised her brows.

He scowled, a moody look that made him look vaguely familiar. "Nine months? That's kind of a while."

"Is it?" Chase flicked off the burner with a little too much force. He jerked up his sleeve and shoved his arm in front of Travis's face, showing him the cigarette burns. "The baby's father had these all over his fucking back, his cheekbone had been broken in two places, and his left foot didn't even fucking work anymore, all because his daddy was as bad as ours. The baby's father, my best friend, is dead, but the bastard who messed him up isn't. Mira's spent the last eight years caring for her paralyzed mother. Every last cent she had went into taking care of her, and now she's got a child to protect. And you want to put a fucking time limit on the protection we give the two of them? Did all your limousines make you forget exactly how shitty life is as a kid without anyone to protect you?"

Travis stared at Chase's arm for a long moment, and when he looked up, his expression had changed. He looked cold and hard, as if he were ready to strike out at the first person who looked at him the wrong way. She wondered where *his* scars were. "I'm in," he said, his voice hard. "It doesn't get to happen again."

His voice was so unrelenting, that she knew he wouldn't change his mind. Suddenly tears filled her eyes, and she didn't even know what to say.

Travis looked at her, and his eyes narrowed. "You have a phone?"

She lifted her chin, refusing to let him see that she was almost ready to cry just because the two of them were willing to stand by her. "Yes, why?"

"Get it."

She pulled it out of her back pocket. "I have it. Why?"

"Put my number in it. If you can't reach Chase, you call me. Just put it under Travis Stockton, not Turner, just in case anyone sees your phone." He rattled off his phone number, but she was so surprised she forgot to type it in.

He frowned at her. "What?"

"You're Travis *Turner*? The famous country music star?" She'd heard of Travis Turner many times, and some of his songs were on her play list. "No wonder you looked familiar." She actually felt a little bit fan-girl for a moment.

Chase plunked a plate with part of an omelet down in front of her. "He's Travis Stockton," he said firmly. "Travis Turner is a stage name because we're a bunch of anti-social hermits who don't want the public in our business." He gave Travis another plate, and then filled the last one for himself.

Travis nodded at her phone. "Put the number in your phone, Ms. Cabot. I want it in there before I leave."

She quickly typed his number in her phone. Travis *Turner's* mobile number was in her phone? How insane was that? "I won't share it."

"I know." He took a sip of his coffee. "That's why I gave it to you." He picked up his coffee and omelet. "Front porch," he announced. "It's a damn fine day." He headed out the door. She grabbed her plate to follow him, but Chase stopped her with a hand to her arm.

Her belly clenched at his touch, and all thoughts of Travis-the-superstar fled until all that remained was Chase. She swallowed and forced herself to look up at him. With Travis in the room, she'd been able to avoid intimacy with Chase, but now that it was just them, the night of lovemaking with him flooded her mind and senses. Heat radiated from her skin, and she felt her cheeks flush with embarrassment and more than a little desire. "What is it?"

He slid his hand through her hair, and cupped the back of her neck. "I haven't given you a proper good morning, yet," he said.

She swallowed. "Good morning—"

He bent his head and kissed her. It wasn't a platonic, "hey, we're roommates now," kind of kiss. It was a kiss intended to shred every last one of her defenses, and to plunge straight to her core and ignite the same firestorm of passion that he'd unleashed last night. She had no defenses against him, and she sank into him as he kissed her. His mouth just tasted so good, and the strength of his body as he pulled her into his arms was irresistible.

She sighed in capitulation, and kissed him back.

The kiss turned carnal within seconds, and she felt his hands on her hips, drawing her against him as he backed her against the counter. God, not in the kitchen! She pushed at his chest, and was surprised when he stopped.

He broke the kiss and pulled back just enough so he could look at her. Without his cowboy hat, he looked younger. His dark brown hair was disheveled from a night of lovemaking, and his jaw was dark with whiskers. "Nine months," he said. "I have nine months."

"Nine months to do what?" Make love to her until she died of ecstasy? Because right now, she felt like that might be an okay way to meet her demise.

"To figure this out." He kissed her once more, breaking the kiss before she had time to respond. "Travis is waiting. Let's eat." He gave her a wink that made her belly flip over, then he grabbed both their plates, forks, and napkins, and headed out the door. "Grab our coffee, will you?"

He didn't wait for an answer. He just walked, leaving her with a body that was still tingling from his assault.

What? She was so not okay with those terms. "Chase!"

He paused at the door, turning back to look at her. "Yeah?"

"Don't kiss me again."

His eyes narrowed thoughtfully, as he turned back toward her. She stiffened as he walked back over to her, still holding the plates. "Why not?"

She raised her chin. "Because I can't do that. I can't be sleeping with you and trying to establish my life. You're just too…overpowering."

"Mira—"

She held up her hand to silence him. "What were you going to say when I walked in? If I hadn't announced I wasn't going to marry you, what would you have said? Were you going to risk the ranch and your brothers to marry me?" Whoops. She hadn't meant to ask that. She didn't want to hear him say it. "Never mind." She grabbed the coffee mugs and brushed past him, heading out to the porch, ignoring his shocked look at her bold question.

She waited for him to call her back and answer her question.

He didn't.

He could have stopped her if he'd wanted to answer.

He hadn't, which means she knew what he would have said.

He had been planning to choose his brothers, which was exactly why she simply could not kiss him again.

Taylor was right.

She did like him, far too much.

Chapter 11

A week later, Chase was tired, sweaty, and his hip hurt like hell from being tossed from his newest horse too many times. He raked the back of his hand across his brow, reining in his mount as dust kicked up at the end of his driveway. He shaded his eyes, watching the approaching vehicle. The moment he saw his red pickup, the tension that had been caked on him all day eased from his tired muscles.

Mira was back.

She hadn't left him.

He knew that she'd committed to staying at the ranch until the baby was born, but every day that she left in search of a job, he found himself on edge until she reappeared. Tonight, she was late, and his tension had been mounting with each passing hour of her absence.

Needing to connect with her, he reached down to unhook the corral gate, then slipped Red through the opening. He urged the horse into a lope, arriving at his front door just as Mira stopped the truck. She'd left the house while he'd been feeding the horses breakfast, and it was almost seven o'clock now. It was the fourth day in a row that she'd been gone all day, and he was getting cranky about it.

Ever since the morning when she'd announced she wasn't going to marry him and had laid down the law of no more kissing, she'd been as elusive as a hare, sidestepping him every time he tried to talk to her about anything significant. She was cordial, but there was a distance that he didn't like.

Yeah, he understood why she'd pulled back. He knew he'd failed the test when she'd asked him whether he would have married her over Travis's concerns. He should have said yes, but he didn't lie, no matter what. He had no idea what his answer would have been if she hadn't taken control, but he knew that he liked coming in from the barn at night and seeing her curled up by the fire reading. In the short time she'd been living with him, he'd gotten used to making dinner for two people. He even enjoyed testing recipes he thought she might like. It hadn't been so bad having a woman in his house, but the truth was, it wasn't enough to simply have her there. He wanted her to be *his*.

He wanted her accessible to him like she'd been when he'd first met her at that church, when she'd jumped up and hugged him, and let every emotion she felt show on her face. He needed her to look at him as if he mattered, and he craved the freedom to touch her whenever he wanted, even if it was simply to tuck a strand of hair behind her ear when her hands were full. Cohabitation wasn't enough, not by a long shot.

Today had been the longest day yet. She'd been gone for twelve hours, and he'd been getting worried. He'd dialed her cell phone three times to check on her, but had never pressed "Send." He didn't know if she would be okay with him checking up on her, and he was skittish as hell about driving her further away. All he knew was that he wanted her home, where he could keep an eye on her and make sure she was okay.

And now she was back.

He reached down from his saddle and opened her door, swinging it open with an agile move from his mount. "Hi." He couldn't keep the smile off his face, he was so relieved to see her.

She beamed up at him, and for a split second, he was stunned by how beautiful she was. He'd never seen her smile like that before, and it was as if the sun itself had poured itself into her. "I got a job!" she announced.

He blinked. "You did?" Tension locked around his gut. Yeah, he wanted her to get her life going, but a job gave her independence from him. "What kind of job?"

"Managing O'Doul's hardware store. Apparently Howard, who was running it, fell into a canyon after drinking too much."

He frowned. "Howard's a lush."

"Yes, well, now he's in a body cast, and they needed someone." She jumped out of the truck, still grinning. "I know absolutely nothing about screws or types of wood, but apparently, I'm charming enough that Mick figured I might steal business from Stevens Hardware Supply, which apparently is his biggest competitor." She looked so happy that he wanted to break out the champagne and raise a toast to her...at the same time he wanted to handcuff her to him so she couldn't leave. "He said if I like the job, I can keep it even after Howard recovers. Apparently, this was Howard's last chance. How about that?" Her smile widened. "Less than a week of job hunting, and I'm employed. How awesome am I?" She held her arms over her head and did a little hip-swaying dance that was ridiculous, adorable, and sexy as hell at the same time.

"Mick's a good guy, but not easily impressed. You did good." Chase had to give her credit. O'Doul's was one of the better gigs in town. With three locations in the state, Mick could even afford to pay health insurance to his full-time employees. "Nice job."

"Thank you." She gave him a sweeping bow that made him want to reach over and haul her into his arms for the kind of kiss he'd been fantasizing about constantly ever since she'd put the brakes on their relationship.

He didn't reach for her, though, afraid of pushing her away. Apparently oblivious to how hard his cock was and how much effort it was taking not to drag her into his arms, she reached into the back of the truck and hauled out some brown paper bags. "Do you know Eva Carter, who works at the café across the street from O'Doul's? Well, she has an apartment over her garage, and the tenant is moving out at the first of the year. She's so nice. She reminded me of my friend, Taylor, from back home. I'll bet I could rent the space from her. She said she's not going to re-rent the apartment because her current tenant is a complete scumbag and she's tired of dealing with renters, but I bet she'd rent to me, don't you think?"

A cold, bitter feeling settled in his gut. "That place only has a space heater. You can't live there with a baby. Winter is brutally cold in Wyoming."

"Oh...a space heater?" She frowned. "She didn't mention that." She wrinkled her nose. "Well, still, it shows me that there are some options out there, you know? Everyone is so nice in this town." She grinned. "You have no idea what it's like to walk down the street and have people smile at me. After all those years taking care of my mom, no one here is looking at me with this great veil of sadness, and no one sees me as the daughter of the local sheriff. It feels good to be able to start a new life without any baggage following me."

He smiled, the tension in his gut easing at the genuine joy on her face. "There are good people in this town," he acknowledged. Some bastards too, but he wasn't going to bring that up. Mira made him want to stop thinking about the crap, and that felt good. He swung down off his horse to take the paper bags from her. "I'll get these. What's in them?"

"So, I also stopped at the grocery store. Apparently, I'm deficient in iron, so I need more red meat. Burgers tonight." She handed him the bags, and turned to gather more.

He frowned. "Deficient in iron? What are you talking about?"

She grabbed her purse, slung it over her shoulder, and picked up one more grocery bag. "Well, I went to see Doctor Murdoch today. I hadn't been to a doctor yet, and I wanted to set up a baseline. She's so fantastic. Anyway, I'm a little anemic, so I need to fix that. Other than that, I'm in great health. The baby is totally fine. I don't have to go back for a month, but I just wanted to establish a relationship with her, in case anything went wrong, you know?"

Something twisted in his gut, and all his amusement vanished. "You went to the doctor today? To check on your pregnancy?"

Her smile faded at his tone. "Was I not supposed to do that?"

"No, you should. It's just..." Shit. Why was he so pissed that she hadn't asked him go along with her? "If it's my baby, then I need to go to your appointments with you." Yeah, that was it. For appearance's sake, he needed to accompany her. "I didn't even know you were going."

She bit her lip, and she lifted her chin in a hint of

defiance that sent waves of apprehension tumbling through him. "It's not your baby."

Her words were like a sharp hit to his gut. Yeah, he knew it was true, but he felt like she was slipping out of his fingers, and so was the child. "If my name is on that birth certificate," he said evenly, carefully selecting his words, "it's my baby to the world. Anyone who knows me is well aware that I'd be there with you at every appointment. It's how I am. In addition, I've committed to that baby's well-being, and I want to be there, because I want to make sure everything is okay."

The smile completely vanished from her face, and he saw fear flicker in her eyes. "If you can't even let me go to an appointment by myself, how would you let me move out with the baby, then? Would you do that? If that's not your style, then how are you going to do that?"

Shit. He felt like things were spiraling. "Irreconcilable differences," he said. "If we can't make it work, then that's the way it is. But right now, you're living with me, and we're a happy couple. So, yeah, I need to go."

She fell silent, and tension seemed to build between them. After a moment, she looked at him. "After my parents' car accident, I felt like my entire world collapsed. I had nothing to lean on, and it was absolutely terrifying. I've had to learn to be strong, and I feel like I'm pretty good at it. But every night when I go to bed, and I lie there thinking about how I'm single and pregnant, I'm terrified. I don't know how I'm ever going to do this on my own, Chase. If you start coming to appointments with me and acting like a devoted dad and partner, I'm going to get used to having you to lean on. Then when I'm on my own again, I don't know if I'll be able to do it. I can't rely on you, and then suddenly not have you there. It's too hard."

Chase swore under his breath and set the bags down. He took her bag and set it beside his, then took her hands. They were trembling and cold, and suddenly he felt like such an ass for being pissed that she was out there in his town, building her life. "You need to understand something, Mira. I will do *anything* for those who I've committed to. For my whole life, it's been only my brothers and AJ. And now it's you and that baby. You're in my circle of protection, and no matter what you do, you'll never be outside of it. You don't have to do this on your own, and it doesn't make a difference whether you're living here or not. I'm here for you and the baby, all the way through."

Tears brimmed in her eyes. "It's not the same thing, Chase."

"What's not the same thing?" He didn't understand how he was failing her.

She carefully extracted her hands from his. "Having you to back me up is wonderful, but it's different than having a partner who is there just for you, someone who is that special confidant who always puts you before anyone else. Going to the doctor's appointments is so personal. Sharing it with you would make it feel…well…it would feel like we're a couple, not simply that you're a great guy who has my back. I'm not made of steel, Chase. I would love to have someone by my side, so if you play that role, it's going to be too hard for me to remember that it's all a lie."

He ground his jaw. He didn't quite grasp the difference of what she was saying. He had no experience, either as an observer or a participant, in the kind of relationship she was describing. He just knew that he wanted to be a part of this with her. "I'd like to go." Was that better? Asking instead of demanding?

Something flickered in her eyes, a vulnerability that made his protective instincts flare up. "Chase, you aren't hearing me."

"I'm trying. I don't have background in this stuff." His horse nudged at his shoulder impatiently, reminding Chase that he still needed to feed him. "I want to go with you," he repeated. Instinctively, his gaze flicked to her belly. "I want to know that the baby's okay, too, you know. The kid doesn't have a dad. He's going to need someone."

The corner of her mouth curved up. "He might be a she."

"Girls need dads too." He frowned, suddenly thinking back to the days when he was in high school. "They need dads with big guns actually. I don't want anyone to mess with her." His gaze settled on her face, and he noted the shadows under her eyes and the weariness of her shoulders. "Or you."

His words fell into the silent chasm between them. After

a moment, she managed a smile. "I'll go make dinner while you feed Red." She picked up two of the grocery bags, then turned and hurried into the house, without even looking back, leaving all his promises and offers dangling in the cool evening air, untouched and unacknowledged.

Grimly, he stared after her as the screen door swung shut behind her. What the hell was he doing wrong? The further she drifted from him, the more he wanted to pull her back. He was beginning to think that his agreement to her proposal that they didn't have to get married hadn't been the best decision. If they were married, he'd at least feel that he had some way to hold onto her.

Red nudged him, and he rubbed the horse's nose. "I think you're lucky you've been gelded," he muttered, as he swung back into the saddle. He turned the horse back to the barn, half-wishing that gelding really would solve his problem...

Or not.

He wasn't ready to give up yet, and when he got Mira back, he was going to need all his parts functioning just fine.

Because he would get her.

He *had* to get her.

🐾 🐾 🐾

Mira braced her hands on the dashboard of Chase's truck, peering at the old farmhouse as his truck bounced up the dirt driveway. "I really think this is a bad idea. I don't think I can lie to Gary." She'd managed to put off the dinner invitation that Gary Keller had issued at the airport when she'd arrived, but when he'd found her at the hardware store earlier in the week, he'd cornered her and she'd had no escape.

And now they were here, about to disillusion one of the nicest men she'd ever met.

"You don't need to lie." Chase put his truck into park, his muscles flexing beneath his denim shirt. He was showered and freshly shaved, and he smelled amazing. He looked younger with his clean shave, and a part of her wanted desperately to run her hand over his jaw. What would it feel like to have him kiss her when his face was so soft?

He raised his brows at her, then lightly grasped her wrist. She was too surprised to pull away, and then, when he pressed her hand against his face, she didn't want to pull away. She slid her fingers along his jaw. "So smooth," she whispered.

"You don't have to hold back," he said, his gaze riveted to her face, and his voice deliciously husky. "You can touch me anytime you want."

Sudden desire rushed through her, and she quickly pulled her hand away. She'd been at the ranch for three weeks, and it had been increasingly difficult to keep her distance from Chase. He was charming at dinner, gruff and cranky before his coffee, and ridiculously sexy in his dusty jeans and cowboy hat whenever he came in from the barn. He didn't appear to have anyone else on the ranch helping him, and he worked literally from sunrise to sunset training horses, caring for them, and keeping the physical structure in good repair.

He reminded her of her dad, in a way, with his unflagging, steady energy to do his job. He never seemed to get flustered when a horse was difficult, and she'd never seen him lose his temper with an animal or anyone else. He was dependable and solid, and she was already starting to rely on him.

His constant, unabashed efforts to seduce her didn't help. She was attracted to him, and it was getting harder to remember to keep her distance. She had to keep reminding herself that he'd refused to choose her over his brothers, so she knew that she would never come first to him. Not that she wanted him to walk away from his family, but she couldn't marry him, or anyone, unless she knew that she would come first if she needed it.

He smiled slightly, the corners of his mouth curving up in a most insanely tempting fashion. "Did I mention that you look sexy as hell in those jeans?"

Heat flooded her cheeks. "I don't think so." She knew he hadn't. She clung to every compliment he gave her, even though she pretended not to hear most of them.

He leaned closer, his fingers gliding over the nape of her neck. "You look sexy as hell in those jeans, sweetheart." His breath was warm against her mouth, and her heart started to race.

"Don't call me sweetheart," she whispered.

He cocked an eyebrow. "Why not?"

"Because I like it." The admission slipped out, and she bit her lip, but it was too late to take back. Chase's face softened, and a hungry gleam appeared in his eyes. Oh, God. He was going to kiss her, wasn't he? He was going to kiss her, and she was going to let him and—

"Chase!" The front door of the gray farmhouse swung open with a bang, and Mira leapt back from Chase, both relieved and horribly frustrated by the interruption. She didn't want to have time to think about kissing him. She wanted it to just happen without her making the decision that she wanted it, because she couldn't make that decision.

Chase didn't look annoyed, however. He was studying her with a thoughtful look on his face, as if he realized that she would have let him kiss her, and he was contemplating exactly what he was going to do with that bit of information.

"You two ever going to get out of that truck?" A red-haired woman in blue jeans and cowboy boots was striding energetically toward the truck. The wrinkles on her face suggested she was in her seventies, but her flaming red hair was fit for a teenage rodeo queen. "It's about time you brought Mira around."

Mira quickly turned away from Chase, wishing that the moment had never happened. She wasn't sure which moment it was that she regretted. Was it the fact she'd almost kissed him, or the fact that she'd been interrupted before it had happened? She didn't know. God, she was so confused.

Taking refuge in their visitor, she opened the door and climbed out of his truck before Chase could make it around the truck to escort her, as he liked to do. "Hi," she said, forcing cheerfulness into her voice. "You must be Martha Keller."

"I am!" Martha swept Mira into a bear hug that surprised her, but felt amazing. "It's so good to see you, my darling." She tucked her arm through Mira's and winked at Chase. "Did you bring my pie, young man?"

Chase grinned, a devilish grin that was so sexy that Mira actually felt a little weak in the knees. "Would I ever let my favorite lady down?" He reached into the backseat and pulled out three pies that he'd baked last night, even though he'd been so tired that he'd nearly fallen asleep in the bowl of apples. Mira had helped him, and it had been fun cooking together. A lot of fun. "Two apple and one blueberry."

"Three pies? For that you get a second helping." Martha beamed at Chase as he leaped ahead of her so that he could hold the front door open, flirting with the older lady as she ducked under his arm.

Mira was startled by Chase's warm affection with Martha. He was so doting and sweet it was a little heart melting. It was a side she hadn't seen of Chase, or maybe a side she hadn't let him show. Either way, it was not what she needed to see. Endearing was not a quality she wanted to add to his list of attributes.

Gary was waiting for them with a roaring fire, some delicious wine, and a cheese plate containing more delicious cheese than she'd ever had in her lifetime. His hug was as warm as his wife's, and Mira felt her tension rising. How could she lie to these people?

Ten minutes into pre-dinner conversation around the fire, it became too much for Mira to cope with. Gary and Martha were so warm and caring that they reminded her of her parents. It was so cozy and homey, a domestic scene that she hadn't been a part of in so long. The camaraderie between Gary, Martha, and Chase was so evident, making her increasingly aware that her sense of belonging over the past few weeks had been such a superficial farce.

This was the kind of home she'd grown up in. This was the kind of warmth she craved. But this wasn't her world. It was a lie, a fabrication set up to protect a baby. What would Martha and Gary think of her when they found out the truth, that she'd been knocked up in a grief-induced one-night stand, and Chase was playing the hero for a child who wasn't even his? All this would be snatched away from her, and she'd be alone before she'd even had a chance to become a part of this world. Nausea churned in her belly. "Excuse me. May I use your bathroom?"

At Martha's direction, Mira stumbled to her feet and made it to the room in question. She was just shutting the door when Martha appeared over her shoulder.

Mira jumped, startled by the presence. "I'll be right

out—"

"Oh, nonsense." Martha took her by the elbow and propelled her right past the bathroom and into the kitchen, plunking her down on a stool at the counter. "You don't need to go to the bathroom, and we both know it. Sit, girl, and talk to me."

Mira stared at her. "Talk? About what?"

"About what? Really?" Martha picked up two potholders and opened the oven. She retrieved a roast, keeping her voice deceptively casual as she addressed Mira. "Oh, how about the fact that you're pregnant, but barely even talking to Chase? Is that a good place to start the conversation?"

Chapter 12

Mira felt her cheeks flame up. "What?"

Martha set the roast down on the stove and gave Mira a look. "How big do you think this town is? You're living with Chase. You were all in love when you greeted each other in the airport. You're seeing a doctor because you're pregnant. Despite all that storybook romancing, you and Chase aren't even sitting on the same couch in my living room. What's going on?"

Oh, God. This was what she'd been worried about. How could she lie to this lovely woman? "I just... I don't..." What to say? She hadn't been expecting Martha to know *everything*.

Martha jammed two meat forks into the roast and hoisted it onto a cutting board. "Those Stockton boys have issues," she announced, her voice warm with affection. "I'll be the first to tell you that they all deserved to be in jail at some point in their lives, but they're cleaning up well." She handed Mira a paring knife and three fresh tomatoes. "Slice."

Mira immediately began to cut, grateful for the distraction. "Yes, well, they aren't real high on the idea of a woman in their space."

"Of course not. They learned not to trust them." Martha wagged a baster at Mira. "Looks like you got the job of teaching them that not all women are she-devils from hell."

"That's not my job—"

"What?" Martha slammed the baster on the counter, making Mira jump. "Chase has never so much as let a woman breathe on his truck, let alone move into his house. He might not be able to show it, but he's head over heels for you. He's the oldest in that family, and he's the one who kept the boys together when all that hell was going on. He's got the word 'responsible' carved all the way to the marrow of his bones, but that's not all life is." Martha leaned forward, her eyes twinkling. "He needs to learn that life is also about long, moonlight kisses, late night conversations under the covers, and the kind of intimacy you can get with only that one special someone."

Mira bit her lip against the sudden longing in her chest. "I know that's important, but—"

"Then show him."

"No!" Mira set down her knife. "I already like him. A lot. But he's going to break my heart, and I can't go through that again."

Martha raised her brows. "You're so sure he's going to break your heart? And why is that?"

"Because his brothers have to come first."

"It's a different kind of first," Martha said, shrugging off her concern. "There's space for lots of people to come first."

Mira thought back to her college fiancé, and his demands, and she knew Martha wasn't entirely right. Sometimes, choices had to be made. "Chase and I had the same best friend, but we didn't meet until recently. He still sees me as the woman that my friend described. I don't even know if he sees me for who I am in real life."

Martha cocked her head. "Fantasy versus reality? You're not sure you measure up?"

"I know I don't. Who would?"

"Don't sell him short, Mira. Chase is no fool, and he's too gun-shy to shack up with a woman unless he knows in his gut that he's right about her."

A tiny, tiny flicker of hope fluttered inside Mira's chest. Was it really possible that at some point, Chase had begun to see the real her? But that wasn't the entire issue. "He feels very responsible for the baby," she said quietly.

"I'll bet he does."

She looked at Martha. "If I let myself fall in love with him, how would I ever know if he married me for the baby, or for me?"

"Ah..." Martha leaned back against the counter, folding her arms over her chest. "And therein lies the problem, doesn't it? You got pregnant too early, before you two were able to solidify what you had together."

Mira shrugged. "It hasn't been very long." It hadn't, but at the same time, she still felt like he'd been a part of her heart forever.

"Huh." Martha picked up a white serving bowl and began to scoop potatoes out of the dish the roast had been in. "Then, I think it's time for you and Chase to start dating."

"Dating?" She shook her head, trying to ignore the flicker of anticipation at the idea. "I'll be honest, Martha, I don't feel like there is a place for me in his life, not with all his brothers. I'm trying to save some money, and then I'll move out after the baby is born. Right now, we're just cohabitating for convenience." There, she'd said it, as close to the truth as she could afford to get.

Martha raised a silvery eyebrow. "Is that how you want it, my dear? Do you see Chase as nothing more than a sperm factory?"

Mira burst out laughing. "A sperm factory? No, I don't think he's a sperm factory."

"Do you think he's a handsome, caring, honest, dependable man who made your entire world turn upside down when he made love to you all night long?"

For what felt like the thousandth time in five minutes, Mira felt her cheeks heat up, and this time, there was no way to deny the ache in her chest for him.

Martha clapped her hands in delight. "That's a yes, if I've ever seen one." She leaned forward, resting her elbows on the counter. "Girl, you need to stop being a pathetic martyr. Yes, so, you've got a baby to complicate things. So what? Trying to protect yourself from hurt will just leave you a bitter, old lady who lives with cats who urinate all over her basement and a child who pretends he isn't related to you. Is that really the life you aspire to?"

Mira blinked. "No, not really."

"Then go date Chase. Seriously. It's not that complicated." Martha set a gravy boat in Mira's hand. "But first, serve up the gravy. I'll give you a can of whipped cream to take home for a private dessert." She winked, ducking out of the way as Mira burst out laughing.

Whipped cream and Chase?

Martha was insane.

But as Martha opened the fridge to retrieve the salad, Mira couldn't help but notice a can of whipped cream sitting on the top shelf.

No.

She couldn't do that.

She wouldn't.

Urinating cats were better than having her heart shattered, she was sure of it.

❦ ❦ ❦

Dinner had been awkward.

Chase wasn't going to lie.

The entire night, Mira had sat on the edge of her seat, looking like a mouse about to bolt.

Gary had pulled him aside and lit into him that he wasn't treating Mira right, and he had a headache from the lecture that Martha had given him to start dating Mira.

Dating her.

Dating her.

Chase looked over at Mira. She was leaning back against the seat, her eyes closed, the bag of leftovers clutched to her chest. It wasn't even nine o'clock yet, and she was already beat.

He frowned as he turned into his driveway. "You feeling okay?"

She nodded, not even opening her eyes. "Martha thinks we should go on a date. She thinks there's magic between us that we're destroying by being stubborn and afraid of being hurt."

He rubbed his jaw as he pulled the truck into his driveway. "She said the same to me."

Mira opened her eyes and looked at him. "What do you want, Chase?"

Her expression was soft and vulnerable, as if she were too tired to keep up the façade she'd been perpetuating all evening.

Her dark eyelashes framed her vibrant blue eyes, making her appear vulnerable. She looked utterly feminine, and his instinct to protect thundered through every part of his body. He eased the truck to a stop in front of the house, and turned to face her, resting his arm along the back of the bench seat, behind her. "What I want is for you to be in my bed every night, and at my breakfast table every morning." There. He'd said it. He couldn't believe he'd admitted it aloud, but he had. The words felt weighty and significant, damned terrifying if he was honest, but he didn't want to take them back. He wanted them out there. He wanted her to know.

She raised an eyebrow. "That's it?"

He frowned at her weary, unimpressed response. Didn't she understand the magnitude of what he'd just said? He'd admitted he wanted her to be part of his personal life, immersed in his personal space, the space he guarded from everyone. "That's a lot."

"It's not enough." With a shuddering sigh, she opened the car door. "There's too much at stake to risk it, Chase. What if we try, but we decide we hate each other? This baby will need both of us, so maybe it's best to just keep things even so that we can support each other as needed?"

"What? No way." He jumped out of the truck, jogging around to catch the door before she could get out. He held out his hand to help her down. "I want more."

She didn't take his hand, helping herself down instead. "What exactly is it that you want? More what? More sex? More intimacy? A great big family of love with your brothers?"

He swore under his breath. "I'm not the kind of guy your dad was, Mira. I don't bring that to the table. I have no clue how to have a family, and my brothers have to come first. I owe them, but I also want you. You matter. A lot."

She nodded, giving him a forlorn smile that tore at his heart. "I get it, but coming in second isn't what I want. I want it all."

He sighed, deflation settling deep in his chest. That was it. The truth. He'd laid it all out there, and it didn't matter. It wasn't enough. "Then I'm not your guy." But for the first time in his life, he wished he could be.

ช ช ช

Mira bolted upright in bed, certain that something was terribly wrong. The house was silent, almost eerily so, but the lights in the barn were blazing. She rolled over to check her phone, and saw it was two in the morning. What was Chase doing? Riding?

She hurried to the window and looked out. The barn doors were wide open, but there was no activity. Fear rippled through her, and she had a sudden feeling that something was very wrong.

Without hesitating, she yanked on her jeans and boots, grabbed a sweatshirt, and then raced down the hall. She flung the front door open and hurried across the dried-out grass to the barn, rushing through the open door.

Horses were up, with their heads out the doors. The barn was immaculate, without even a stray piece of hay in the corner. Pride of ownership gleamed from every surface, and her heart tightened at the sight. It was obvious how much Chase cared about the ranch. She'd never been in the barn, because she'd spent her days at work, trying to keep herself emotionally divested from the ranch that she was going to have to leave.

But now that she had seen it, she knew that she'd made a mistake in not coming in before. This place was Chase. This amazing stable defined who he was. The only way she would ever have answers about him was to see what made him thrive.

She realized suddenly that he wasn't around. "Chase?"

"Mira?" His voice was tense and strained, echoing from the last stall.

She hurried down the aisle, noticing now that the last door was open. She reached it, and then gasped when she looked inside. Chase was gripping the halter of a beautiful black stallion, who was trying to lie down. The animal's flanks were coated in sweat, and his nostrils were flared as he fought for breath. "What's wrong?"

"Spy has colic," Chase said tersely. His face was lined with tension, and he looked fearsome as he gripped the horse's halter. "Stomach ache," he clarified. "He wants to roll, but that could twist his intestines and kill him. I need to keep him on his feet."

Urgency surged through her, and suddenly, all the distance she'd tried to erect between them dissolved. "What can I do?"

Sweat was pouring down his temples, and he shook his head. "I've got it—" Just then, the horse groaned and his knees buckled. Chase swore and shouted at the horse, dragging on his halter to try to keep him up.

Instinctively, Mira ducked past Chase into the stall and shouted at the horse, shoving against his hip and trying to startle him. Their joined efforts worked, and the horse lurched back to his feet again.

Chase dragged the horse's head to the side, pulling him to the left to try to get him off balance enough to take a step. "Stay beside him," he commanded. "Keep working it. I'm going to try to get him to walk out of here." He tugged on the lead shank, and Mira got behind the horse, clucking as she dragged off her sweatshirt, and waved it behind Spy.

The animal lurched forward, his front hooves making it past the stall door. Chase shouted with victory, and together they got the animal moving forward. They made it down the aisle, but the horse was still fighting, still trying to go down with each step. Each time his knees began to buckle, she shouted and flapped her sweatshirt, while Chase urged him on in front.

"Outside," Chase said. "Let's get him to the ring."

Together, working as a unit, they got Spy to the corral, but it was a battle for every step. The air was cool, but the horse was still drenched in sweat.

"I gave him some medicine," Chase said. "If we can keep him moving until it kicks in, he should be okay. Come on, Spy!" He tugged on the horse as he tried to go down again. "Shit, come on, boy. You can do this!"

They got him going, and then one minute later, the horse dropped to his knees before they could stop him. He rolled onto his back with a groan, kicking his feet in the air as if he were itching his back, instead of risking his own life. Mira's heart dropped, and she and Chase leapt at Spy, shouting and pushing at him.

"Get up," she screamed. "Come on!"

For an agonizing moment, Spy continued to roll, and then he lurched to his feet with a groan, staggering as he tried to regain his balance. "Good boy!" Chase urged him forward, and Mira stayed by the horse's side, each of them working together to try to keep him moving.

As the horse stumbled forward, Chase looked over at Mira. His face was gray with worry. "Good job back there, Mira."

She nodded. "No problem."

They fell into a grim, tense partnership, working together to keep the horse moving. Twice, he managed to get down and start to roll, but both times they got him going again. After what felt like an eternity, Mira finally noticed that Spy was moving less laboriously now, and he wasn't trying to stop anymore. She looked over at Chase, who was rubbing the horse's ears and talking softly to the animal as they walked, his voice soothing and calming. He was so nurturing, that her own heart tightened. She'd never seen him be so soft, and it was amazing to see the big, strong cowboy being tender. "Chase?"

He glanced over at her, and she saw his face was lined with dirt and grime, with streaks down his temples from the sweat. "He's getting better," he said. "Can you see that?"

She nodded, relief rushing through her. "I didn't know if I was imagining it or not."

"Nope. He's made it through the worst." Relief was heavy in his voice, as was exhaustion. "I think he's going to make it."

She smiled, joy rushing through her. "We did it, eh, boy?" She rubbed her hand over Spy's coat, which was caked with sweat and dirt. His skin was cold, and she realized the sweat was beginning to dry. "Should I get a blanket or something for him?"

Chase hesitated, and then nodded. "I think it's safe for you to go into the barn. Thanks. There's a sweat sheet on a rack outside his door. It's a cotton blanket with holes in it. It keeps him warm, while letting the air circulate to dry him."

"Got it." Mira patted Spy once again, and then hurried into the barn. As she reached the barn door, she glanced back over her shoulder at the ring. The sun was just beginning to rise, casting the arena in a faint orange hue. She watched Chase run his hand down Spy's neck, and the horse lightly nudged Chase's hip. Her throat tightened with pride. She and Chase had done that. Together, they'd helped that horse live. What an incredible night.

Smiling for the first time in what felt like forever, she turned and hurried into the barn, humming to herself.

Chapter 13

Chase leaned over the stall door, resting his arms on the wood as he watched Spy doze peacefully in the back corner. The animal's head was down, and he was exhausted, but his body was relaxed.

The worst was over.

He was going to make it.

"I brought you coffee." Mira leaned over the door beside him, holding a steaming mug. "Thought you might need some caffeine."

"Thanks." He glanced over at her. She was covered in sweat and dirt from the long night, and there were shadows beneath her eyes, but there was a radiance on her face that nearly glowed. "You were great. I don't think I could have done it without you."

She smiled, and mimicked his position, resting her arms over the top edge of the door as she watched Spy rest. "Could he really have died?"

"Yeah. It was bad." Chase let out a breath, finally able to acknowledge the depth of what had been at stake last night. "He's my breeding stallion," he explained. "I paid a lot of money for him when he was a colt, but it was far less than he's worth. The guy who owned him was short on cash, and I was in the right place at the right time. He's my future. I could never afford to replace him if he'd died last night. The entire future of this ranch is riding on him." Instinctively, in a move that was so natural he didn't even think about it, he draped his arm over

Mira's shoulders, drawing her against him as they watched Spy. "Thanks for your help, city girl."

She relaxed against him, and he could tell she was as weary as he was. "I'm glad I was here."

"Me too." As he stood with her tucked up against him, Chase had a sudden feeling of contentment. Mira had been a star all night, fighting as hard as him to save Spy. She'd never complained, and had never shown a sign of fatigue, even when she'd worked tirelessly beside him to help with the morning feeding. Not a single one of his brothers had ever been here to help him, but Mira had been by his side all night, without hesitation, and her satisfaction in saving Spy was evident.

He realized suddenly that she fit on the ranch. She fit in his life. She was an asset, not a liability. Mira, the Deep South lady he'd coveted for so long, wasn't who he'd thought at all. Yeah, she had the huge heart he'd always expected, but she was also gritty, strong, and tough enough to fight off death.

Was she also tough enough to survive him and his brothers? Was he tough enough to survive her? Shit. He didn't even know how everything was supposed to fit together anymore. He'd had a plan for his life, and now things were skewing in different directions, ones he wasn't prepared for.

His phone rang. He pulled it out of his pocket and saw it was Zane. He moved his thumb over the "Send" icon to answer, then realized Zane was probably calling to give him grief about Mira.

He didn't want to hear it.

He didn't want his brothers in this moment.

He turned off his phone and slid it back into his pocket, Gary's words echoing in his mind about how he needed to treat Mira better. He thought of Martha's orders to start dating her. Maybe he would try. Maybe he was supposed to try. "You hot?"

She glanced over at him. "Hot, sweaty, and dirty, yes."

"Want to go for a swim? I know a place. Just for an hour, then we'll be back to check on Spy. It'll work better than caffeine to pick you up."

She eyed him for a moment, those sexy blue eyes studying him. He tensed, his entire body on edge, waiting for her to accept his offer. *Say yes, Mira. Say yes.*

After a moment, she nodded. "Okay."

"Okay." He couldn't suppress his grin, or the rush of energy that flooded his body. "Two horses or one?"

She raised her eyebrows. "Two."

Two? Bummer. Looked like he still had some work to do.

But she'd said yes.

It was a start.

�� �� ��

"I am so not jumping off this rock." Mira stared uneasily over the edge of the boulder that loomed above the natural pool nestled in the cliffs near Chase's house. The boulder was at least fifteen feet above the water, and despite Chase's suggestion, there was no chance she was jumping off there.

Maybe in her youth, but now? She'd probably need a wheelchair if she did it.

Chase walked up beside her. He'd already shed his jeans and shirt, leaving on only a pair of black boxer briefs that didn't hide the fact that he was walking around with an erection. He didn't seem to care that she could tell, so she tried to ignore it.

Not so easy, when she could remember lots of details about that particular part of his anatomy.

His body rippled with muscle, and his neck and arms showed the layers of grime where his collar and shirt sleeves had ended, exposing his skin to the dirt of the previous night. He looked sexy beyond words, a rugged cowboy who was a part of the earth that he rode on every day.

Suddenly, she didn't feel like a woman who wanted to park her butt on the top of the rock and sit. She wanted to be the woman who jumped out there with him.

Chase raised his eyebrows. "You stay out all night battling colic, but you're afraid of a little jump? The water's deep. It's safe."

She grimaced, still wearing her jeans, boots, and tank top. Why hadn't she thought of a bathing suit when Chase had suggested swimming? He'd had the horses saddled up and ready in minutes, and she'd been too busy second-guessing her acceptance of his invitation to actually consider the logistics of swimming.

Dirt caked her body, and the water was so clear she could see all the way to the rocks on the bottom. A waterfall was cascading on the far side of the pool, and the high red rock surrounded it, an oasis of perfection in the middle of a harsh landscape. In truth, it looked unbelievably appealing, but to rip off her clothes and charge off the rock was so not her. At least, it wasn't the grown-up her. As a youth, she used to swing out in a tire swing she and AJ had tied to their tree and careen into the river, but that was a long time ago.

Chase stepped in front of her, and held out his hands, his eyes twinkling. "Come on."

She bit her lip. "Leaping off massive cliffs into tiny pools isn't really my thing." She peered past him. "Is there a way down on the side? I can meet you down there." Then, at least, she could swim.

"It's worth it." He wiggled his fingers, clearly trying to tempt her. "Do you trust me?"

His question jerked her attention back to him. She'd used those very words with Taylor such a short time ago when she'd justified packing her life up and moving out to Wyoming. She'd barely even met him at that point, and yet she'd boldly announced how much she trusted him.

How ridiculous to trust someone who was a virtual stranger with her life and her baby's. But now, staring into his blue eyes, she realized the answer was still yes. She did trust him. This time, it was real trust, not trust built simply upon a legend created by their shared mutual best friend. She'd seen Chase care for his horse, bond with his brothers, and stand by her. It was Chase she trusted, the real life man. Slowly, she nodded. "I do."

A smile flashed across his face. "Then come with me."

"Oh, jeez. Really?"

He grinned wider. "Come on, babe. You'll love it."

She made a noise of exasperation, even as her heart was starting to hammer in anticipation. "Okay, fine. But if I break both my legs and wind up in a body cast, you have to be my manservant for the rest of my life." She poked at his chest, and he caught her finger.

"I'll even massage your numb, lifeless feet," he said. "And I'm great at massages. It would be worth it."

"I doubt it." She took a deep breath. Her heart was pounding, but a part of her really did want to jump. "Give me a sec." Trying not to think about what she was doing, she stepped back from him and unfastened her jeans. Her cheeks burned as she peeled her pants off, glad she'd grabbed her pink low-cut bikinis instead of her white, cotton oh-so-comfy ones. And heaven help her if she'd put on a thong. A little bit of modesty was a good thing, right? Yes, she was well aware that he'd seen her completely naked, but that time, she'd been stripped bare by his roving hands while he was seducing her in the dark of night with tempestuous kisses and whispered temptations. Peeling off her clothes in the broad sunlight, while standing on a barren rock with Chase watching her, was completely different.

She tossed the jeans aside and turned back to face him. Her heart immediately started pounding when she saw the heated expression on his face. His gaze seemed to bore into her, and she caught her breath. "Don't." Even as she said it, another part of her was screaming for him to *do, do, do*. Her body remembered exactly what it was like to have his hands on her, and her heart missed that intimacy between them.

Chase didn't leap across the rock and sweep her up in his arms. In fact, he said nothing. He simply held out his hands to her again in an invitation that suddenly seemed much more personal than it had a few minutes ago.

She decided to leave her tank top on. In her middle-of-the-night rush to the barn, she hadn't put on a bra. Yes, Chase had been best friends with her breasts, but in the bright light of morning, standing on a rock ledge with the man who was turning her life upside down, she needed a shirt. "You swear I won't land on a rock or something?" Her hand went protectively to her belly, and the tiny swell that was beginning to show.

Chase walked over to her and put his hand over hers. His palm dwarfed hers, sending heat pulsing through her. "I swear I won't let anything happen to either of you."

She nodded, her heart pounding at how close he was. She could see scars on his chest, and she wondered what those had been from, what horrors he'd endured when he'd received them. "Okay."

He smiled and took her hands, walking backward as he drew her toward the edge of the rock. "I used to come here all the time when I was a teenager. After Old Skip worked me all day, I'd get an hour off, and this was my spot. My brothers came here too, when they took their turns working at the ranch. We called it Stockton Rock. It was usually cold as hell, but we swam anyway. We got lucky today with this weather. It's a rare gift for it to be this warm here."

The warmth in his eyes as he spoke about his brothers made her smile. "How did you manage to stay so close to your brothers when you grew up in a rough situation? Where did you learn about that kind of loyalty?"

He shrugged. "I was the oldest. They needed me to protect them. It worked out okay." He dropped her right hand and turned to face the pool, still clasping her left hand as they stood together. "We'll jump side by side. On three. One."

She tightened her grip on his hand, peering down at the still water. "Um...okay."

"Two."

Did she really want to do this? She didn't. She really didn't think she did. "Chase—"

"Three." He jumped.

With a small yelp, she leapt with him, carried far out over the water by the force of his leap. For a split second, she lost her balance, and then he steadied her with their clasped hands. She had a moment of experiencing the sheer beauty of freedom as they sailed through the air, and then they plummeted into the water. The cold water sucked the breath from her, shocking her system as she went under.

She seemed to sink forever, a slow, peaceful descent into water so clear she could see Chase grinning at her through the bubbles rising around them.

She finally stopped descending, giving her the chance to kick to the surface. She broke through, and gasped in the fresh air as Chase surfaced beside her. He flipped his wet hair out of his eyes, his grin so boyish and charming that she found herself laughing at him. She felt energized and brave, filled with life she hadn't felt in so long.

He grinned. "Fun, wasn't it?"

She nodded, treading water. "It was awesome. Can we do it again?"

He threw back his head and laughed, a gorgeous, irresistible laugh that made her belly curl with delight. "Of course. Follow me, my princess." He stroked his way across the pool toward the base of the rock and grabbed an outcropping.

When she reached him, he grabbed her hand and hauled her against him. "One kiss per jump. It's the toll." He kissed her once, a hard, fast kiss that was over just as her toes were starting to curl. "Now, up you go." He pointed out the footholds, and then she grabbed the rock.

To her surprise, there was a natural path of foot and hand holds up the side of the rock, and she found herself at the top before she'd even realized she was climbing. Chase was right behind her, water streaming over his bare chest, making it glisten in the sunlight.

He was unbelievably sexy, and the way his gaze raked across her made her feel just as desirable. Her shirt was plastered to her body, and she could feel that her nipples were hard from the cold water.

"Aren't you hot in that shirt?" he asked. "You look hot."

She grinned at the double word play. "I'm keeping it on." She turned away from him, aware of his heated gaze on her almost naked bottom. "You coming?"

"Wouldn't miss it." He caught her hand, and they stood side by side again. "On three?"

"No. Now!" She let go of his hand, ran two steps, and leapt into the air, sailing far out into the pool. The wind was rushing by her, flinging her hair aside as she waved her arms for balance. Again, a moment of perfect suspension, and then she plummeted into the water. The cold closed in around her again, but this time it felt like it was cleansing all the silt from her body and her soul. She felt like she was a child again, leaping out in the river with AJ, using the rope swing they'd hung themselves. She'd felt so free and happy back then, and she felt the same way again: young, carefree, and connected with the man she was with.

There was a loud splash as Chase plunged in beside

her, and he caught her ankle as he went past, jerking her down toward him.

She had only a split second to protest, and then she was in his arms, being assaulted by his kisses as he kicked them both to the surface. They broke the surface of the water, and she pushed off him, laughing as she caught her breath. "Let's do it again!" She stroked toward the rock, laughing as Chase caught up to her and then effortlessly passed her, reaching the rock while she was still several yards out.

He pulled himself halfway out of the water, and it streamed in sensual rivulets over his body. His biceps flexing from gripping the rock, he swung out over the water, extending his hand toward her. "Time to pay the toll, my pretty."

She laughed at his wicked voice. "This is a really expensive theme park."

"You're in Wyoming. We're the land of pricey resorts." He caught her hand and pulled her in for another kiss.

It lasted longer this time, and got a little bit steamier. By the time the toll was satisfied, there was no way to blame her perky nipples on the cold water. "Should we do flips this time?" She scurried up the rock, laughing as he sped up past her, apparently finding a second path in the rocks.

"You can flip?" he asked.

"Yep. I did gymnastics as a kid, and some cheerleading." She reached the top of the rock and shook her hair out as she walked over to the edge.

"Cheerleading? You seem much too serious for cheerleading," Chase said as he walked up beside her. "I could see you being editor of the school newspaper."

She grinned. "I was that as well, but yes, cheerleader. I liked the flips." She cocked her head. "Didn't you play football?"

"I did. College and high school." He studied her. "I think football players are supposed to date the cheerleaders. Want to share an ice cream sundae with me on Sunday afternoon?"

She burst out laughing. "I want my own ice cream." She patted her belly. "I have to eat for two, you know."

"Damn. And here I thought I'd just come up with a brilliant way of getting close to you. I'm going to have to work on my skills." He managed to look cranky, which just made her laugh even more.

"Ready?" She turned toward the water, taking a breath to calm herself and focus. It had been a long time since she'd been upside down. She flexed her muscles, activating memories long stored.

Chase was still beside her. "Together?"

She glanced at him, and something tightened in her chest. "Side-by-side flips? You don't think we'll kill ourselves?"

"Nope. I don't."

She nodded, a sense of rightness settling over her. "I don't either. Side-by-side then."

"You call it."

"Okay." She flexed her hands. "On three. One."

He moved a few inches away from her, giving them both space.

"Two."

They both bent their knees slightly, stabilizing their balance.

"Three!"

She took three steps, swung her arms, and launched herself off the rock, tucking her chin. To her delight, her body rotated just as she'd intended, and she had executed a complete somersault before her feet even hit the water. Chase flipped in perfect synch with her, grinning at her as they went upright. She let out a whoop of laughter, throwing her arms above her head in victory as her feet broke the surface of the water and she plunged beneath the surface.

Perfection, in every way.

Chapter 14

The moment was heaven.

Chase stretched out on the blanket he'd brought with him, the rough surface warm against his back. Mira lay against him, using his stomach as a pillow as she pointed out shapes in the clouds.

He grinned contently as he played with her drying hair. He was valiantly trying to discern the animals she could see in the sky, but all he could see were floating balls of white fluff, constantly changing shapes.

It wasn't that he had no imagination. It was that all he could think about was the woman who'd spent the last hour leaping off the rock, doing more acrobatics than he could ever hope to do without breaking his neck, though he'd certainly tried. He'd crashed more times than not, completely schooled by her talent.

But it had been hilarious.

He couldn't remember the last time he'd laughed so hard. Mira's laughter had been infectious, each of them igniting more humor in the other, until finally, exhaustion had done them in. Well, not him, but he'd been carefully tracking her energy level, aware that her body was supporting two.

The moment he saw her energy dip and her shoulders start to slump, he'd suggested a break, and she'd agreed right away.

And now...what had been high-octane fun had morphed into quiet, peaceful intimacy that was equally perfect. She fit, he realized. She fit the ranch, she fit the horses, and she made him happier than he'd ever been.

He reached down and placed his free hand on her belly. There was a slight swell now, but it was still, devoid of any telltale movement. "When can you feel it start to kick?"

She went still, and he felt her stiffen slightly. "Around four to five months, I think. A while."

"I bet that's wild." He rubbed his thumb over her belly, almost unable to believe that a live human being was forming inside her body. He didn't want her to feel threatened by his touch. He wanted to be the one to ease her stress, not magnify it. "Pretty amazing, isn't it?" He kept up the slow, deliberate caress on her belly.

She relaxed slightly. "It is."

They were both silent for a moment, but it was no longer a tense silence.

"Chase?"

"Yeah."

She put her hand over his. "I think you'll be a great father."

His hand stilled on her belly. "You do?"

"I do." This time, it was Mira who began a slow caress, tracing her fingers over the back of his hand. "Even if we don't get married, I'm going to put you in my will as the baby's guardian. I can't think of anyone else I'd rather have look out for it if something happens to me. Is that okay?"

A ball seemed to lodge itself in Chase's throat. "Yeah, sure. Of course it's okay."

"Good." A faint smile played at the corners of her mouth, a smile so sweet that he found himself wanting to lose himself in it.

He grinned, untangling the ends of her hair. A lock fell free and floated over his chest, across a long scar from the horsewhip his father had found at the town dump one day. His smile faded, and that old, familiar fear clamped across his chest. As idyllic as this moment was, it didn't hide the truth of her life, and of the demon chasing her and the baby. He knew suddenly that it didn't matter what his brothers thought. Mira and her baby deserved to be protected, and he was all they had. He was their protector, end of story. He knew it, without any doubt whatsoever, whatever the repercussions were with his brothers. "Mira?"

"Hmmm..." Her eyes fluttered closed, and he felt her head become heavier against his stomach as she began to doze off.

"I think we should get married."

Her eyes snapped open, and she turned her head to look at him. "Why?"

He shrugged. "It feels right."

She smiled slightly, and his heart seemed to stutter in his chest at her relaxed smile. "It's felt right all along, hasn't it? You think it's all because of AJ?"

He took time to consider her question, then finally he gave her the truth. "I don't know how much of it is the last ten years, and how much of it has been the last few weeks. I don't think I can divide it." He lightly squeezed her belly. "I just know that I want to protect both of you." His gaze flicked to his scarred forearm. "We can't leave anything to chance."

She stared up at the sky, watching the clouds. "What has changed with your brothers?" she asked. "I can tell you meant it just now, when you said we should get married."

"Nothing has changed with them, but I've changed. I know it's right, and if I know it's right, they'll come around. You saw Travis. He understood."

"He understood for a few months of free room and board. Not for the full nine months, let alone marriage."

"It was a start. We've all been knocked around by our father. They'll get it." He knew they would, because they had to. "There's no way on this earth that I can do anything but commit every last resource I have to you and the baby."

He saw a tear trickle out of the corner of her eye, but she didn't look at him. "Do you love me, Chase?"

"I've always loved you." The words were automatic and natural, a truth that he'd lived with for over a decade.

She turned her head to look at him again. "Not like that. Do you love me so desperately that you feel like you'll never be whole again unless I'm by your side?"

Fear clamped down on him, even though a part of him

burned to say yes, to acknowledge that she'd described exactly what he felt like, putting into words that which he couldn't articulate himself. But he didn't. Because he knew he couldn't. Instead, he shook his head. "I can't do that. I can't even let anyone that close, even if I want to." But if he were capable of letting someone matter that much to him, it would be her.

"I see." She closed her eyes, putting distance between them, distance that made him want to shout in denial.

Swearing, he caught her hand, drawing her attention back to him. "Don't you understand, Mira? I know I can't give you promises of soul-searing love, but I'm giving you every last thing I have to give. Whatever love I'm capable of, it's yours. My money. My home. My family. My brothers will become yours. I'm offering you my circle of protection. It's everything to me. It's all I have to give, and it's yours."

He knew it wasn't enough, not for Mira the woman, but maybe, just maybe, it would be enough for her as a mother who needed to protect her child.

Mira bit her lip. "Chase—"

"Can you afford to say no? What if Alan comes for you? What if he finds you living in town, and your only safety is my name on the kid's birth certificate? A name on a line isn't going to be enough, Mira. Are you willing to risk it for the baby?" He knew he was being unfair, pushing her at her most vulnerable, but he didn't know what else to do. All he knew was that he *had* to make her a part of his world. He knew that he alone wasn't enough, but his protection might be. It *had* to be. "You know we get along. We have great sex. We fit okay, and the baby will be safe."

Gone was the hesitation that had plagued him at first. He knew, without a doubt, that Mira was the missing piece of his life, the very thing he'd been waiting for all these years. She made him laugh. She made his house feel like a home. She enriched the life he wanted to live.

His brothers would get on board, one by one. She could be the anchor that held them all together in a way he could never do, because he couldn't articulate or express the warmth that she could. "Marry me, Mira."

She didn't answer, and he felt his soul freeze, hovering

in terrified anticipation of what she might say. Had he pushed her too far to the edge? She had a job now, and was on her way to supporting herself. Soon, she wouldn't need him, except to deal with Alan.

She sat up, facing him, her blue eyes searching his face. "Chase—"

The sudden roar of a motorcycle broke through the moment. They both turned to see a bike hurtling across the plains toward them. It took Chase only a split second to realize it was Zane.

Alarm ripped through him, and he lunged to his feet. What in the hell was his brother doing out there on his bike?

Mira grabbed her jeans and yanked them on. "Who is it?"

"My brother." Chase jerked his own pants on, watching the dust spiral from Zane's tires as he sped toward them. "He never comes out here. Something's wrong." Instinctively, he shaded his eyes to look toward his ranch, half-expecting billows of smoke to be filling the air, but the sky was blue.

The relief that his ranch wasn't on fire was fleeting, replaced by the gnawing realization that it had to be something else equally wrong. He jerked on his shirt and shoved his feet in his boots as Mira got dressed.

The horses were dancing in agitation as Zane roared up. Chase suddenly recalled that he'd silenced a call from Zane just before they'd headed out to ride.

He grabbed Mira, pulling her back as the back tire came to a stop inches from her bare toes. "What's wrong?"

Zane jerked his helmet off and dragged his forearm across his sweaty forehead, his face lined with absolute fury as he shot Mira a look so deadly that Chase stepped in front of her. "What's going on?" Chase asked.

His brother jerked his gaze off Mira. "Steen's been stabbed. Some altercation in the prison yard. They think he's going to die. We can't get in to see him, because you're the only one on his visitor list. I've been trying to reach you all fucking morning, and you've been out here with *her* while your own brother is dying? What the fuck, man? We have to go!"

Chase felt the bottom drop out of his gut. "Son of a

bitch." Without hesitation, he swung his leg over the back of the bike as Zane gunned the engine. "Can you take the horses back?"

Mira's face was ashen. "Of course," she said. "I'll take care of everything. Go!"

Chase just had time to shout his thanks over the roar of the engine, and then the bike was hurtling across the high desert, bouncing over ruts as they raced back toward the ranch in a race for the life of one of the few people in the world who mattered to him, who had been dying alone while he'd been swimming with a girl.

❧ ❧ ❧

Steen looked like he was already dead.

Stunned by the state of his younger brother, Chase sank down next to the hospital bed. Despite his attempts to visit, Steen had refused to see him for over two years. His head was shaved, several new scars marked his skull, and his skin was ashen. Tubes were coming out of his arms, and his bare torso was wrapped in bandages. Around his wrist was a handcuff, locking him down to the bed like he was a fucking criminal who would rip off his tubes and start shooting up the hospital.

Of anyone who he thought would wind up in prison, it wasn't Steen. Son of a bitch. "Steen." Chase leaned forward in his chair, whispering urgently. "You with me?"

"He goes in and out of consciousness." A nurse walked up, carrying a clipboard. Behind her, Chase could see the police officer on duty to guard his brother. "You must be Chase Stockton."

"Yeah, what's going on?"

She smiled. "Excellent. I'm so glad you're here. Steen was asking for you when he first came in for surgery, before he lost consciousness. We tried to call at the time, so he could at least hear your voice, but we were unable to get through. We had to go ahead with the surgery. There was a lot of damage, and he's already showing signs of infection. We're doing what we can, but he has to want to live in order to fight through it. He has a long recovery ahead even with the right attitude."

Guilt shot through Chase. How long had Steen been lying here, dying, while he'd been screwing around with Mira? Shit. "When did this happen?"

She looked at her chart. "He was stabbed just before six o'clock. He was in surgery by six thirty. We tried to call several times yesterday evening but we weren't able to go through."

Chase ground his jaw. It had probably happened right after they'd left to go to dinner with Gary and Martha. He'd never checked the messages on his landline, which was the number that the prison had. *Shit.* "Can we get his other brothers in?" He thought of Zane and Travis, sitting out in the waiting room of the hospital, desperate for news, unable to come in because Steen had refused to name them on his list of approved visitors. They were still trying to reach the others, calling them in. Every Stockton they'd reached was on his way. The brothers were finally coming together, but it was for the wrong reason.

"If it appears that he's close to death, yes, they can come in. Right now, we're waiting. You're the only one who's approved." The nurse checked the machines. "We were hoping you could get here earlier. The first few hours are critical. It's all about a will to live, and Steen, quite frankly, doesn't have it. He awoke briefly, just long enough for us to remove the breathing tubes, but we haven't been able to rouse him since." Her voice was clinical and non-judgmental, simply educating him as to the current situation so he'd be prepared. "Talk to him. Hold his hand. Play songs that matter to him. It sometimes works." She sighed. "Prison sucks the will out of many of the inmates. He may simply want to go, so be prepared."

Fear clenched Chase's gut and he took his brother's hand. "Steen, man. You can't check out. You have less than five months left in that shithole, and then you're coming home. You and me, bro, at the ranch, like old times, with the horses. Got a new young one that I'm saving for you. He's had a tough life and won't trust anyone. He needs you." All the Stocktons were horse people, but Steen had a special touch that the rest of them didn't have.

Steen didn't respond, not even a blink of his eyelids.

"His name's Superman. I figured he needed a badass name, because he's got a long way to go. I can't even get near him. Someone beat the hell out of him, and he's still losing weight. He *needs* you, Steen."

There was still no response, and Chase bowed his head, fighting off the grief. He'd tried so fucking hard to hold his family together, and now he was losing Steen, for good, for real, forever. "Come on, man. I got this big ranch, and I need help on it." He swore under his breath. Steen, of any of his brothers, had suffered more at the hands of their stepmothers and their father. He'd wound up in prison because a woman he'd loved had betrayed him. There was no one who had less faith in women than Steen, and now he was dying because of it.

Grimly, Chase realized that there was no way in hell Steen would come back to the ranch if Mira were there, no matter what the reason for her presence.

If he even lived.

⁂ ⁂ ⁂

Exhausted beyond words, Mira sank down on the couch in Chase's living room, her muscles actually shaking with exhaustion. She'd fed all the horses, walked Spy and made sure he was still recovering, cleaned the stalls, and watered the horses.

It had taken all day, and it was almost six now. There had been no word from Chase all day, and she hadn't dared call him, not after the look of absolute horror on his face when he'd realized that Zane had been trying to reach him while he'd been with her. The accusation in Zane's lethal stare had clearly stated what he thought about Chase being with her when their brother was dying.

No room for her. *No room at all.*

Mira rested her head against the back of the couch, staring at a photograph of a young Chase and two other teenage boys. They were wearing cowboy hats, and holding the reins of three scrappy looking ponies. Hoodlums in cowboy boots, she was sure. Was one of them Steen?

God, she would never forget the depth of anguish in Chase's eyes when Zane had told him that Steen was dying. His fear had plunged right into her heart. She knew that terror. She'd felt it the day she'd gotten the phone call that her parents had been in a car accident. The hospital had said the same words about her own father, that they didn't think he'd live through the night.

He hadn't.

She knew the shock of losing a loved one in an instant. She knew it too many times over.

Again and again, she'd replayed their car accident in her mind, wondering if it would have been different if she hadn't gone to college, if she'd stayed home, if she'd called her parents that night and made them three minutes later. No matter how many times she revisited the situation, she was never able to make the accident go away. It had taken time, but she'd eventually accepted that she couldn't blame herself for it.

But she'd seen the look on Chase's face, the stricken horror at the realization that his brother had been dying, but he hadn't answered his phone because he'd been with *her*.

If Steen died, a part of Chase would always blame her. And if he didn't die, Chase would realize that it had been a close call. There was no room for her and them in his life. After tonight, Chase would be sure to always put them first. *Always*.

Tears filled her eyes as she looked around the room. She had become accustomed to the ranch, and it had started to feel like home. Some of her books were on the shelves, and her magazines were on the coffee table. Her sweatshirt was draped over the armchair, and a picture of her parents was on the mantle next to Chase's pictures. The fridge now held her favorite kind of yogurt, organic milk, and flaxseed meal for her oatmeal, and there was now fabric softener in the laundry room.

At some point, this ranch had become home, and Chase was a part of it. She hadn't even been aware of it, until now, until she was facing a future without it. She'd assumed she had time to find her way. She'd rested comfortably on the knowledge that Chase would fight for her and the baby, that she didn't need to commit to him because he would wait for her.

But now that opportunity was gone. She'd hesitated, and the window had closed. After spending the night helping Chase save Spy's life, and then playing at the swimming hole, she'd realized that she wanted to be with him, that she wanted to find a way to make it work. Yes, she knew he was damaged and bruised when it came to relationships, but there was such beauty in his soul and in their connection, that she'd realized she had to be brave enough to try.

And now...what would happen after today? Had she lost her chance?

Her phone rang suddenly, jerking her out of her reverie. Was it Chase? Hope leapt through her. She jumped up and raced across the room, sweeping it off the kitchen counter. Her heart fell when she saw Taylor's name on her caller ID, not Chase. With a sigh, she declined the call and walked back over to the couch.

Her old life seemed so far away now. She didn't want to go back there.

Her phone started ringing again, and again, hope leapt through her as she looked down. Taylor again. Fear trickled through her at the repeat call. With foreboding weighing in her heart, she answered the call. "What's up?"

"Did you get my message? Tell me you left."

"Left? What message? I didn't see one from you." Tires rolled on the gravel outside, and she leapt up. "I have to go. I think Chase is back."

"No! Don't answer it! Alan found you! He found the record of the pregnancy test! He's on his way to the ranch!"

"What?" Mira's heart dropped and she raced to the window. A long, black limousine was pulling up in front of the ranch. "Oh, God, he's here."

"Get out the back door," Taylor said. "You have to go."

Mira watched as the rear door of the car opened and Alan got out, along with two other men in suits. Lawyers? "Oh, God," she whispered. "Where would I go? He'd find me."

"Don't answer any questions!" Taylor said. "You'll need a lawyer. Don't let him bully you!"

The doorbell rang, making Mira jump. She backed away from the door, clutching the phone. Dear God, why hadn't she married Chase already? Why had they waited? "I have to go. I have to call Chase."

Someone pounded on the door, and she ducked into the kitchen, leaning against the fridge as she tried to catch her breath, pressing her hand to her stomach. She wasn't prepared to face him. Dammit. She shouldn't have underestimated him. Her hands shaking, she dialed Chase's number.

It went straight into voicemail, and she realized he probably had to turn it off in the hospital. She immediately hung up. Could she really bother Chase when his brother was dying?

"Mira Cabot! Open the door!"

She closed her eyes, trying frantically to decide what to do. Call Chase again? Add to his stress? But then she thought of his reaction when he'd realized he hadn't been there for Steen. It was in his blood to take care of those in his circle, and she knew that the baby was in that circle. Regardless of whether there was a place for *her* in his life, she knew that he would do anything to protect the baby. She had to give him the chance. Ignoring the furious pounding on the door, she dialed his number again. "Chase," she said into his voicemail, her voice shaking. "Alan's here. He found out I bought the pregnancy test before you came to town. I don't know what to do. Call me, as soon as you can. And, I hope Steen's okay. I've been thinking about you all day."

She hung up, trying to calm her mind enough to think clearly. She could call the hospital, but she had no idea what facility his brother was in.

Footsteps sounded on the back porch, and she blanched when she saw shadows fall across the kitchen window. Before she could move, a face appeared in the glass, and she found herself staring straight into the bitter, angry eyes of her baby's grandfather. His gleam of satisfaction twisted right in her gut, and she instinctively covered her belly with her hands.

His gaze followed her movement, and then he smiled. "Open the door, Mira." He held up a manila envelope. "I have a document for you to read and sign."

She knew what that document was.

It had to be a waiver turning guardianship of her baby over to Alan, and she knew that he would have a way of forcing her to sign it right then and there. He had something on her, something she wouldn't be able to defeat, because he wouldn't have come until he had everything in line. What would it be? Her parents were dead. Taylor? Chase? What did he have on them? What card was he going to play? What knife was he going to plunge in her belly and twist until she caved?

Frantically, she dialed the only other phone number she knew in town.

Gary Keller picked up on the first ring. "Coming for dinner tonight, my dear?"

Before she could say another word, the back door crashed open, and the man who had beat his son so badly that he'd never walked right again strode into her kitchen.

It was too late.

Chapter 15

"Chase?"

He looked up in surprise as Zane and Travis walked into Steen's hospital room. For a split second, relief rushed through him, and then the reality crashed down on him. "Why are you here? They said you couldn't come in unless he was dying— "

Fuck.

He looked down at Steen, at the machines pumping life through him, and he felt his world begin to crush in on him. "They came and got you?"

Zane looked ashen, and Travis had dark shadows beneath his eyes, even more so than when he'd been at the ranch a few weeks ago. "They said he's giving up." Zane punched his fist against the wall, leaving a dent.

"What the hell, Steen? Why aren't you trying?" Zane dropped his muscled frame into a folding chair, and braced his forearms on his thighs, staring at their brother. Steen's muscle had wasted away, and his chest wasn't even moving perceptibly. "Steen," he said urgently. "We need you, man. Don't give up. It's just a knife wound. You've healed worse than that."

Still no response from their brother.

Zane and Chase exchanged grim looks. "I've said everything I can think of," Chase said. "I don't know what else to say."

Zane ran his hand through his hair. "It's Rachel, isn't it? He gave up the day all that went down."

Chase ground his jaw at the name of the woman who

had landed Steen in prison. "Yeah. He changed that day. You could see it in his eyes. They went dead."

"Well, fuck it." Zane hunched forward. "She's just a woman, Steen. Forget her. You want to give her the satisfaction of dying? Your best payback will be to go live and reclaim your life."

Still nothing from Steen.

Travis leaned against the wall, keeping back. "He looks like he's been sick. That can't all be from the last twenty-four hours, can it? He's thin as hell."

"I don't know. I haven't seen him in two years." Chase looked around at his brothers. How long had it been since the four of them were in the same room together? Years, and years. It had to come to this to get them together? It was what he'd been striving for, but hell, not this way. "What about the others?"

"Quintin will be here tonight. Logan's coming in tomorrow. Maddox and Ryder should be here any minute. I can't find Caleb. His number has been disconnected. You got a more recent number?"

"I don't know." Chase dug his phone out of his pocket and tossed it at his brother. "You can check the one in my phone and see if it's different." He looked at Zane, who had been in a coma in high school after a motorcycle. "You think he can hear us? Does he know we're here?"

Zane shrugged. "I don't remember anything from when I was out. If I heard you guys, I don't remember. All I remembered was you standing over me when I was on the side of the highway, shouting at me not to die or you would come to hell and kick my ass." Accusation flashed in his eyes. "You had that chance with Steen, to tell him not to give up, but you didn't answer your phone when they called. If you'd talked to him then, he'd have known we cared. But no one was there, and now he's given up."

Chase gritted his jaw, guilt wrenching away at him. "I know."

"What the hell, man? What were you doing with her at that pool?" Zane shook his head in disgust. "I went through the house looking for you. Her shit's everywhere. It's like she's claimed the place."

Images of Mira's fuzzy pink blanket draped over the back of the couch popped into Chase's mind, and a sense of rightness settled over him. He liked her belongings in his house. It made the house feel less empty. Suddenly, a yearning to talk to her rushed over him. He was in over his head, and he wanted to hear her voice. She'd lost her father, and she'd somehow kept her mom from giving up after the accident. Maybe she would have an idea. He suddenly wanted to talk to her, to get her advice, to hear her voice—

"Hey, Chase?" Travis interrupted. "Mira called and left a message. You want to listen to it?"

"Yeah." Instinctively, Chase reached for his phone, but he paused when he saw Zane's hostile glare.

"Really?" Zane challenged. "You're going to take her call while Steen could be taking his last breath? Dad put his women before us. Don't do it. Don't fucking be him, Chase." There was a hard edge to his voice, but beneath it was something stronger, the weight of a childhood they had all suffered.

Chase swore under his breath. Maybe Zane was right. Maybe Steen just needed it to be about him right now. But hell, he didn't know, and he couldn't afford to make a mistake. He needed to reach Steen, and he didn't know how. He looked over at Travis, who was holding out the phone. "She's been through something like this. Maybe she can help."

Travis's eyebrows went up. "Call her then."

"Help? Really? You think a woman can help Steen? A woman destroyed him." Zane's voice was bitter. "What the hell happened to you, bro? Since when do you call upon women as your savior? We're all we need. Us." He gestured to the three of them. "A woman is the reason Steen's given up in the first place, and now you want to bring one into this room?"

Chase ground his jaw, and shook his head at Travis, knowing that an argument with Zane wasn't what Steen needed to recover. "I'll get it later. Just check Caleb's number."

Travis's eyebrow went up. "You didn't take the hospital's call, and that was a mistake. You sure you want to skip this one?"

Chase frowned, studying his brother, fighting to think clearly. Right now, all he wanted to do was get on that phone and talk to Mira, but Zane's words made sense too. "You think

I should?"

"I think that you made a promise to her kid, and that means you always take the call. You take mine, you take Zane's, you take Steen's, but you also take hers. I made a promise to her as well, and if you don't take the call, then I will." He held out the phone. "You or me."

Zane sat up, looking back and forth between them. "What are you talking about Travis? You're in with her too?"

"It's not about her. It's about that kid who is going to end up like us if we don't step in, so yeah, I'm in with her too." Travis took the phone back, and touched the screen. "I'll listen to her message." He began to put the phone to his ear, and Chase lunged to his feet.

"I'll do that." He grabbed the phone from his brother and put it to his ear, walking a few feet away to listen to her message. The moment she said his name, he knew something was terribly wrong, and his heart clenched in fear.

By the time she finished her message, he was already racing toward the door. He'd just reached it when Zane barked out his name. "Where the hell are you going?"

Chase stopped abruptly and looked back at the room. He looked at Zane, with his angry scowl. He looked at Travis, who appeared exhausted and drained. And he looked at Steen, who was dying in front of him.

If he left, Steen might die, and if so, he'd die without Chase by his side. He'd never know if staying could have given Steen the motivation to fight for his life. He'd hold his brother's death in his hands for the rest of his life.

If he stayed, Mira and the baby would be Alan's forever. He knew the old man would waste no time. The trap would be sprung within moments.

And yet, he had to choose.

❧ ❧ ❧

Zane stood up and walked over to Chase. "Don't you dare leave."

His muscles straining with the need to run to Mira, Chase met his gaze. "The baby's grandfather is at my house. He found her. He's going to claim the baby."

Zane stopped, his eyes flashing with sudden anger. "He's there? At the ranch?"

"Yeah." Images of what was going down flooded Chase's mind, and panic surged over him, so intense he could barely think.

Travis swore. "You gotta go."

"What about Steen?" Zane said, not moving out of the way.

All three brothers looked at him. He was so still, he looked as if he were already dead. His face was sunken, his skin pale, his arms limp. He looked beaten, not just from the stabbing, but from the last four years in prison. Sudden anger flooded Chase, and he looked at his brothers.

"I've been mortgaged up the ass on that ranch for five years," he snapped. "I've been holding over a thousand acres for you guys to come home to, and no one ever does. Steen won't even fucking let me visit him." He strode over to the bed and grabbed his brother's shoulders. "You fucking gave up before you even got stabbed, didn't you? Did you jump in front of that knife just to get it over with more quickly? Well, fuck that!" He released Steen and whirled around to face Zane and Travis, who were gaping at him as if he'd lost his mind. "Mira is the only one who has moved into that house and let me help her."

Zane's face darkened. "We don't need help, Chase. We're not kids anymore."

"No, you're not. I get it." He looked around the room at his three brothers, his family, the only people who had ever mattered to him. "But you know what? It's not just that. I've sacrificed everything to hold onto that damned ranch for you guys, for me, and for us. None of you have dropped a dime or broken a sweat over there. Mira was up all night with me saving my best stud, even though she's pregnant." As he spoke, he realized it was true. For the first time in his life, he had an equal relationship. "She's there for me as much as I'm there for her, and I'll be damned if I'm going to let her down."

He spun toward the bed and leaned over his brother. "Listen to me, Steen. I love the hell out of you, but you've been wasting away for too damn long. If you want to die, that's your choice. I can't stop you, and neither can the others. If you want to live, we're here for you, but you have to make the choice yourself, because I need to go save a life. Yours is up to you." His throat tightened as he set his hand on his brother's shoulder. "I love you, bro, no matter what you choose, but right now, it's up to you."

He squeezed Steen's shoulder, and then turned away. Zane was blocking the door, but Travis was nodding. "You gotta go," he said. "I'll keep you posted."

Chase nodded and strode toward the door. "Move, Zane."

"It's your *brother*."

"As you said, he's a grown man, and he has to make his choice. I can't hold his hand anymore. I can't hold any of yours." He grabbed his cowboy hat off a hook by the door and jammed it on his head. "I can't change the past, but right now, I can change the future for one kid, and that's what I'm going to do."

Travis pulled the door open and stepped aside. "Keep in touch."

"Will do." He slammed his hand on Travis's shoulder, and then, after a moment, the brothers embraced. It was quick, but real, a bond that would never die.

He raced out the door, and he didn't look back.

He wanted to. Hell, he wanted to look back at the brother he might never see alive again, but he didn't.

He knew what he had to do.

🐾 🐾 🐾

Mira pressed her phone to her chest as Alan walked into the kitchen, his smoothly polished black shoes clicking on the floor that belonged to cowboy boots, not dress shoes. Her heart thudding almost uncontrollably, she went still, watching him approach. "What do you want?" she asked, somehow managing to keep her voice steady.

He was wearing a custom suit, and his gray hair was perfectly coiffed. His skin had a slight grayish tint to it, and it was sagging more than it had the last time she'd seen him. He looked old, but deadly. "I want my grandchild."

Oh, God. Her stomach dropped to her feet. "What are you talking about?" She met his gaze, not looking away.

"You're pregnant with AJ's child." Anger flashed across his face, but he quickly masked it. "Do you really think you could hide it from me by coming out here?" His voice was cold with loathing.

She schooled her features into a blank look, still trying to calm her mind. Panic wouldn't serve her. "Pregnant with AJ's child?" she repeated. "What in the world are you talking about?"

This time, he couldn't hide the flash of anger, and he stalked across the room toward her, his fingers curving as if he intended to grab her.

She quickly stepped around the granite island in the middle of the kitchen. "Don't touch me," she snapped. "This is my house, and you're trespassing. Leave now."

"It's not your house. It's Chase Stockton's, and he still owes a considerable amount on his mortgage."

His mortgage? Could he take Chase's ranch? No. That was impossible. He was bluffing. "I live here. You don't. Leave." She looked at her phone, saw that she was still on the call with Gary, and spoke again, more loudly. "I am going to call 9-1-1 if you don't leave here in one minute—"

Alan moved suddenly, lunging across the island and grabbing her arm. He ripped the phone out of her hand and threw it across the room. It shattered against the stone fireplace, and he grabbed her arm, his fingers digging into her skin like talons. "Shut the hell up, Mira. I'll give you one chance to make the right choice." He shoved the envelope at her, pressing it against her breasts. "For one million dollars in cash, you will assign me guardianship of my grandchild. The moment it's born, you walk away, and never come back."

Her mouth dropped open. He actually believed she would abandon her own child for money? Obviously, he did, which showed exactly where he placed the value of his own child in that hierarchy. "First of all," she snapped. "I would never trade money for my child. Second, it's not AJ's baby. It's Chase's, and we're getting married." Her voice didn't waver, and her gaze was unyielding.

For a moment, Alan's eyes narrowed. She could tell

she'd taken him by surprise, and she waited, resisting the urge to babble in defense of her lie. She'd learned from her dad that liars usually talked too much, wrapping themselves up in fabrications that unraveled when more information was revealed. People who told the truth let the facts speak for themselves.

So, she said nothing else.

"A DNA test will clear up that situation, won't it?"

Crap. How dare he be intelligent enough to know about basic science?

He jerked his chin toward the back door, and she was startled to see that his two suited escorts were now in the doorway, waiting for his command. "Find out how old an unborn baby has to be before we can do a DNA test. I'm sure we don't have to wait until it's born."

Bastard! Of course he'd want a DNA test. "You can't run one without my permission, and I'm not giving it to you."

"You're unfit to be a mother," he said, his fingers still digging in. "I have reams of evidence of you buying illegal drugs, coming home drunk, and using your dying mother's pain killers to fund your own habit." He released her to pull a document out of his envelope. "I have over twenty affidavits from people who will attest to your substance abuse problem, as well as evidence that you were defrauding the insurance companies to steal money from your mother's medical funds to pay for it."

He slapped the document in her hands, and she looked down, her heart sinking when she saw the names of assorted prominent people from town listed, and their quotes. How much money had he paid them? Were there so many people willing to sell themselves for money? Apparently, there were. "They lied."

"They swore under oath." Alan leaned forward. "You have two choices, Mira. Take a million dollars cash and disappear. Or you can fight me, and I'll destroy your reputation until the courts ban you from ever coming near the child again. That kid will grow up knowing that his mother was an addict who thought her next high was more important than her own kid. I can do it. You know I can."

Her mind started to spin, and she felt dizzy. She wanted to protest that Chase would never let it happen, and that Alan couldn't violate the sanctity of the marriage vows, but the words died in her throat. If she roped Chase in deeper, he'd destroy Chase as well. He'd take the ranch, destroy his reputation, and steal everything that mattered to him. Especially because it *was* AJ's child and that might give Alan power she didn't want him to have.

"If you sign the papers giving me guardianship, I'll tell the kid that his mom was a good woman who died in a plane crash. He'll never know otherwise."

Never know her own child? Or have it grow up thinking that she was an addict? "Chase is the father," she managed. "Not AJ. You have to leave."

Alan grabbed the front of her shirt and jerked her over to him. "You will sign the papers, Mira. If the DNA test shows Chase is the father, then I'll walk away and tear up the contract, because I don't want his filthy spawn. You can keep the money. If it's AJ's kid, then the deal is a go."

"No!" She tried to twist out of his grasp, but his grip tightened. "I'm not signing anything!"

Alan snapped his fingers, and one of the other men walked up. He was holding a tablet computer. Silently, he turned it so that Mira could see what was on the screen. It was a detailed email outlining countless instances of substance abuse, including an incriminating paragraph about how she was pregnant with the heir to one of the most dominating empires of the south, and how the baby's future was at risk because of her substance abuse problems. The recipient of the email was the editor-in-chief of a major national newspaper, and the producer of a national investigative television show. "I have twenty-two more emails ready to send right now to other media outlets. The campaign will begin this instant. Once word gets out about how messed up you are, you'll have *no chance* to ever see the kid again, and you'll be locked down in my house until the baby is born."

Oh, *God*. "You're going to look like a fool once the DNA test says it's Chase's child." Her breath was tight in her chest, and she was having trouble getting oxygen. "And it's all lies, so I can sue you for libel and slander. No one will publish that. They'll all be liable."

Alan smiled. "They're only lies if you can prove they're lies. I have proof that it's all true, and I can afford to fight a very lengthy legal battle in the process. Can you?"

She felt sick. "You're the bastard," she snapped. "If you drag me into a court battle, I swear I'll expose you for the father you truly are. I've seen AJ's scars, and I know his foot was messed up because of what you did to him." His face darkened with rage, and she leaned in toward him, anger surging through her. "I guarantee I'm not the only one who knows you beat him, and I'm guessing that your other son has told an awful lot of therapists that the reason he's such a mess is because his daddy beat the hell out of him. Is that worth it, Alan? You really want to go there? Because *that* is the truth, and we both know it, and I *will* make sure it gets out."

White-hot anger flashed over his face, and sudden fear ripped through her. She'd pushed the monster too far.

She had no time to back up before his fist came up and hit the side of her face.

No one helped her when she fell.

His two escorts simply walked out of the room, shut the door behind them, and left her alone with a bastard.

Chapter 16

She wasn't answering her phone.

Sweat trickled down Chase's spine as his truck hurtled down the highway toward his ranch. Mira's phone was going directly into voicemail, and he was still twenty minutes away. What if she stood up to Alan? What if she pissed him off?

Shit!

His phone suddenly rang, and he lunged for it, nearly losing control of the truck in his frenzy to get it. One glance told him it wasn't Mira, but he answered it anyway. "Maddox! Where are you?"

His brother, who he hadn't spoken to in several months, answered. "Heading toward the hospital. We're about forty-five minutes away. I have Ryder with me. How's Steen? Tell me he's gonna be okay." The edge to Maddox's voice bit deep, and Chase knew that the bond that tied the Stocktons together was soul deep.

He was going to have to ask his brother to break that bond. "How far are you from the ranch?"

"A couple minutes. Why? You need something?"

"There's a woman there. She needs help. I'm fifteen minutes away. You have to go help her."

There was a short silence. "What?"

"A woman. Mira Cabot. Get over there now!" His fingers were tight on the steering wheel, and Chase wanted to leap through the phone and grab his brother by the throat.

"You want us to go help a woman instead of coming to

see Steen? What the hell? I thought he was dying."

"He is."

"Well, shit, Chase, why are you—"

"There's a bastard there who's going to beat her up! Get the hell over there! She's under my protection and she's pregnant with the guy's grandkid. He's like Dad, and he wants to hurt that baby!" And Mira. Son of a bitch. Alan wanted to hurt Mira as well.

There was more silence, and then he heard Maddox talking to Ryder. Chase gritted his teeth, pressing the accelerator even harder, but even he couldn't make the truck fly. "Travis and Zane are with Steen. I told them I was coming to help her. Come on, man. Do this for me." He couldn't keep the urgency out of his voice. "I can't get there in time."

Maddox came back on the phone. "The bastard's dead. We're on it."

Relief rushed through Chase. "Thanks."

"Tell Steen that if he dies before we get there, we're going to hunt him down in the Afterlife and make him pay," Maddox added. "Got it?"

"Got it." He hung up and immediately called Travis. When his brother answered, he gave him the message for Steen.

Something had to reach his brother. Maybe that was it.

⁂ ⁂ ⁂

Pain rang through Mira's head as she dragged herself backwards, trying to get away from Alan. "Every time you hit me, it digs your hole deeper, proving what you did to your sons," she snapped. "Get out while you can, Alan."

His face was grayish and pinched as he advanced upon her. "No, bitch. I've had enough of you interfering in my relationship with AJ. He rejected me because your family told him to. Your piece of shit father tried to steal my son, and you helped. Your entire family took him from me." He kicked aside a chair that went spinning across the kitchen floor. It slammed into the wooden cabinets with a sickening thud that made Mira jump. "It's over now. I'm taking what's mine."

Mira scrambled to her feet, staggering as a wave of

dizziness hit her. Pain raked through her abdomen, and sudden fear knifed through her. What if he made her lose the baby? "Stop it!" she shouted, keeping the island between them. She pressed her hand to her belly. "Don't you dare touch me again," she snapped. "You want to hurt the baby?"

He lunged across the table and grabbed her hair. "Any grandchild of mine is tough enough to handle a few bumps."

She yelped and grabbed his hand, trying to stop him from pulling her hair, but he dragged her around the island anyway, jerking her to him. "Sign the papers," he snapped. "You have no idea what I'm capable of."

"Yes, I do." She slammed her elbow into his gut.

He grunted and released her hair. She immediately broke for the back door, her feet slipping on the polished wood. She grabbed the doorknob, but Alan caught her arm just as her fingers closed around it. He jerked her back, just as she heard shouting from outside. "Help!" she shouted. "Help me!"

There was more yelling, and she recognized Gary's voice, among others. She realized he'd come to help her, but Alan's men were blocking his path. "Gary!"

Alan threw her onto the couch, and she landed so hard she couldn't breathe. She just lay there, fighting for breath as Alan walked up and crouched beside her. Outside, the shouts continued, but no one came in to help her. She couldn't even yell for help. All she could do was try to regain her breath.

Alan's face was pale, deathly pale, his features contorted into a diabolical rage. He set the papers on the couch by her face, and shoved a pen into her hand. "I have dozens of witnesses who will swear you signed this of your own free will," he said, his voice pinched with anger. "I can keep this up all night, and if my grandchild doesn't survive it, then it's on you, not me."

She closed her eyes as a wave of nausea washed over her. She realized he was telling the truth. He would rather win than have his grandchild survive. He hated her and her family for the fact AJ rejected him, and it was finally his chance for payback. If she kept fighting, she would lose the baby. If she gave up, the baby might survive, and she might be able to fight back in courts.

She opened her eyes to look at Alan, and her heart fell.

He had power and connections beyond comprehension, and she had nothing. Was there really a chance she could defeat him in a legal battle? She knew with sinking certainty that he'd never let it get that far. He'd never let her expose who he was. After the baby was born, there would be another night. Another visit. This time, with no witnesses. A night she wouldn't survive. "Did you kill my father?" The question popped out unexpectedly, as if she'd known it as a truth all along. "Did you cause that car accident?"

Alan stared at her for a long moment. He didn't answer, but she saw the truth in his eyes.

He'd killed her parents out of spite, out of hate, out of a psychotic insanity about his son, and now he was ready to do the same to her.

❦ ❦ ❦

Chase gunned the engine as he raced up his driveway, and his gut dropped when he saw Maddox and Ryder in a brawl outside his front door. Gary was slumped on the ground, not moving. Both his brothers were in a hard-fought hand-to-hand battle against two guys in suits who knew how to fight. It was clear his brothers were trying to get into the house, and the men were blocking them. Neither suit was Alan, but a long, black limousine was sitting ominously in front of the house.

Chase knew Mira had to be inside the house with Alan. Fear ripped through him, and he gunned the engine and jerked his steering wheel to the right. The truck plunged over the edge of the driveway and bounced across the rutted ground toward the back of the house. It bounced over rocks, careening dangerously to the side, but Chase didn't even slow down.

The truck skidded around the corner of the house, and Chase plowed down a birdbath before slamming on the brakes. The truck crashed into his gas grill, knocking it over as Chase leapt out and vaulted onto the back porch. He exploded through the back door into the living room.

Mira was on the couch, and Alan's face was twisted in rage as he drew back his fist to hit her.

"No!" Chase leapt across the room and tackled the

older man, throwing him back against the wall before he could land the blow. They crashed into the built-in shelves, and books rained down upon them.

He threw aside a hardcover book as it cracked against his temple and leapt to his feet. "Mira!" His heart seemed to freeze in his throat as he took in her bruised face and her bleeding lip. He vaulted over the coffee table and landed beside her, going down on one knee.

She managed a smile, but her eyes were pinched with pain. "Thanks for coming."

"I was late. Shit. I was late." Guilt poured through him, as he pressed his hand to her forehead. Her skin was cold, but sweat was trickling down her temples. He saw her hand pressed to her belly, and terror congealed in his gut. He set his hand over hers. "Tell me, hell, he didn't hit you in the stomach, did he?"

She shook her head. "No, not yet. I think the baby will be okay."

Chase felt his chest constrict, as he wrapped his arms around her, helping her sit up. Just as she sat up, she looked past him, and her eyes widened.

Chase spun around immediately, rising to his feet as Alan grabbed the fireplace mantle and dragged himself to his feet. His skin was ashen, and his cheeks were sunken. He looked like a man who'd been to hell and had never found his way back. Disgust poured through Chase for the man who was the replica of his own father, a bastard to the end. "Assault and battery is going to get you prison time, you piece of shit."

Alan grabbed his left shoulder, as if he'd hurt it in the fall. "I'll buy your mortgage, Stockton. You'll lose the ranch. You want to risk that?"

Chase froze. "What?"

"Your mortgage. Lenders sell them all the time." Alan tried to stand up more erectly, and his face pinched with pain. "I can own you by the end of the day."

His ranch? *His ranch*? Could Alan really find a way to take it?

Mira's fingers slipped into the waistband of his jeans, and she pulled herself to her feet. "Stay out of it, Chase. It's my battle. Don't risk the ranch."

Movement outside caught his eye, and Chase glanced out the front window. He could see Maddox fighting. Blood was trickling down the side of his face. His brothers were out there taking hits for him, because he'd asked them to. Could he really sacrifice his ranch, their ranch?

Then he looked down at Mira. Her jaw was clenched with pain, but there was a fire in her eyes, and he knew she wasn't going to give up. She was a fighter who had lost her family and her home, but she wasn't going to step down.

He realized suddenly that this was what family was about. Family wasn't a ranch. It was his brothers stepping in to help him, defending a stranger because he'd asked. It was Mira, willing to take whatever Alan dished out to protect her baby. It was the fact that every one of his brothers had rushed back to town when Steen needed them, without hesitation. Family was defined by the people who stood together against all odds, and it didn't matter whether they were standing on a ranch, or in a gutter somewhere. It was all the same.

It wasn't about a ranch, and it hadn't ever been. The front door suddenly flew open. Maddox and Ryder rushed inside, both of them battered, bruised, and bleeding. The brothers stopped when they saw Chase, but when they noticed Mira's black eye, their eyes narrowed in open hostility.

Chase nodded at them, and then slung his arm around Mira's shoulder, pulling her against him. "You can try to take the ranch," he said evenly to Alan. "I don't give a shit. But you need to know that you will *never* get through me to Mira or our baby."

Out of the corner of his eye, he saw Maddox and Ryder's faces go blank in shock at his announcement. He tensed, ready for them to resist, the way Zane and Travis had. But to his surprise, they walked right up, flanking him and Mira. Their cowboy hats were dirty, their faces were bruised, and knuckles were bleeding. They looked as mean as their father ever had, and Chase knew they could fight just as dirty.

"You have to go through me, too," Maddox said, wiping the back of his arm across a stream of blood trickling down his forehead.

"I'm in," Ryder agreed. "Don't touch what's ours."

Alan looked back and forth between them, then he glanced toward the door, where his men were limping in with torn suit jackets and more damage than either Maddox or Ryder had sustained. "This isn't over," he snapped.

"Yes, it is!" Mira pulled out of Chase's grasp and walked over to him. "Let it go, Alan. You almost destroyed AJ, and you're doing the same to your only living son. Get help. You won't ever get my baby—"

His lip curled in distaste. "I will. You wait." He lurched over to the coffee table, walking crookedly, as if he were drunk. He swept the computer off it. "I'll still send the email, Mira."

Mira stiffened, and Chase didn't need details to understand the threat. He strode over to Alan, and stopped beside Mira, angling himself between the bastard and Mira. "You don't get it, old man. You can blackmail her or any of us all you want, and we won't give in." He took Mira's hand, squeezing tightly. "We stand by each other, and every piece of crap you throw at us will have to go through all of us. You'll never do it."

"I have money," Alan snapped.

"Yeah, but I have more." Travis walked in the front door, wearing his pristine white cowboy hat and his pressed jeans. He looked every bit the country music superstar he was, and Chase grinned.

Mira gripped his hand. "Travis," she hissed. "Don't. He can ruin you."

Travis shrugged. "My pop tried to ruin me. He failed. Bullies suck." He walked up beside Mira, facing Alan. "We know what you're like," he said simply. "We don't like people like you."

Alan's upper lip sneered in distaste, and he looked at all of them, as if assessing whether he could take on all the Stocktons at once.

He couldn't, and Chase saw the moment the bully realized he was outnumbered.

Without another word, Alan spat on Chase's boots, and then turned and walked toward the door.

Mira's fingers tightened in Chase's, and he glanced down at her. Her face was pale as she watched Alan go, and he knew she was thinking that it wasn't over. He pulled her close and pressed a kiss to the top of her head. "You're not alone."

Tears shimmered in her eyes, and she nodded once, still not talking as she watched Alan lurch toward the door. He careened into one of his men, who caught him. As they helped him toward the door, Chase began to realize that something was wrong. Really wrong.

Alan collapsed before he made it through the front door.

⚜ ⚜ ⚜

"He's gone. Cardiac arrest." The paramedics passed the verdict on to Alan's men, who took the news of their boss's demise with stoic silence as they turned away and pulled out their cell phones.

Mira's heart, however, felt like it had been eviscerated. *Alan was dead.* She watched numbly as the paramedics pulled the sheet over Alan's face. Dead. Alan was *dead.* She was stunned, unable to tear her eyes off the shadowed figure beneath the stark white sheet. She could still see the ashen color of his skin as he'd fallen. She could still feel the hate from his bloodshot eyes burning into her as he fell, using the very last moment of his life to punish her with his loathing.

Her father had died in front of her. Her mother had died in front of her. And now Alan. Three deaths. Three times, she'd watched the life, the spirit, bleed from the body of someone, leaving behind nothing but an empty shell. Experiencing death again was like reliving her parents' death, a gaping wound flooded with tears, loss, and anguish. But at the same time, it was different, so different, because losing her parents had been like losing a part of herself. Watching Alan die was… "I feel happy," she whispered, horrified that she could feel joy upon someone else's death. "I just watched a man die, and I feel…happy."

"It's okay." Chase put his arm around her, pulling her tight against his side. "He was a sick bastard who hurt you and those you loved for a long time. You're finally free of him. Don't feel guilty."

She dragged her gaze off the stretcher and looked up at Chase. His face was grim as he watched them load the stretcher onto the ambulance. "Chase?" she whispered.

He looked down at her, and smiled, a smile that was

loaded with the weight of death, but one that held the same relief she felt. "I'm not going to lie, Mira. I'm glad he's dead, and he got what he deserved. He owned his life, and he owned the way he died. He brutalized my best friend, stalked you, and he would have hurt a lot more people. The sun's going to shine brighter tomorrow because he's not in this world. I'm not going to waste a second mourning him." He touched her chin, his fingers so soft and gentle that they seemed to pull her back from the edge of her grief. "And you shouldn't either, okay?"

She nodded. "I know, but it's still—" She took a trembling breath, unable to articulate the miasma of emotions swirling through her.

"You're safe, sweetheart. Do you realize that?" Chase palmed her belly, his fingers spread across her stomach like a shield. "Do you understand? This little baby is safe, for the rest of his life. The enemy is gone. *Gone.*"

Tears suddenly filled her eyes, and her hands started to shake. She was safe. Forever. Alan could never come after her, and he could never hurt her child. The danger was *over.*

"Hey, it's okay." Chase pulled her into his arms, and she buried her face in his chest, clinging desperately to his strength. She wrapped her arms around his waist and held tight to the only stable thing she had in her life while the tears poured forth. They were tears of loss for AJ and her parents. They were also the cathartic release of a fear that had gripped her since she was a child and acquired him as an enemy after befriending AJ, a fear that had been tightening around her neck with each passing minute…and now it was over. *Over.*

Chase pressed a kiss to the top of her head, holding her tightly, until the strength and warmth from his body eased her trembling. She squeezed her eyes shut, breathing in his woodsy, masculine scent as the tears began to fade, replaced by a new, fragile sense of hope, of new life.

"Well, I think that's it for now," the sheriff said as the doors to the ambulance clanged shut.

Mira pulled back from Chase and looked around at the scene she'd been too upset to notice. The Stockton brothers were standing in grim silence, and Gary was sitting on the front porch, holding a frozen steak to his head. He'd been knocked out by one of Alan's men, but he'd recovered and refused to go to the hospital.

These men were the victors, the ones who had triumphed, the ones who deserved to win. Her heart softened for these men who had come to her rescue, strangers who hadn't hesitated to take on an enemy more powerful than they.

The sheriff tilted his hat back on his head and walked over to Chase. He'd already grilled them all on the situation, including failing to convince anyone to go to the hospital or press charges for assault, so there was no drama left. Mira and Chase hadn't mentioned the email threat, and neither had Alan's men. It didn't matter anymore, now that Alan was gone. It was all just…over. The officer was in his thirties, and his short brown hair reminded Mira of photos of her dad when he'd first made sheriff, back when she was a little girl. He'd been so proud in that photograph, a man ready to save the world. Then his life had been stripped from him too early because he'd dared to stand up against Alan. He would be proud of her, she realized. He would have been so proud of her refusing to give in to Alan, of aligning herself with Chase, of finding the strength to battle Alan for her baby. She smiled, almost feeling her dad smiling down upon her.

Sheriff Wilson extended his hand toward Chase. "Let me know how Steen is."

"You bet. Thanks." Chase kept one arm around Mira, tucking her tightly against his side as he shook the sheriff's hand.

The sheriff tipped his hat to Mira. "Welcome to town, Mira. I'm sorry it took this for us to meet." He gave her a little wink that was so much like her dad that tears suddenly burned in her throat.

"Thanks," she managed, trying desperately to hold her emotions together.

He eyed Chase's brothers. "I hope you ruffians stay in town for a while this time. It's been too long." To her surprise, he grabbed Travis's hand and yanked him into a bear hug. He did the same with Maddox and Ryder. There was no mistaking the bond between the men, making her wonder what past the men shared with the sheriff.

He saluted the brothers, then got into his truck and drove off, his tires spitting up dirt as he held his hand out the window in silent farewell.

Silence descended upon the small group. Mira looked around at them, the heroes who had been willing to fight for her. How had she been so lucky as to acquire such a formidable army to fight for her? "I don't know how to thank you all," she said, clearing her throat. "The way you came to help me—"

"It's no big deal," Ryder interrupted with a shrug, shifting uncomfortably. "It's how we work." He jerked his head at Travis. "Call Zane. See how Steen is." His attempt to change the subject was obvious, a man who wanted no thanks for being a hero.

"I'm on it." Travis stepped away from the group as he pulled out his phone.

As he did so, Mira saw Maddox and Ryder studying her. They were both tall and rugged, with heavy whiskers and jeans that were dusty and worn. They looked like men who had been out on the range when they'd gotten the call, throwbacks to the old west, to the days when men and their horses defined loyalty and teamwork.

"She's pregnant with your kid?" Maddox asked Chase. His dirty blond hair was brushing against the collar of his shirt, and his leather jacket was creased and old. "You called it 'our' kid when you were talking to the old man."

Chase didn't answer. He didn't give the party line they'd been planning for so long, about how the baby was his. Instead, he looked at Mira. She knew what he was thinking. With Alan dead, there was no longer a threat to her baby. There was absolutely no need for Chase to declare himself the father.

She didn't need a protector now.

It was over.

She was free...and suddenly felt like crying. She didn't need Chase anymore...but she did. How could she let him go? He was a part of her on so many levels. But how could she ask him to burden himself with her? Now there was no need. He deserved his freedom.

So, she lifted her chin and smiled at the Stockton brothers. "I really appreciate all your help. You guys go see to Steen. I'll clean up here and watch the horses until you get back." She glanced at Chase. "I should pack my stuff—"

"Let's go for a walk," Chase interrupted.

Mira shook her head, wanting them to leave. Everything had just shifted for her and she needed time to process it. Alan was gone, and her baby was safe. *Safe.* She had to look ahead to a life as a mom, starting her own family, without being forced to play house with a man who didn't love her, who was committed to her only out of a sense of obligation. "No, it's okay. I'm fine. You need to go back to Steen—"

Chase was already shaking his head. "No. We need to talk." He took her hand and started walking toward the barn. "I'll be back in a few," he informed his brothers. "Mira and I need a moment."

Travis grinned, watching them. "What about your brother?" he called out, his phone still in his hand. "You going to walk out on Steen for a girl?"

Chase paused, and looked back at his brothers. "I'll never walk out on any of you. Ever."

Satisfied, Travis nodded, as did Maddox and Ryder. It was all Mira needed to hear. She knew what Chase was going to say. She felt like her heart was fragmenting into a thousand pieces, and she knew she would never let him say the words.

She had to say them first.

Chapter 17

Tension flooded Chase when Mira pulled her hand free even before they reached the barn. She turned to face him just inside the doors, her hands settling on her hips. "Listen, Chase," she said, her voice as steady as he'd ever heard it. "There's no need for you to do any more for us. Now that Alan's gone, we're all set. Thurston won't want any competition for the family business." She put her hand on her baby bump. "We're all set now," she repeated.

He ground his jaw, fighting against his reaction to drag her into his arms and kiss her until she took her dismissal back. "I think you should stay for a while, at least until you're sure you're okay."

She smiled, but there was sadness in her eyes. "Thank you and your brothers for saving me today. I really mean that. But I know there's no room for me in the Stockton world. I need to be in a place where I belong, and where everyone is fully invested in me." She shrugged. "That's what I grew up with, and that's what I need."

"How can you say that? Everyone showed up here for you. There is room—"

She put her finger across his lips, silencing him. "Chase," she whispered. "You don't need to protect me anymore. It's about your family, and it always has been. I need to find my way now. You guys were here for me tonight when I really needed it, but I'm okay now. You don't need to do any more for me."

Words flooded his mind, demanding that he claim her,

that he refuse to let her walk away, but he couldn't articulate them. They just died in his throat, fading away into the same ugly place where the memories of his childhood lay haunting him. "Where are you going? Back home?"

There was a visible hesitation, and he felt his heart leap.

"I don't know," she said. "I might stay in town for a while. I've made some good friends, and there's nothing really left for me back home." She wrinkled her nose. "Just memories that hurt, you know?"

He thought of the night he'd made love to her so many times. He thought of the midnight ride to see the wolves. He remembered swimming with her that morning, an idyllic moment that felt like an eternity ago. He could picture her crazy hair when she stumbled into the kitchen for breakfast every morning. Every image was burned indelibly into his mind, and he knew they'd be there forever, a constant reminder of the moments that had given him the first peace he'd ever had. "Yeah, I know about memories that hurt."

She patted his arm. "Okay, so I'll just start to pack my stuff. I know it's everywhere in the house. I'll stay until you're back from the prison, so you can focus on him, okay?"

He wanted to say more. There were a thousand words rushing through him, words he didn't know how to say. "Do you want to go?" The question slipped out before he could stop it, and he grimaced. It was clear she was ready to leave, and he wasn't going to beg. When women wanted to leave, it never worked to talk them out of it. He knew that from the hell of his childhood.

She went still, watching him warily. "Go where? To see Steen?"

He leapt at the idea, grasping at it greedily. "Yeah. They say he's given up and isn't trying to live. I know you somehow helped your mom keep going even after the accident, so I thought maybe you could reach him." He didn't even bother to consider what his brothers would think if he showed up with her. He just knew he wanted her there. He wanted her with him. He needed her to be a part of whatever he was going to have to face in Steen's hospital room. "He's dying, Mira, and we can't save him."

Some of the stiffness faded from her shoulders, and she touched his hand. "I doubt I can reach him—"

"Will you try?" He flipped his hand over and cradled her fingers in his. "Please?"

She nodded. "Of course. What about the horses?"

"Gary will be in charge." Hope leapt through him. It felt so right to be bringing Mira back with him. "Let's go."

She looked past him, her gaze settling on his brothers, who were huddled in deep conversation. He felt her hesitation, and he swore under his breath. "I need you, Mira." The words came out rough, barely muttered under his breath, but when she looked at him, he knew she'd heard him.

Without another word, she squeezed his hand and started leading him back toward his truck.

⁂

Mira had never been around so much testosterone or so many pairs of Wranglers in her life, especially in such a small, confined, somewhat hostile space. There were six Stockton men hovering around Steen's bed. Chase and Travis, along with her gallant rescuers, Maddox and Ryder, who were both sporting bruises and moving stiffly from the fight they'd endured on her behalf.

Her throat clogged when she looked at their injuries. They were complete strangers who had jumped in to help her, simply because their brother had asked them to. Such loyalty and commitment to each other was so amazing, and it reminded her of what she'd had with her own parents. She missed that feeling of connection, and a sad envy wrapped around her for the tightness of their bond.

They'd been joined by Quintin, whose tall, lean body reminded her of a wild stallion surviving on guts and courage out on the range.

Lounging against the wall, and giving her the most hostile glare, was a man Chase had called Zane. Unlike the others who were wearing cowboy boots and hats, Zane was in motorcycle boots, and a black leather jacket. He looked fierce and angry, and most of it was directed toward her.

Each of the brothers was well-muscled, carrying the air of a man who had been to hell and back, and would never forget it. Travis at least had a decent smile, but even he wasn't smiling. They all looked worried, almost scared, barely talking as they took over the area around the bed.

As she stood in the doorway, watching them, her heart tightened for what they had endured, and how they'd forged unbreakable bonds with each other for survival. Chase was arguing in low tones with Zane, and she could hear her name being batted around while he tried to convince his brothers to let her talk to Steen.

Her gaze slid to Steen, and her heart seemed to freeze in her chest. With the tubes and the bandages, and his sunken face, it was like seeing her father again in that bed, dying. Tears suddenly filled her eyes, and she put her hand over her mouth, fighting against the surge of emotion. She started to turn away, but then warm arms wrapped around her.

She looked up as Chase pulled her against him, ducking his head so that his face was beside hers. "I'm so sorry, sweetheart," he said quietly. "I didn't think about the impact it would have on you. I shouldn't have asked you to come. I'll take you home."

His voice was so tender, his concern so genuine, that it broke through the vise closing around her heart. She closed her eyes and rested her head against his chest, feeling the rise and fall of each breath and the steady thud of his heart. He held her tightly, pressing soft kisses to the top of her head, not asking anything of her, just offering his support.

Ever since the accident, she'd had to be so strong, and now, suddenly, Chase was there to hold her. The warmth of his body enveloping hers seemed to infuse her body with strength, taking the edge off the grief. She gripped his shirt, focusing on the feel of him, on the strength of his body.

As he held her, she began to understand the depths of what had happened. His brother, his beloved brother, was truly on the edge of death, and yet he'd left the hospital to come to her aid. Travis had come. Ryder and Maddox had come. These men, who claimed to have no room in their lives and hearts for anyone except their brothers, were liars.

They had room. They just didn't know it. They were

born protectors, each and every one. They thought they had space only for each other in their sphere of protection, but they were wrong, and they'd already proved it.

And Chase...her dear, sweet, Chase. He'd been her protector since the very first moment, and AJ had known that.

Tears brimming in her eyes, she pulled back from Chase enough to look at him. His blue eyes were weary, and his face was lined with a lifetime of worry. She smoothed her fingers over his dark whiskers, each coarse strand like a promise of his strength. He'd been broken by women, and she knew he might never be able to cross that line and give her what she'd wanted: the superficial trappings and declarations of love.

But he gave her more. He gave her actions that spoke far more than words would ever speak. He was the man she'd been waiting for all this time. Did he love her? Or had his frantic, heroic rescue been because of the baby who reflected his own past?

She didn't know, but she needed to find out. If there was a chance, she would be brave enough to take it.

Chase frowned. "You want to leave?"

She shook her head. "I want to stay and talk to him."

The intensity of relief and gratitude that flooded his face made her heart turn over. This man cared, more than anyone would ever know, except, perhaps herself.

"But before I do," she said quietly, soft enough that the words were for him, but not so quietly that the rest of the room couldn't hear. She wasn't going to hide it, and she wasn't going to protect the others. "I have to tell you something."

She felt the attention of the room shift onto her, and Chase stiffened. She saw his jaw tighten, and his eyes cooled, putting distance between them. God, she knew it was a risk, but she was going to say it anyway. "I know that we got together because of the baby," she said. "I know that changes now that Alan's dead, but I just want you to know that I've fallen madly, deeply, truly in love with you. I don't need Alan and his threats to make me want to marry you. I think you'd be the most amazing father this child could ever have, and its uncles would be more than a mother could ever ask for. I would still marry you, if you wanted, and I would marry you for real."

Chase's face went impassive as he blocked his emotions from her.

Was he afraid of what she offered? Or did he want nothing of it? She stood on her tiptoes and clasped his face, forging onward with what she needed to say. "I know you might not love me like I love you, but I want you to know that you are worth all my heart. I love you, and my love will be with you no matter where our lives lead." There was utter silence in the room as she pressed a kiss to his mouth.

He didn't kiss her back, and her cheeks were flaming as she pulled back. His eyes were searching hers, brimming with emotions so turbulent she couldn't decipher them. She waited for a heartbeat, but he said nothing.

She turned away, feeling like her heart was shattering as she walked past the towering, silent masses of Stockton muscle and sat down on the edge of Steen's bed.

No one said a word as she leaned forward and placed her hands on Steen's cheeks. She leaned over and pressed a kiss to his forehead. "If you die now," she said softly, "you'll miss out on the chance to know what it's like to be truly loved by someone who will treat you well. And somewhere out there is a woman who needs you to hold her at night, to protect her, and to love her. If you die, then she'll never have the chance. She needs you, Steen. She needs you to get out of this bed, get out of this prison, and to rescue her, because there's no one else who can do it except for you. She's out there, right now, in this very moment, and she needs what only you can give her."

She took his inert hand and sandwiched it between her palms, pressing tightly. "Do you feel this?" she asked him. "This is what it feels like to be safe. She needs that from you, and she will be the one who will save you right back." She pressed a kiss to the tip of his finger, and couldn't stop the tears that started to fall. "Don't miss out, Steen. Life is so short, and opportunities are so fleeting. Don't miss her."

She bowed her head, trying to fight back the sobs. It was as if all the emotions that had been trapped inside her since her parents' death, AJ's death, the battle with Alan, and her feelings for Chase had suddenly surged to the surface, no longer willing to be crushed by sheer willpower.

Someone moved, and she looked up into Zane's face.

He'd sat down across from her, and she realized he'd heard everything she'd said.

"You tried to use a woman to save him? And love?" He sounded pissed, but also disbelieving.

"Yes." She kept holding Steen's hand.

"A woman is what destroyed him. That's what women do."

She met his gaze. "Don't be an ass, Zane. Not all women are evil, and you know it. So back off and let your brothers live a real life, even if you won't do it yourself." She knew it was probably a mistake to stand up against one of Chase's beloved brothers, but she didn't care. Someone had to, and it was going to be her, because they needed a protector, and she was going to claim the role.

⚝ ⚝ ⚝

Mira had just called his brother an ass?

Yeah, she had.

Chase grinned at the sudden irritation on Zane's face, and his brother looked over at him. "For real?"

"Yeah." He started walking across the room, ignoring his brothers, heading right toward her. Mira glanced over at him, and her eyes widened when she saw him coming.

Travis and Maddox moved out of his way, and he reached her in several short strides. He pulled her hand free of Steen's and knelt in front of her. The words that hadn't come before were tumbling through him, alive and vibrant, desperate to be spoken. "You're right," he said.

She frowned, her beautiful, tired face wary. "About what?"

"What you said to Steen."

Disappointment flickered across her face, and she lifted her chin. "It's what I believe."

"Well, it's true." He pressed a kiss to her palm. "I'm not going to lie, Mira. My brothers and I are fucked up when it comes to women."

She gave him a look. "Yes, I know that."

"But you've broken through that."

She blinked. "What?"

He chuckled, suddenly feeling the happiest he could ever remember being in his life. *She loved him.* "I've been waiting for you for ten years, Mira. Not just the fantasy woman, but the real life woman who leaves her coffee mug on the bathroom counter, and gets cranky when she gets hungry. I love the woman who can call my brother an ass when he's being one. I love the woman who's brave enough to ignore a room full of cynical Stocktons to give my brother the one message that none of us would have been able to give."

Some of the wariness left her face, and he saw hope in her beautiful eyes. Hope that he loved her back?

Hell, yeah, he did.

He shifted his weight so that he was on one knee, and he took her other hand, so he was holding both of them. He wanted this moment to be perfect, but he wasn't a poet, and he wasn't a romantic. All he could offer was himself. "I offered to marry you to protect the baby, but it was always about you. As Zane told me a thousand times, there were other ways to help you, but marrying you was the only one that felt right, because it was the only one that was right." He put his hand on her belly. "I love you, Mira, all on your own, and I've fallen more in love with you every day that we've been together. I want to be your husband, to be this baby's father, and to be a family."

Tears shimmered in her eyes. "But what about your brothers?"

He didn't even bother to look at them. He'd gotten his answer when Maddox and Ryder had headed toward the ranch at his request. It might be rocky, but his brothers would accept her because he loved her. "They're good."

She started to look toward Zane, but he caught her chin, directing her back toward him. "No, sweetheart. This is about us. You and me. It's no longer about anyone else." He took the plastic straw that he'd filched from the hospital tray and bent it into a disjointed circle. "I promise I'll get you a real one as soon as we leave here, but I want this done right." He held it up. "Will you marry me, Mira Cabot? I can't promise to be poetry and romance, but I promise you that I'll stand by you and love you every second of every day for the rest of my life. I love you with every last bit of my heart and soul, and I offer you my everything."

For a long moment, she said nothing, her eyes searching his desperately. He let her see the truth of his words, his promise of everything he was capable of giving. Would it be enough for her?

The silence in the room was overwhelming, everyone focused on her.

Finally, she held up her hand. "Yes," she whispered. "Of course, I'll marry you. It's always been you, Chase. Always. Since the first time AJ told me that his new roommate had told him that he should come to football tryouts with him, because his damaged foot would work the same in cleats as anyone else's. It just took ten years to find you."

Emotions flooded him, and he slipped the straw over her extended ring finger on her left hand. "AJ, the matchmaker."

She beamed at him. "He'd be happy right now."

Chase pulled her into his arms. "He'd be saying, 'it's about damned time,' and I tend to agree." Then he kissed her, the first kiss of the rest of his life.

When she melted into him, absolute rightness flooded him, and he knew that he'd finally found where he was supposed to be. He'd keep every scar on his body and soul, because without them, he'd never have ended up where he was, with Mira in his arms, loving him every bit as much as he loved her.

Love was a hell of a risk, except when it was with the right woman. Then it was the best, safest, purest emotion a man could ever have.

As for his brothers...well...he had a feeling that their time would come.

෫ ෫ ෫

He needed to do something.

It was important.

He didn't know what it was, but it was pressing at him relentlessly.

It was difficult.

Impossible.

But he had to try.

Try.

Try.

There were voices in the distance, ones he recognized. And another. A woman. He had to talk to her. There was something he needed to say.

The urge grew stronger, pulsing through him, driving him. He became aware of a great weight pressing down on him, trying to hold him back. *No!* He screamed his outrage, fighting to get past it. He had to tell her. It had to be now. He felt like he was swimming through mud, fighting for breath that didn't want to come to him. He could do this. *He had to do it.*

Light suddenly burned his eyes. It was bright. Too bright. He tried to block it by closing his eyes, but he didn't want them closed. He needed to see. Shapes began moving, shifting in and out of focus. Shadows mixing with the light. Where was she? He tried to call her, but he didn't know her name.

Suddenly, a face came into focus in front of him. He recognized it. "Chase?" His voice was raw, and his throat hurt, as if he hadn't spoken in so long. Was it really Chase there with him?

His brother's face morphed into shock. "Steen?"

Yeah, yeah, it was really Chase. "Where is she?"

There was noise in the room, and suddenly there were faces crowding his vision. He recognized all of them. Ryder. Maddox. Travis. Zane. Quintin. They were crowding him, grinning those shit-eating grins that he remembered. "Where is she?" he asked again.

There was a shuffle, and then Chase pulled a woman forward. She was pretty. Dark blond hair. Blue eyes. She sat beside him. "I'm Mira."

Yes. Her voice rippled through him, and he took a deep breath at the familiar sound. Excruciating pain tore through his stomach from the attempt to inhale, and he couldn't hold back the grimace of agony. He shook his head at Chase's concerned look, trying to focus on the woman. "I heard you."

She nodded. "I know."

"What did you say?" He felt like she'd said something

important, something slipping away at the edges of his memory, elusive but critical. Shit. His stomach hurt. And his side. He felt like he'd been sawed in half and left to rot on the side of the road. His vision began to fog, but he fought to stay conscious. He had to talk to her.

She smiled then, a smile so kind that he wanted to smile back through his cracked lips. "When you're ready to remember, you will."

"No." Desperation rushed through him, and he tried to reach for her hand, but he couldn't seem to move his arm. Pain tore through him again, and he pressed back in the bed, going utterly still as he waited for the pain to abate. *Jesus.* He clenched his teeth, fighting not to breathe and make it hurt more.

"I've got you, bro." Chase took his arm, moving it carefully until Steen's hand was in hers.

Steen forced his eyes open so he could see her. "I need to know. What did you tell me?"

She glanced at Chase, then leaned forward. "The day you walk into the kitchen of the ranch a free man, I will tell you."

"Free man?" he echoed. For a moment, he didn't know what she was talking about, and then his life came rushing back to him. Prison. The stabbing. He looked down and saw his body bandaged up and tubes coming out of him everywhere. Right. He'd forgotten. All the energy left him, and he sagged back into the bed. The pain from his wounds burned through him, and he wondered whether he'd ever be able to take a deep breath again. .

Chase leaned over Mira's shoulder, and Steen noticed that his arm was around Mira's shoulder and she was leaning into him. There was an intimacy between the two of them that made him think of Rachel, and pain echoed in his chest. "Steen," Chase said. "You have less than five months until you're out. This shit will be over, and you can start again."

"For what? I—" He cut off the familiar refrain when he saw the expression on Mira's face. "What?" She knew something. What did she know?

"Give it time," she said softly. "You'll figure out why you decided to live." She leaned forward and pressed a kiss to his cheek. He closed his eyes, stunned by how incredible it felt to be touched so softly, and so intimately. He went utterly still, afraid to break the spell, afraid to move, afraid of never feeling that kind of touch again. The pain that had been gripping him so fiercely eased slightly, allowing him just enough room to inhale slightly.

"Careful, buddy," Chase said. "She's mine."

Steen opened his eyes as Mira pulled back. She held up her left hand, which had a straw wrapped around her ring finger. "I'm marrying into your family, Steen. Zane is pissed, and most of your brothers are afraid of me. It seems as if you like me, so do me a favor and get healed, okay? I need you at the wedding so that Chase isn't the only one on my side. Got it?"

"Married?" He looked at Chase, who was grinning the biggest smile he'd ever seen in his life. Even as he studied his brother, he felt weariness stealing over him, and his eyes growing heavy. Shit, he was tired. He needed to sleep. He could feel his body screaming at him to let it heal, and he knew he had to shut it down. His eyelids began to drift shut, and his finger slackened in Mira's hand.

"Damn right," Chase said. "I need you there. You coming?"

Forcing his eyes open Steen looked at Mira again, and then he looked at each of his brothers, who he hadn't seen in years. He'd cut them out when he'd gone to prison, and yet there they were, all of them present, crowding his bed like they didn't give a shit about what'd he'd done. Only Caleb and Logan were missing. All the rest were there. Something rolled over inside him, something that had been dead for a long, long time. "Yeah, okay," he said, returning his gaze back to Chase and Mira. "I'll be there. At your wedding. But you're going to have to wait. Gotta get better. I'm not coming in a wheelchair." Pain stabbed through him again, and he gritted his teeth.

Chase's smile widened, and the others all seemed to take a universal deep breath. "You promise?"

He met his brother's gaze, knowing that in their world, a promise meant everything. "Yeah," he said. "I promise."

Sneak Peek: A Real Cowboy Knows How to Kiss

A *Wyoming Rebels* Novel

It was Steen Stockton.

Erin couldn't believe the man who was standing before her. After all her years of fantasizing about him, wondering what had happened to him, searching the web for information about his football career after he'd blown out his knee in college, he was standing right in front of her.

An old, faded cowboy hat was pulled low over his forehead, almost shielding his dark eyes from her view. His face was clean-shaven, his jaw angular and refined. He was wearing a black tee shirt, black jeans, and boots that would fit more with a motorcycle helmet than a cowboy hat. His shoulders were still wide and his body angled down to a V toward his narrow hips, but he was lean, too lean, and his cheeks were sunken, as if he'd been in a bad place for a long time. He was pure male, well over six feet tall, and his muscles were hard and cut beneath his shirt, despite his leanness.

He was no longer a boy, but the man she'd envisioned. He was pure, raw heat, with a languid grace that she knew hid his lightning-quick reflexes and innate physical grace. For the first time in years, she felt a pulse of physical attraction. Involuntarily, her gaze flicked to his mouth. His lips were pressed together, as if he were trying to contain the words that wanted to escape. Sexy and silent, just as he'd always been, only now, he was so much more.

In the face of the sheer strength of his presence, she suddenly felt like the ugly, geeky fourteen-year-old again, hopelessly outclassed by the only person she'd ever known who lived life on his terms and didn't care one bit what anyone else thought of him.

He frowned. "You okay?"

Erin suddenly realized she'd been gaping at him. Horrified, she snapped her mouth shut, trying to regain some semblance of self-respect. "Yes, fine. Thanks. It's so incredible to see—"

"You need some help with your engine?" he interrupted, cutting off her sentence before she could finish commenting how good it was to see him.

It was her turn to frown now. Did he not recognize her? After all these years of fantasizing about him whenever she'd needed to escape from the reality of her life and marriage, he didn't even *remember* her?

Desolation flooded her, the kind of utter loss that happens only when a dream is shattered, a dream that had all its power because it was pure fantasy, and therefore could never be destroyed. And yet, in one instant, he'd shattered it, because *he* was reality now, standing in front of her. Steen had been the only one who'd ever looked *at* her, instead of *through* her, but it apparently hadn't meant anything to him, at least not enough for him to remember her.

She lifted her chin resolutely. It didn't matter. She knew that her imagination had elevated him into the perfect man, and just because the real life man didn't even *remember* her, it didn't change the fact that he'd been her salvation, her escape over all the years. She knew he was a good guy, and it wasn't his fault that she'd been such an insignificant blip in his life that he didn't remember her.

He tipped his cowboy hat back, giving her a clear view of his eyes for the first time. They were haunted. Deeply haunted. She was shocked by the change in them from the jaunty, arrogant boy she'd known in high school. There was no humor in his gaze. No life, even. Just emptiness. She'd never have believed anything could take him down, but something had, something that had broken the spirit of the man she believed in for so long, the one who had lived in her heart for over a decade. Her heart tightened, and instinctively, she reached out, touching his arm. "What happened to you, Steen?"

Steen froze, and his muscles went rigid under her touch, making her realize that she'd overstepped her boundaries in a major way. She quickly jerked her hand back. "Sorry, I didn't mean to—"

"You recognize me?" he asked.

She blinked. "What? Of course I do. How could I not?"

Did that mean he recognized her? She wanted to ask, but she didn't dare. His gaze was too intense, and his silence was too unyielding.

After a few moments, she began to shift uncomfortably. She cleared her throat, and tried to change the subject to one that wasn't quite so incredibly awkward. "So, um, you know engines? Is that right?"

"Yeah." He still didn't take his gaze off her face, which she found both completely intimidating and wildly intoxicating. She used to catch him watching her when they were in school, but his face had always been inscrutable and distant. Now, however, there was so much intensity burning in his eyes that her heart started to race. No longer were his eyes empty and apathetic. They were simmering with heat, and all of it was directed at her.

So much for the fantasies not living up to reality. Even in her dreams, he'd never made her feel the way he was making her feel in this moment, like she was the only thing in his world that had ever mattered. Flustered, she pulled her gaze off him. "Well, um, here." She grabbed Josie's notebook from the engine. "I have this diagram of what I'm supposed to do if Faith dies, but I can't figure it out."

"Faith?" He still didn't take his eyes off her, not even to look at the notebook that she was waving at him.

"My car. Josie's car. Do you remember Josie? She was my only friend...I mean, she was my best friend in high school. Anyway, she's a vet out here, but she had to go to Chicago to help her mom through surgery, so I'm out here for a few weeks taking over her clinic while she's gone. So it's her car, and I don't know how to use it and—" She stopped when the corner of his mouth tipped up in a slight smile. "Sorry. I'm babbling."

"You used to be so quiet," he said. "I think you spoke more words just now than you uttered during your entire high school career."

"I used to be so quiet?" She stared at him as the meaning of his words sunk in. He remembered her from high school? The liar! *He remembered her!* Elation flooded her, and she couldn't stop the silly grin. "I'm still quiet," she said. "That was just a momentary babble because I'm nervous. So, don't get used to it. I'm not suddenly going to become a talker."

His right eyebrow quirked. "You're nervous? Why?" As he spoke, he plucked the forgotten notebook out of her hand and walked around her toward the engine.

"Because you make me nervous."

He glanced over at her as he leaned over the engine. "Me? Why?" There was an edge to his voice that was like steel.

"You always have." She leaned against the side of the truck and folded her arms over her chest, watching him as he looked back and forth between the notebook and the engine.

He tossed the notebook over his shoulder and braced his hands on the truck, his gaze methodically scanning every inch of the engine. "Why?" He repeated the question, not even bothering with polite preamble. He wasn't even looking at her, but she felt his intense awareness of her.

"Because you're you."

"That's not an answer." He bent over and fiddled with something in the shadowy recesses of the engine.

Her heart began to pound as silence built between them. She knew he was waiting for her answer, and a part of her wanted to give him the absolute truth. She'd never see him again after she left in three weeks, right? After so many years of suppressing every emotion and trying to be the woman that everyone in her life wanted her to be, now was her chance to speak up, to admit who she was, to let it all out. To take a chance. That's why she'd come out to Wyoming, right? Because she'd been dying inside, and she'd been desperate to find some kind of kick in the pants that would get her heart beating once again.

He twisted something and moved a wire, still waiting for her answer.

After a moment, he looked up. "She's all set," he said, his voice rumbling through her. His gaze was boring into her. "You're good to go." He waited a heartbeat, and she knew this was her last chance to speak up. In a split second, he was going to lower the hood, and she was going to drive away, and he would walk out of her life…again.

Sneak Peek: A Real Cowboy Rides a Motorcycle

A *Wyoming Rebels* Novel

He was tired.

He was cranky.

He was wet.

Zane Stockton idled his motorcycle outside his brother's ranch house, narrowing his eyes at the darkened windows. Gone was the time when he'd let himself in and crash. There was a woman in there now, and that changed all the rules, especially when it was two in the morning.

He probably shouldn't have come tonight, but he was here, and he was done being on the road for now. Rain had been thundering down on him for hours, and he was drenched all the way to his bones. He just wanted to sleep and forget about all the crap that had gone down today.

Trying not to rev the engine too much, he eased his bike down the driveway past the barn and turned right into the lean-to beside the bunkhouse. He settled his bike and whipped out a couple towels to clean it off, making sure it was mud-free before calling it a night.

He grabbed his bag from the back of the bike, scowling when he realized it had gotten wet, then sloshed across the puddles toward the front door of the bunkhouse. He retrieved the key from the doorframe, and pried the thing open.

It was pitch dark inside, but he knew his way around and didn't bother with a light. He dropped the bag, kicked off his boots and his drenched clothes, then headed for the only bed that was still set up in the place, ever since Steen and Erin had rearranged it for their own use during their temporary stay there. At least they'd upgraded their lodging so the bunkhouse was now available again for use by the family vagrant.

Zane jerked back the covers and collapsed onto the bed. The minute he landed, he felt the soft, very real feel of a body beneath him, including the swell of a woman's breast beneath his forearm. Shit! "What the hell?" He leapt to his feet just as a woman shrieked and slammed a pillow into the side of his head.

"Hey, I'm not going to hurt you! I'm Chase's brother!" He grabbed the pillow as it clocked him in the side of the head again. "Stop!"

There was a moment of silence, and all he could hear was heavy breathing. Then she spoke. "You're Chase's brother?" Her voice was breathless, and throaty, as if he'd awakened her out of a deep sleep, which he probably had. It sounded sexy as hell, and he was shocked to feel a rush of desire catapult through him.

Shit. He hadn't responded physically to a woman in a long time, and now he'd run into a woman who could turn him on simply by *speaking* to him? Who the hell was she? "Yeah," he said, sounding crankier than he intended. "Who are you?"

"You're Steen?" He heard her fumbling for something, and he wondered if she was searching for a baseball bat, pepper spray, or something that indicated she hadn't been nearly as turned on by his voice as he'd been by hers.

"No, a different brother," he replied, his head spinning as he tried to figure what was going on, and why he was reacting to her so intensely. "I'm Zane. Harmless. Good guy. No need to decapitate me."

There was a pause in her movements. "I wasn't going to decapitate you. I was looking for my shirt."

"Your shirt?" he echoed blankly. "You're not wearing a shirt?" He hadn't noticed much bare skin for that brief moment he'd been on top of her. How had he missed it?

"I'm wearing a camisole, but it's not exactly decent. Give me a sec." A small laugh drifted through the darkness. "You're such a guy. Of course you'd fixate on the possibility of me being naked. Do all men think only of sex?"

He grinned, relaxing. He'd startled her, but she'd regrouped quickly, and he liked that. She wasn't a wimp who was running to the door screaming. "What's your name?" he asked.

"Taylor Shaw. I'm Mira's best friend from home. I surprised her for a visit, but it turns out, there's no space in the house."

"Nope. Not anymore. I'm displaced too." He suddenly wanted to see her. "You decent yet?"

"Yes, but barely—"

He reached over and flicked on the small light by the bed. The soft yellow glow was less harsh than the overhead light, but it still took his eyes a moment to adjust to the brightness. When they did, he saw Taylor sitting on the bed, curly blond hair tumbling around her shoulders in a disheveled mess that made her look completely adorable. Her eyes were green, fixed on him as she squinted against the sudden light. He could see the curve of her shoulders beneath the light pink, long-sleeved shirt she was wearing. The faint outline of a white camisole was evident beneath her shirt, not quite obscuring the fact that she wasn't wearing a bra. Her gray yoga pants were frayed at the knee and cuff, but they fit her hips with perfection. She looked like she'd just tumbled right out of a bed, and she was sexy as hell.

But it was her face that caught his attention. Her gaze was wary, but there was a vulnerability in it that made him want to protect her. He had zero protective instincts when it came to women…until now, until he'd met this woman who'd tried to defend herself with a pillow.

Then her gaze slid down his body, and his entire body went into heated overdrive. It wasn't until her eyes widened in horror when her gaze was at hip level that he remembered something very important.

He was naked.

Sneak Peek: No Knight Needed

An *Ever After* Novel

Ducking her head against the raging storm, Clare hugged herself while she watched the huge black pickup truck turn its headlights onto the steep hillside. She was freezing, and her muscles wouldn't stop shaking. She was so worried about Katie, she could barely think, and she had no idea what this stranger was going to do. Something. Anything. *Please.*

The truck lurched toward the hill, and she realized suddenly that he was going to drive straight up the embankment in an attempt to go above the roots and around the fallen tree that was blocking the road. But that was crazy! The mountain was way too steep. He was going to flip his truck!

Memories assaulted her, visions of when her husband had died, and she screamed, racing toward him and waving her arms. "No, don't! Stop!"

But the truck plowed up the side of the hill, its wheels spewing mud as it fought for traction in the rain-soaked earth. She stopped, horror recoiling through her as the truck turned and skidded parallel across the hill, the left side of his truck reaching far too high up the slippery slope. Her stomach retched as she saw the truck tip further and further.

The truck was at such an extreme angle, she could see the roof now. A feathered angel was painted beneath the flood lights. An angel? What was a man like him doing with an angel on his truck?

The truck was almost vertical now. There was no way it could stay upright. It was going to flip. Crash into the tree. Careen across the road. Catapult off the cliff. He would die right in front of her. Oh, God, *he would die.*

But somehow, by a miracle that she couldn't comprehend, the truck kept struggling forward, all four wheels still gripping the earth.

The truck was above the roots now. Was he going to make it? *Please let him make it—*

The wheels slipped, and the truck dropped several yards

down toward the roots. "No!" She took a useless, powerless step as the tires caught on the roots. The tires spun out in the mud, and the roots ripped across the side of the vehicle with a furious scream.

"Go," she shouted, clenching her firsts. "Go!"

He gunned the engine, and suddenly the tires caught. The truck leapt forward, careening sideways across the hill, skidding back and forth as the mud spewed. He made it past the tree, and then the truck plowed back down toward the road, sliding and rolling as he fought for control.

Clare held her hand over her mouth, terrified that at any moment one of his tires would catch on a root and he'd flip. "Please make it, please make it, please make it," she whispered over and over again.

The truck bounced high over a gully, and she gasped when it flew up so high she could see the undercarriage. Then somehow, someway, he wrested the truck back to four wheels, spun out into the road and stopped, its wipers pounding furiously against the rain as the floodlights poured hope into the night.

Oh, dear God. He'd made it. He hadn't died.

Clare gripped her chest against the tightness in her lungs. Her hands were shaking, her legs were weak. She needed to sit down. To recover.

But there was no time. The driver's door opened and out he stepped. Standing behind the range of his floodlights, he was silhouetted against the darkness, his shoulders so wide and dominating he looked like the dark earth itself had brought him to life.

Something inside her leapt with hope at the sight of him, at the sheer, raw strength of his body as he came toward her. This man, this stranger, he was enough. He could help her. Sudden tears burned in her eyes as she finally realized she didn't have to fight this battle by herself.

He held up his hand to tell her to stay, then he slogged over to the front of his truck. He hooked something to the winch, then headed over to the tree. The trunk came almost to his chest, but he locked his grip around a wet branch for leverage, and then vaulted over with effortless grace, landing in the mud with a splash. "Come here," he shouted over the wind.

Clare ran across the muck toward him, stumbling in the slippery footing. "You're crazy!" she shouted, shielding her eyes against the bright floodlights from his truck. But God, she'd never been so happy to see crazy in her life.

"Probably," he yelled back, flashing her a cheeky grin. His perfect white teeth seemed to light up his face, a cheerful confident smile that felt so incongruous in the raging storm and daunting circumstances.

But his cockiness eased her panic, and that was such a gift. It made her able to at least think rationally. She would take all the positive vibes she could get right now.

He held up a nylon harness that was hooked to the steel cord attached to his truck. "If the tree goes over, this will keep you from going over."

She wiped the rain out of her eyes. "What are you talking about?"

"We still have to get you over the tree, and I don't want you climbing it unprotected. Never thought I'd actually be using this stuff. I had it just out of habit." He dropped the harness over her head and began strapping her in with efficient, confident movements. His hands brushed her breasts as he buckled her in, but he didn't seem to notice.

She sure did.

It was the first time a man's hands had touched her breasts in about fifteen years, and it was an unexpected jolt. Something tightened in her belly. Desire? Attraction? An awareness of the fact she was a woman? Dear God, what was wrong with her? She didn't have time for that. Not tonight, and not in her life. But she couldn't take her gaze off his strong jaw and dark eyes as he focused intently on the harness he was strapping around her.

"I'm taking you across to my truck," he said, "and then we're going to get your daughter and the others."

"We are?" She couldn't stop the sudden flood of tears. "You're going to help me get them?"

He nodded as he snapped the final buckle. "Yeah. I gotta get into heaven somehow, and this might do it."

"Thank you!" She threw herself at him and wrapped her arms around him, clinging to her savior. She had no idea who he was, but he'd just successfully navigated a sheer mud cliff for her and her daughter, and she would so take that gift right now.

For an instant, he froze, and she felt his hard body start to pull away. Then suddenly, in a shift so subtle she didn't even see it happen, his body relaxed and his arms went around her, locking her down in an embrace so powerful she felt like the world had just stopped. She felt like the rain had ceased and the wind had quieted, buffeted aside by the strength and power of his body.

"It's going to be okay." His voice was low and reassuring in her ear, his lips brushing against her as he spoke. "She's going to be fine."

Crushed against this stranger's body, protected by his arms, soothed by the utter confidence in his voice, the terror that had been stalking her finally eased away. "Thank you," she whispered.

"You're welcome."

There was a hint of emotion in his voice, and she pulled back far enough to look at him. His eyes were dark, so dark she couldn't tell if they were brown or black, but she could see the torment in his expression. His jaw was angular, and his face was shadowed by the floodlights. He was a man with weight in his heart. She felt it right away. Instinctively, she laid a hand on his cheek. "You're a gift."

He flashed another smile, and for a split second, he put his hand over hers, holding it to his whiskered cheek as if she were some angel of mercy come to give him relief. Her throat thickened, and for a moment, everything else vanished. It was just them, drenched and cold on a windy mountain road, the only warmth was their hands, clasped together against his cheek.

His eyes darkened, then he cleared his throat suddenly and released her hand, jerking her back to the present. "Wait until you see whether I can pull it off," he said, his voice low and rough, sending chills of awareness rippling down her spine. "Then you can reevaluate that compliment." He tugged on the harness. "Ready?"

She gripped the cold nylon, suddenly nervous. Was she edgy because she was about to climb over a tree that could careen into the gully while she was on it, or was it due to intensity of the sudden heat between them? God, she hoped it was the first one. Being a wimp was so much less dangerous than noticing a man like him. "Aren't you wearing one?"

He quirked a smile at her, a jaunty grin that melted one more piece of her thundering heart. "I only have one, and ladies always get first dibs. Besides, I'm a good climber. If the tree takes me over, I'll find my way back up. Always do." He set his foot on a lower branch and patted his knee. "A one-of-a-kind step ladder. Hop up, Ms.—?" He paused, leaving the question hovering in the storm.

"Clare." She set her muddy boot on his knee, and she grimaced apologetically when the mud glopped all over his jeans. "Clare Gray." She grabbed a branch and looked at him. "And you are?"

"Griffin Friesé." He set his hand on her hip to steady her, his grip strong and solid. "Let's go save some kids, shall we?"

Sneak Peek: Fairy Tale Not Required

An *Ever After* Novel

A car door slammed, and Jason tensed. Shit. He wasn't in the mood to be sociable right now. If the little old lady from his fantasies had finally shown up with a plate of cookies, she was too damn late. She was just going to have to leave them on the porch.

Jason sheathed the blade of the utility knife back into the casing, waiting for that inevitable ring of the doorbell. How many times had he answered his door to find another note of condolence or another casserole after Lucas's death, and then Kate's? Well-meaning acquaintances who thought that a smile and a slab of meatloaf would ease the gaping void in his soul. He'd stopped answering the door, because there was no way to pretend to be appreciative when all the darkness was consuming him.

And now, after fighting like hell to get past that, after scraping his way back into a place from which he could function, all those emotions had returned, brought on by the overwhelming silence of his house. That same silence that had flooded him when he'd come back home after watching his son die at the hospital and felt the gaping absence of Lucas.

Silence fucking sucked, but a doorbell was no better.

But the doorbell didn't ring, and the car didn't drive away.

Scowling, Jason walked across the landing to peer out the back window at the driveway.

Astrid Munroe's rusted junker was in his driveway. *Astrid.* He'd forgotten she was coming.

Adrenaline rushed through him, breaking him free from the tentacles of the past. His heart suddenly began to beat again, thudding back to life with a jolting ache. He tossed the knife aside, spun away from the window and vaulted down the stairs, taking them three at a time, almost desperate for the air he knew Astrid would feed back into his lungs.

He jerked the back door open and stepped out onto

the front porch, unable to keep the hum of anticipation from vibrating through him. "Astrid?"

Her car was empty, and she was nowhere in sight.

Trepidation rippled through him. Another woman dead? He immediately shook his head, shutting out the fear that had cropped up out of habit. Instead, he quickly scanned his property, knowing she had to be there somewhere.

But there was no Astrid. Frowning, Jason jogged down the pathway that led around the house toward the lake front, urgency coursing through him to find the one woman who had brought that brief respite into his life, that flash of sunshine, that gaping moment of relief from all that he carried. Where was she? He had to find her. *Now.*

Jason was almost sprinting by the time he rounded the rear corner of his house and saw her. The moment he saw her, he stopped dead, utterly awed by the sight before him.

"Son of a bitch," he whispered under his breath as he stared at the woman who'd rocked his world only a few hours before.

Astrid was standing on one of the rocks on the edge of the lake, silhouetted by an unbelievable sunset. The sky was vibrating with reds, oranges and a vibrant violet, casting the passionate array of colors across the lake's surface. Astrid's hands were on her hips, her face tilted up toward the sky, as if she were drinking the beauty of the sunset right through her skin. Her auburn hair was framed in vibrant orange and violet, a wild array of passion that seemed to mesh with the wild woods around her.

Her sandals were on the ground beside the rock, her bare toes gripping the boulder. She was wearing the same jeans and tank top as she had earlier, despite the slight evening coolness cropping up in the air. It was as if she hadn't bothered to notice, as if she couldn't deign herself to succumb to something so mundane as a cool breeze.

She was above it all, and Jason felt the tightness in his lungs easing simply from being in her presence. *Astrid.*

He knew then that he hadn't come to Birch Crossing for the town, or for the plate of cookies, or even for the damn pizza store he was planning to open. He had come for her. For Astrid. For the sheer, raw passion that she exuded with every breath.

She was the epitome of freedom, of passion, of life. Rightness roared through him at the sight of her on his land, basking in the sunset, breathing in the air that he suddenly noticed. The fresh, clean scent of woods and crystalline water filled him, as if Astrid's reverence of their surroundings had brought his own senses back to life.

She was beautiful. Not simply beautiful. She was beauty itself, the definition of all that it could be in a person's wildest, most desperate imagination.

Yearning crashed through Jason to lose himself in her, to use her vibrant energy to wipe away the smut covering his soul and give him the chance to breathe again, to find his path in this second chance that he'd tried to give his son. He was captivated by her, even the way she ignored protocol and had helped herself to his rock and the sunset, not even bothering to ring the doorbell. She was a free spirit, a woman who didn't fit into the town and didn't care.

He wanted that freedom. He needed to get caught up in her spell. He would never survive if he didn't find a way to forget, even for a minute, all the burdens crashing down on him. There was no choice, no other path, no other option, than to lose himself in the aura that was Astrid. To remember that there was something else in life beside the darkness that consumed him.

"It's beautiful, isn't it?" She didn't turn around, but her voice drifted to him, a melody that seemed to crawl under his skin and ignite flames within him.

"Yes, it is." He began to walk toward her, tentative, almost afraid of spooking her and losing the moment. But he couldn't keep from approaching her. He was drawn to her as if she were a magnet, calling to his soul, to the part of him that had once been alive. His need for her was pulsing through every cell of his body, so intense that it almost hurt, as if something inside of him was fighting its way to life after an eternity of being dead.

"This is the best place in town to watch the sunset. Is that why you bought it?" She spoke softly, almost as if she were afraid to disturb the beauty of the sunset.

"I haven't noticed a sunset in years," he admitted as he reached her. He stopped beside the rock, suddenly uncertain of how to approach. Of what to do next. Of how to get closer. "I bought the house because it has lake front, and I thought Noah would like it."

Astrid turned her head slightly to look at him, and he caught his breath at the sight of her face. The sun was casting a soft glow, illuminating her face so that her eyes seemed to vibrate with depth and passion... He realized suddenly that there was none of the levity in her expression that he'd seen before. Just pain and emotion, fighting to be free. His chest tightened for the agony he saw in her face, for the depth of trauma that seemed to echo what beat so mercilessly in his own soul. Outrage suddenly exploded through him, fury that someone had inflicted such damage on this angel that she could harbor such pain. Astrid was so free, so untamed, that she should be gallivanting across the surface of the lake, not looking at him as if her heart had been carved right out her chest.

"You don't notice sunsets?" she asked.

He barely heard her words or registered his response to her. All he could think about was the woman before him, the depth of her spirit, his need to somehow chase away the shadows and bring back the spirit that he knew was coursing through her veins. "No. I wouldn't have noticed this one if you weren't out here."

She shook her head, and that teasing glint sparkled in her eyes again, making his stomach leap. *Yes, Astrid. Come back to me.* He moved closer to the rock, ruthlessly drawn toward her.

She grinned at him. "Well, you've got some learnin' to do, Sarantos, if you're going to be living in this here town. Sunset appreciation is mandatory for all residents, and you'll be quizzed every morning at Wright's when you show up for your coffee." She held out her hand and beckoned with her fingers. "Up," she ordered.

Jason grinned at her bold command, and he immediately set his hand in hers. Electricity leapt through him as his skin touched hers, and she sucked in her breath at the contact. Wariness flashed in her eyes, and Jason sensed she was about to retreat.

No chance.

He wasn't missing this moment.

He immediately tightened his grip on hers and hauled himself up onto the rock beside her. The peak of the boulder was smaller than he'd expected, bringing them dangerously close to each other. For a moment, neither of them moved. He just stared down at her, and she gazed at him, her brown eyes wide and nervous. Her pulse was hammering in her throat, and he instinctively pressed his index finger on it, trying to ease it down. "Your heart is racing."

Those dark, expressive eyebrows of hers shot up, and she lifted her chin. "Beautiful sunsets get my adrenaline going."

"Do they?" They were so close to each other that he could feel the heat from her body. "Shouldn't they calm your soul and ease the stress from your body?" He moved closer, easing across the boulder. "Are you afraid of me, Astrid? I won't hurt you."

She blinked, and he saw doubt flicker across her face again. "Don't touch me," she whispered.

Instead of moving his fingers away from her throat, he traced her collarbone. Goosebumps popped up on her skin, and she sucked in her breath.

Awareness leapt through him at her transparent response, at the realization she was as affected by the touch as he was. Sudden desire blasted through him, raw, physical need that leapt straight to his loins. Jason froze, shocked by the pulse of physical need that shot through him. Son of a bitch. He hadn't responded to a woman in years. *Years*. "Jesus, Astrid," he whispered. "What is it about you?"

She shook her head once, her eyes so wide that he could read every nuance of her emotions. Unexpected, powerful desire, coupled with a fear so deep that it came from her soul. Excitement. Anticipation. Uncertainty. Vulnerability. "It's not me," she whispered. "It's you."

He spread his hand over the back of her neck, basking in the sensation of her skin beneath his palm. She felt so alive, vibrating with life, and yet at the same time, her skin was so delicate and soft that protectiveness surged through him. A need to be the strong male and take care of her, in the way that his former wife had never allowed him to do. His fingers tightened on her neck and he drew her closer. "No. It's both of us."

Astrid braced her palm on his chest, blocking him. "Don't," she said. "Please, don't."

"I can't help it." He couldn't tear her gaze off her eyes, off the myriad of expressions racing through them. He couldn't breathe. He felt like his soul was screaming with desperation, frantic for one chance, one moment, one kiss with this woman. As if the brush of her lips could save him from the free fall threatening to consume him. "I need to kiss you, Astrid. Now."

Select List of Other Books by Stephanie Rowe

(For a complete book list, please visit www.stephanierowe.com)

CONTEMPORARY ROMANCE

The *Wyoming Rebels* Series

A Real Cowboy Never Says No
A Real Cowboy Knows How to Kiss
A Real Cowboy Rides a Motorcycle

The *Ever After* Series

No Knight Needed
Fairytale Not Required
Prince Charming Can Wait

Stand Alone Novels

Jingle This!

PARANORMAL ROMANCE

The *NightHunter* Series

Not Quite Dead

The *Order of the Blade* Series

Darkness Awakened
Darkness Seduced
Darkness Surrendered
Forever in Darkness
Darkness Reborn
Darkness Arisen
Darkness Unleashed
Inferno of Darkness
Darkness Possessed
Shadows of Darkness
Hunt the Darkness
Release Date TBD

The *Soulfire* Series

Kiss at Your Own Risk

Touch if You Dare
Hold Me if You Can

The *Immortally Sexy* Series

Date Me Baby, One More Time
Must Love Dragons
He Loves Me, He Loves Me Hot
Sex & the Immortal Bad Boy

ROMANTIC SUSPENSE

The *Alaska Heat* Series

Ice
Chill
Ghost

NONFICTION

Essays

The Feel Good Life

FOR TEENS

A Girlfriend's Guide to Boys Series

Putting Boys on the Ledge
Studying Boys
Who Needs Boys?
Smart Boys & Fast Girls

Stand Alone Novels

The Fake Boyfriend Experiment

FOR PRE-TEENS

The *Forgotten* Series

Penelope Moonswoggle, The Girl Who Could Not Ride a Dragon
Penelope Moonswoggle & the Accidental Doppelganger
Release Date TBD

Collections

Box Sets

Alpha Immortals
Romancing the Paranormal
Last Hero Standing

Stephanie Rowe Bio

USA Today bestselling author Stephanie Rowe is the author of more than 40 novels, including her popular Order of the Blade and NightHunter paranormal romance series. Stephanie is a four-time nominee of the RITA® Award, the highest award in romance fiction. She has won many awards for her novels, including the prestigious Golden Heart® Award. She has received coveted starred reviews from Booklist, and Publishers Weekly has called her work "[a] genre-twister that will make readers...rabid for more." Stephanie also writes a thrilling romantic suspense series set in Alaska. Publisher's Weekly praised the series debut, ICE, as a "thrilling entry into romantic suspense," and Fresh Fiction called ICE an "edgy, sexy and gripping thriller." Equally as intense and sexy are Stephanie's contemporary romance novels, set in the fictional town of Birch Crossing, Maine. All of Stephanie's books, regardless of the genre, deliver the same intense, passionate, and emotional experience that has delighted so many readers.

www.stephanierowe.com

http://twitter.com/stephanierowe2

http://www.pinterest.com/StephanieRowe2/

https://www.facebook.com/StephanieRoweAuthor

Made in the USA
Lexington, KY
04 July 2015